INTO DEADLY STORMS

An absolutely gripping crime thriller

JUDI DAYKIN

DS Sara Hirst Book 2

JOFFE
BOOKS

Joffe Books, London
www.joffebooks.com

First published in Great Britain in 2021

This paperback edition first published
in Great Britain in 2023

© Judi Daykin 2021, 2023

Cover art by Dee Dee Book Covers

ISBN: 978-1-80405-910-4

We are such stuff
As dreams are made on, and our little life
Is rounded with a sleep.

William Shakespeare, *The Tempest*

AUTHOR'S NOTE

It has been my great delight to call Norfolk my home for the last forty years. As with all regions, we have our own way of doing and saying things here. If you would like to pronounce some of the real place names in this book like a local, the following may help:

Happisburgh = Haze-bruh
Wymondham = Wind-am
Norwich hides its 'w'
Marlham is a composite of several small towns, but if it existed a local would say Mar-lum

For the benefit of my North American readers the word 'fanny' in this book is the UK usage.

PROLOGUE

The half-naked body lay on the floor. One arm was stretched out in the tray of the shower, the other crushed across his chest and pinned beneath the torso. The legs were splayed on either side of the toilet column, the right foot broken at the ankle. The head nestled in the armpit, face to the vinyl, the visible cheek showing the impact of a bunched fist. Blood ran from a head wound, even though breathing had ceased.

The bathroom was tiny, with barely enough room to turn around even if standing. The body occupied all the floor space, and the door had been rammed open. The handle had splintered the wood of the poorly constructed partition wall, where it was deeply embedded. There was blood on the toilet bowl and a bloody piece of scalp on the porcelain shower tray. Blood had sprayed up the wall and on to a pile of freshly laundered, ancient-looking towels balanced on an old Lloyd Loom basket in the corner.

From the narrow corridor, a scrawny-looking, middle-aged man gazed in trying to decide what to do. The lad had been a cocky little bastard, king of the dunghill that was the local high school. But he'd picked a fight with the wrong person and paid the price.

The man went into the kitchen, reached down a glass from the cupboard and filled it with water. With shaking hands, he took two paracetamol from the packet on the work surface and swallowed them. He needed to clear his head and deal with his painful hand, which was already starting to bruise.

It had been dark when the lad had arrived after school. Christmas wasn't far away, the days were short and there was no street lighting here. In the distance, car headlights turned the corner by the caravan park on to the nearest road. It was after ten now. He knew his neighbours would be heading for bed or watching the late news behind drawn curtains. The remnants of adrenaline from the fight still surged through his veins, as he weighed up his options.

Call the police, tell them the truth and trust them. Or tidy up the mess, dump the evidence and hope that Norfolk police are too inept to connect it to me.

He opened and closed his fist. *Fat chance with either option.*

He took a key from the rack near the back door and went outside to the garden shed. In the light of the single bulb, he rummaged through piles of junk until he found what he was looking for. Armed with an old plastic ground-sheet and a wide roll of gaffer tape, he went back inside. If he was lucky, then he had all night to sort it out. The boy wouldn't be missed until the morning, perhaps not even then if the school weren't being vigilant. The first job was to get rid of the body. Clearing up could come later.

Laying the groundsheet out as wide as he could in the cramped passageway, the man grasped the young man's legs and heaved him out of the bathroom on to the plastic. The body hadn't had time to stiffen, and the skin was clammy. As he arranged the lad neatly, arms folded across the chest like a proper burial, the foot with the broken ankle annoy-ingly flopped to one side. He fastened the wrists and ankles together to keep them still. Next, he wrapped the ground-sheet around the boy until he looked like a giant moth pupa, then taped it shut.

He washed his hands, pulled off his bloodied clothes and threw them into the washing machine along with the towels and lots of soap powder. He turned it on at the highest temperature. It was half past ten.

Climbing over the body, he went into his bedroom and got changed before going outside to reverse the car up as close as it would go to the back door. He turned off the engine and stood beside it for several minutes, straining to listen.

The two homes on either side of him were in darkness. Not everyone stayed here in winter. Of the twenty-six properties on the private road, more than half were holiday homes. The wooden bungalows faced one another in an arc around a large communal green, their private gardens stretching out to the rear. At the edge of the green, the land fell away — sometimes literally — over a small sandy cliff to the beach below.

The man could hear the wind whipping through the marram grass that clung to the margins, and the sea hammering against the curve of the concrete sea defences that rose, Canute-like, between the beach and the ever-eroding twenty-foot bank. It was tempting to drag the pupa over the green and throw it out into the water. But his knowledge of the sea wasn't great. The body might wash down the coast, or back onshore. Besides, it was too far to throw something that heavy. He couldn't take the risk.

Satisfied that he couldn't hear anyone, he dragged the body outside and folded it on to the back seat of his small car. The young man was tall. Though still a teenager, there was a lot of him to manoeuvre. He fetched a couple of old blankets and covered up the bundle, hoping the late hour would be his best protection.

The man got into the car and restarted the engine, pausing to wipe a hand across his sweaty forehead. With a jerky start, he turned the vehicle and headed for the road.

CHAPTER 1

It was a cold, overcast evening. Sara opened the French windows on to the small balcony of her third-floor flat to let in
some air. The clock in the Norwich city hall chimed six. Over
the road, she could hear her boyfriend, Chris, locking up his
coffee shop and setting the alarm. She watched him as he
crossed the road to the flats where they both lived, Chris on
the second floor, Sara on the top storey. She waited for his
footsteps on the stairs and went down to greet him with a kiss.

'How was your day?' he asked.

'Routine. Yours?'

'Busy, very busy, thank goodness.'

Sara looked at the dark circles under his eyes, knowing
how hard he was working to make the best of his business while
customers were plentiful. 'If you come upstairs, I'll cook for us.'

'I've got a rehearsal.'

'Skip it for once.'

'I agreed to do it. I can't let them down, and I'm due
there at seven.'

'It's not like you get paid or anything,' Sara argued.

'I know. People consider it an honour to get into one of
their productions. I might not get cast again if I mess them
about.'

'See you tomorrow, then?'

'Absolutely.' He leaned forward and kissed her. Sara waited until he went into his flat and went back upstairs to her own. She knew Chris was proud of being cast in the Maddermarket Theatre's version of *Romeo and Juliet* and was looking forward to seeing him in it. She was just surprised at how much of his free time it seemed to be taking up. It made her feel that their relationship came out a poor second compared to playing at being an actor.

She was feeling lazy, so she rummaged among the ready meals in her freezer for something to eat. Waiting for the microwave bell, she curled up on her sofa, and opened the latest letter from her solicitor.

Dear Miss Hirst,

Thank you for your patience on the matter of probate regarding your late father's will. Please be assured that we have been doing our best to expedite matters.

I am pleased to say that probate has been granted. You may now have access to the cottage. As you are aware, the contents are left to you as part of the estate.

Sara's father, an East Ender born and bred, had been absent for most of her life. The pressure on his relationship with her mother, Jamaican-born Tegan, had proved too much for the young, mixed-heritage couple in 1980s Brixton. They had fallen out when Sara was still a toddler, after which her father was never spoken of. But he had never forgotten her, and in his will, he'd left her his home — a two-bedroom, end-of-terrace cottage in the small Norfolk coastal village of Happisburgh. The worst of it was that Sara had been expected to arrange her father's funeral. Tegan could not bring herself to help or even to attend on the day, which Sara understood, but also resented. It was too late to hold grudges, she felt, now that the man was dead.

The Norfolk police, on the other hand, had risen to the occasion. Her father had been a long-serving member of the force and Sara's boss, DI Edwards, had pulled out all the stops for him. Two police motorcycles had led the cortège. Officers in uniform had lined the road from the entrance of the crematorium to the chapel porch. Six detectives had acted as pall-bearers and carried her father's coffin on their shoulders. Even Assistant Chief Constable Miller had given an address. Throughout the whole ordeal, Sara had relied on Chris, and her father's former neighbour, Mrs Barker. It was Chris's arm Sara leaned on during the service and Mrs Barker who had hugged away her tears in the chapel grounds. A photograph of the funeral had featured in the local newspaper, with a generous obituary. Sara had a framed copy of the picture on the mantelpiece. It stood next to one she had brought from the cottage, showing her father as a young, ambitious police officer being given an award.

The microwave pinged. Sara pulled out the plastic tray and plonked the lasagne in a bowl. Flicking on the television, she returned to the solicitor's letter.

If you would like to make an appointment, we can go over the final paperwork and hand over the keys. I will be available in our Cathedral Close office until 21 December.

The cottage would be dusty and covered in cobwebs by now. It had been empty for months. Sara wasn't sure she could face going there alone. She tucked the letter from the solicitor back in its envelope and began to eat her unappetising meal. She would think about the cottage another time.

A sudden gust of squally rain rattled through the open window, reminding her that it was winter. Jaunty Christmas street decorations hung below the level of her balcony, twinkling with the damp and swinging in the breeze.

Sod Chris and his rehearsal, Sara thought. *I can watch an old movie on my own. He doesn't like film noir anyway.* With a contented smile, Sara shut out the night and settled in for the evening.

CHAPTER 2

Sophie was the first teacher to arrive at school on Wednesday morning. Geoff, the caretaker, had barely had time to let out the cleaners before she was marching past his tiny office next to the front door.

'Good morning, Geoff,' she called as she signed the attendance register. Her voice was curt and clipped.

He didn't bother to look out of his window, which suited Sophie fine. Let him believe that she was keen and naive because she was young and newly qualified. After all, she only lived around the corner. It took her less than three minutes to walk here.

She dumped her bag of books on one of the easy chairs in the staffroom, hung her coat on the rack near the door, turned on the water heater and headed for the ladies' toilet, handbag over her shoulder. Not wanting to take any chances, she checked the deserted corridor to make sure she was still alone.

Safely inside, she selected the cubicle at the far end against the wall. It was larger than the other two, with a little shelf running just above the cistern and a small floor cupboard. The female teachers left cosmetic bags with sanitary products in them. The unwritten rule was that anything left on the shelf was for emergencies, and could be taken by anyone. If a bag was in the cupboard, it belonged to a given individual, and no one helped themselves to what was inside.

Thank God, she thought.

Sophie locked the cubicle door behind her and paused, hands trembling, listening again for any sound that indicated she wasn't alone. A steady *drip drip* coming from the sink was all she could hear. She upturned the handbag, scattering the contents on top of the cupboard. Her lip gloss dropped with a clatter to the floor and rolled away under the door.

'Fuck it,' she snarled, too impatient to retrieve it immediately.

Sophie shuffled through the remaining contents until she extracted a small leather zip-up bag. Her fingers searched rapidly, but the only thing they pulled out was a piece of clear plastic tube that had once been part of a ballpoint pen. She'd known the bag was empty since first thing that morning.

She reached inside the cupboard and brought out a flowery washbag — her private tampon stash. It was her last resort. She emptied the loose tampons into the mess on top of the cupboard and pulled up the base that kept the bag rigid. Underneath, Sophie found what she needed. There were two wraps left. They were flimsy folds of what looked like the old-fashioned packets of Beechams Powders her grandmother had sworn by. She shook the contents of one wrap into the central fold of the paper, then snorted half up one nostril through the biro tube, swapped sides and snorted what remained up the other.

Her head swam, and her stomach lurched. She slumped down on to the toilet seat, eyes closed to prevent the spinning walls from making her vomit. This had to stop.

As the hit did its job, Sophie began to feel back in control. Very much in control. She took a deep breath and opened her eyes again. She cleaned off her nose, ripped the wrap-paper into tiny shreds and flushed everything away, waiting to check that the evidence had indeed gone down the sewage system. She hid the tampon stash at the back of the cupboard again and dropped the remaining wrap and plastic tube into the leather pouch, which she pushed to the bottom of her handbag, the rest of the contents shoved on top at random. When the toilet cistern stopped filling, Sophie listened again to make sure she was still alone.

She wasn't. A set of heels clipped their way along the tiled floor outside. They passed the door and carried on further into the school.

Hurriedly retrieving the lip gloss from the floor, Sophie washed her hands thoroughly and made her way back to the staffroom. The stimulus from the hit made her confident, ready to deal with her fellow members of staff.

'Good morning,' she said, closing the staffroom door behind her.

A middle-aged woman stood at the water heater, making a drink. Sophie recognised her as Miss Mitchell, the social worker attached to the school. Her clothing was rumpled. She wore an elderly cardigan covered in bobbles from too many washings. Her shoes were worn down at the heels.

Does she dress this way on purpose? Sophie wondered, smoothing her trouser suit back into line.

'Oh! You made me jump,' said Miss Mitchell, looking round for something to mop up the water she'd spilled. 'You're in early.'

'Catching up on paperwork,' said Sophie.

'Me too. Never-ending with this lot.'

'It's not too bad an area, surely?' Sophie asked. She spooned instant coffee into a mug.

'No,' agreed Miss Mitchell. 'This one's not too bad, hence two mornings a week. I have three others to look after, as well. Right, I'm going to catch up with my emails.'

The staffroom was empty again, though it wouldn't be for long. Sophie settled into an armchair. She focused on the selection of carelessly written essays on *Pride and Prejudice* that she was supposed to have already marked. Evenings were not her best time. In fact, these days it was often lost time. Like the bizarre ramblings of the narrator in *Naked Lunch*, her evenings and weekends were full of fantastic trips, sensational highs, hideous monsters and disastrous comedowns. Funny how she always thought of her life in terms of novels.

This room also gave her a kind of anchor. Its familiarity grounded her. Here she could still attempt to work, marking generously the ramblings of these under-ambitious rural teenagers, who grew their vocabulary from Instagram and thought Orwell was something you caught. Buzzing with her boost, topped up with caffeine, Sophie wrote helpful remarks and supportive words in the margins, knowing that they wouldn't be read, but doing her best all the same. Her heart rate settled and her concentration returned. By the time the rest of the teaching staff began to arrive for the day, Sophie could greet them cheerfully, daring to combat the tired attitude of some of the die-hard older teachers.

Let them be cynical, she thought, *I've got kids I can help.*

She repacked her work bag with the completed marking and followed the other staff to the weekly assembly in the main hall. The only cloud on her horizon was the single wrap in her handbag. She'd need that at lunchtime. Then what? With her level of consumption, she couldn't wait until the evening to be sure of more. Gary only came to see her when he felt like it.

See you soon, babe, was all he had left her with on Sunday evening. *Ciao, bella.*

Sophie laughed inwardly at the brief memory. After five months, she still didn't quite know what to make of Gary.

She joined the line of teachers who stood casually around the edge of the hall. While the headmaster droned on at the ranks of bored teenagers, Sophie had time to scan the pupils in Year Eleven for her regular dealer, Callum Young.

CHAPTER 3

It looked as if Detective Constable Mike Bowen had arrived in the office first, which was an unusual state of affairs. His jacket was over the back of his chair and his computer was on. Aggie, their new admin, was starting her computer and looked up when Sara wandered in.

'Mike's gone for the butties,' she said, pulling her cardigan around her tubby middle for warmth.

The heating in the open-plan office, along with the rest of the building, had been turned down this winter. It was a money-saving exercise. So far it hadn't proved too bad, although it wasn't particularly cold outside. Windy and rainswept, yes, but still mild for December. Sara had bought a couple of fancy scarves to help keep the draft off the back of her neck.

The Serious Crimes Unit team had changed since the summer. There was a new young detective constable called Ian Noble. Tall, blonde and gangly, he was enthusiastic and still inexperienced. He reminded Sara of her favourite childhood cartoon character, Inspector Gadget. There was also the civilian admin, Aggie Hewett, who fussed around them all like a mother hen. She was in her mid-fifties, short and homely, and surprisingly good on the computer. She had soon picked up the police database systems and typed so quickly that Sara couldn't follow her fingers.

'I brought something for later.' Aggie gestured to a cake tin on the shelf next to the coffee machine. Aggie's baking was becoming the stuff of legend. Visitors from Vice and Drugs had a habit of popping in for a chat, just in case there was something homemade available. Even ACC Miller was known to drop by and graciously accept a slice.

Sara opened her files, preparing herself for the morning. She and Bowen intended to interview the landlord at a pub in Cromer about a street fight, then follow up on a couple of local suspects. It was hardly riveting work, but at least it got them away from their desks. DI Edwards had taken Noble under his wing, and they had planned to head for the Suffolk border first thing, to investigate a spate of burglaries. She helped herself to a coffee.

'No point in going there too early.' Bowen dumped a bacon roll on her work files. 'Landlords tend not to get up first thing. Unless they have to.'

'By the time we get up there, it will be nearly opening time anyway,' Sara replied as she loaded ketchup on to her bacon. 'We'll go once we've eaten.'

Bowen didn't argue. Spotting the cake tin, he winked at Aggie. 'What flavour today?'

'Lemon drizzle. That's your favourite, isn't it?' Aggie smiled at him.

He nodded enthusiastically. Sara knew he was flirting with the woman, and why not? They were of a similar age. It was more appropriate than the crush he'd had on DC Ellie James during the summer. Sara's arrival on the team back in August had seriously ruffled Bowen's feathers. He had wanted Ellie to have the promotion and made sure he let Sara know about it, in less-than-subtle ways.

However, Ellie had subsequently received her detective sergeant's promotion and been transferred across to the Drugs team some weeks ago. Bowen had come round to Sara being his immediate boss. His long service and sharp observation skills made him an asset, even though he couldn't keep up with Sara when she ran. Since the summer, Sara and Ellie had become friends. They went for the occasional girls' night out, drinking cocktails in some of the fashionable bars in Norwich city centre, pretending not to be coppers for a couple of hours.

'It's the Duke, isn't it?' Bowen was wiping ketchup off his fingers. 'I know the landlord.'

Sara washed her roll down with coffee. 'Of course you do. Is there a landlord in Norfolk that you don't know?'

'One or two.' Bowen grinned. 'I'm not that much of a drinker.'

Sara looked pointedly at his beer belly.

'Oi! This is winter padding.'

Aggie chuckled from the corner. Sara rolled her eyes. 'Let's get going, shall we?'

* * *

They parked up in Cromer. When she'd first arrived, the distances from place to place had taken Sara by surprise. The county was large, and the road system was poor — driving anywhere always took time. The seaside resort was nearly an hour away, and to her surprise, it was busy with shoppers. Cafés with cheerful Christmas decorations were selling coffee and cake to customers bundled in scarves and hats.

'Looks busy,' said Sara.

'Christmas show,' said Bowen. Sara glanced at him with a raised brow. 'They have a lovely little theatre down on the pier. I used to bring my mum back in the day. It's very popular.'

The North Sea wind blustered refreshingly down the narrow streets. The skies were grey, though rain-free, for once. The Duke was on a corner, one street back from the top of the cliff ramps that zigzagged down to the promenade and the pier. As they approached, a young man was unlocking the pub doors to let in a small group of older men, several of them with dogs on leads. They had to be regulars, as the

13

barman began to pull pints without asking for orders. He put their money in the till and allowed each customer to settle in their favourite seats before turning to Sara and Bowen.

'Need to speak to Arnie.' Bowen flipped his warrant card.

'About the fight? He's in the flat.' The barman pointed to the ceiling. 'I'll give him a call.'

Sara expected him to pick up the phone, but the action was literal. He opened a door at one end of the bar, revealing a flight of stairs, and yelled, 'Arnie, it's the police.'

'Send 'em up,' a voice answered. The barman lifted the hatch and directed them upwards.

Arnie led them into the living room, offering seats and drinks, before settling himself. 'Mike Bowen, long time no see.'

'Don't get up this way so much now,' Bowen agreed. 'So, tell me about this incident.'

'You saw the CCTV? I gave it to uniform.'

'Yeah, we might be able to identify them from it. Did you know them?'

'Couple of little toerags from up Runton way, I think. Don't know their names.'

Sara's phone vibrated in her handbag. She checked the screen. With an apology, she went out on to the landing, pulling the door shut behind her.

'Sara, where are you?' DI Edwards asked as soon as she answered.

'Cromer, sir. About the street fight.'

'Best get your skates on,' her boss said. His tone was grim. 'We've got a Code One. A dog walker has found a body, wrapped up and dumped at Stiffkey Woods near Fakenham. I'm about as far away as it's possible to be. I want you to get up there, and I'll join you as soon as I can.'

CHAPTER 4

The steel of the knife glistened against her boyfriend's dark skin, mercilessly sharp against his windpipe. The man holding it vibrated with savage intensity.

Danni recognised the well-built white man. His nickname was Striker. She didn't know his real name, nor had she realised that he worked for the woman standing in the living room doorway. Lisa London, the most feared dealer on the Hayridge Estate, the most notorious housing estate in all of the capital. London lounged against the door frame, a smile creasing her lips. Long, glossy brown hair cascaded down her shoulders. Her figure was slim and tall, her make-up immaculate. After all, she never needed to raise a sweat when Striker did all the dirty work for her.

'Your boyfriend should pay his bills,' said London. 'Ain't that right, Johnny-boy?'

Johnny gurgled, reaching with his free hand towards the blade. Striker twisted the armlock tighter and nicked the neck skin with the knife. A bubble of blood formed on the tip, gleaming like a ruby, and ran down the steel to drip off Striker's fingers. Johnny's hand subsided.

'Danni, isn't it?' London asked. Danni nodded, her mouth too dry to speak. 'Well, Danni, it's like this. Your

Johnny-boy should have been happy working for me. You earned enough, didn't you, boy?'

London drew herself up and walked round to face the young man. With the height of the heels on her red boots, she looked down on Johnny even though he was nearly six feet tall himself. His breaths shortened as London put her face close to his. Striker slowly twisted the blade in his skin. The blood dripped more freely. Johnny moaned but looked London in the eyes.

'Answer the lady.' Striker kicked at Johnny's ankle. 'Be polite.'

Johnny opened his lips, and saliva trickled out of the corner of his mouth. 'Yes. Plenty of money.'

'Exactly.' London leaned in so close, Johnny's spit flecked her face. She ignored it. 'But you decided to branch out on your own account, didn't you?'

'No, no, no,' Johnny stammered in terror. 'Don't know what you mean.'

'Not what I hear, and I know everything that goes on in my patch. Where's my money?'

Danni knew her boyfriend was a low-chain supplier, with a steady flow of customers he met in the square near the shops. It was their only source of income. As far as she knew, Johnny paid for the stuff when he picked it up, and sold it on at a profit, which he was allowed to keep. So what on earth was London going on about? It was true that recently Johnny had been flashing the cash, treating her to new clothes, saying that he'd had a good run and they could afford to go up West to eat in Chinatown.

The tall woman turned to Danni, brushing the spit away from her face. 'So you're going to help repay the debt, little girl.' Danni flinched as London reached up a hand and touched her cheek. 'She's quite pretty, ain't she, Striker?'

The big man grunted. It could have meant anything. Johnny wriggled, only succeeding in tearing the flesh wound wider than before. Striker snorted in amusement.

'Oh, don't worry,' London leered at Johnny. 'This one's not for the whorehouse. She's going on a little trip for me. If she's good at it, then you might find a little bit of the debt has been settled. Meanwhile, it's business as usual for you, Johnny-boy.'

Striker shoved hard, sending Johnny tumbling sideways. His head thumped against the wall, leaving a swipe of blood as he collapsed. The big man turned to land a couple of kicks to Johnny's head, whose eyelids fluttered as he fell unconscious.

'Got to love that Striker,' said London to Danni. She looked at the big man and laughed. 'Not too much football practice this time. I want him earning again by this evening.'

Danni gasped, retreating so rapidly from London she backed up hard against the filthy plate glass window.

'Wanted to be a professional, didn't you, Striker? Tried out for . . . ?'

'Gunners.'

'That's why he's called Striker. Funny how things turn out, isn't it?' London stepped towards Danni. 'Got a coat?'

Danni nodded, tears in her eyes. Fear turned her pallid face more grey than white.

'Get it. I'll give you thirty seconds to pack a bag with some clothes. Then we're gone.'

Striker snapped shut his flick knife. Three strides brought him to where Danni pressed herself against the window. Reaching up, he twisted Danni's long mousey hair in his fist. She squealed in pain as he dragged her into the hallway and pointed to the doors.

'Which?'

She pointed to the bedroom. He kicked the door open and pushed her inside. She staggered to her knees. His bulk occupied the door frame, his arms folded, face impassive, his flick knife still visible in one hand.

'Hurry up.'

Danni shook her head to relieve the smart in her scalp. Leaning on the unmade bed, she levered herself up and grabbed a sports holdall. Her clothes lay scattered on the floor. She only had a few seconds to decide if they were fit to wear and shove them into the bag. Johnny groaned in the living room, and Danni heard a thump. She packed faster, zipping up the bag hurriedly. Striker grabbed Danni's arm with iron fingers and dragged her into the hallway.

'Will you look at that?' London asked as she joined them. 'There's blood on my boot. This yours?'

London dangled a grubby pink parka with a fur-lined hood from two fastidious fingers. Danni stared at the tip of the boot, where a smudge of blood was barely visible against the red leather. London threw the coat at Danni, who caught it clumsily with her free hand, and leaned over to wipe the smudge away with a tissue. She tucked it into the pocket of her skintight black leather jeans and fastened her smart beige coat.

'Best you put it on, then.' London waved at Striker to let Danni go. 'Now, here's what's going to happen. You and me are going to walk downstairs like the best of friends. If anyone sees us, you smile. Got that?'

Dropping her bag to pull on the parka, Danni nodded. The big man picked it up.

'You're a gent.' London smiled at him. 'Ain't he, girl?'

Wide-eyed, Danni glanced at Striker. He pointed the knife at her and flicked out the blade.

'Not that much of a gentleman.' London laughed. She opened the front door to the flat. 'Get in the car downstairs and you won't get hurt. If you try to run, Striker here is as fast as a greyhound, and his bite is much worse than his bark.'

Danni followed the tall woman on to the passage deck outside. The door slammed behind them. London led the way to the staircase at the end of the block and, despite her high heels, descended rapidly to the ground floor where a gleaming black saloon waited, engine running. The driver jumped out to open the rear door. Danni and her bag were shoved on to the back seat. London followed more elegantly. The two men climbed into the front seats, and the door system was locked. The car rolled gently out of the car park and on to the road.

The car accelerated away. God only knew where they were going. Danni offered a silent prayer to a deity she didn't believe in. It was her only hope of getting out of this alive.

CHAPTER 5

Sara rang Aggie for the details as Bowen powered the car up the hill out of Cromer.

'The woods are near Little Kettleford. On the Fakenham road,' said Aggie. 'CSI teams are already en route, as is Dr Taylor.'

Dr Taylor was the police pathologist. Like DI Edwards, he had also been very kind to Sara over her father's death, something she was grateful for. She liked him anyway, for the respect that he showed to the victims and his compassion for their families.

Bowen sped along the A148, around the Georgian town of Holt and out on to the Fakenham road. Little Kettleford was a tiny place, with a pub on one side of the main road and a café on the other. A car park served both the woods and the café. Several CSI vehicles were already in evidence, along with a patrol car and Dr Taylor's car. White-suited SOCOs were unloading equipment, while customers at the café watched with undisguised curiosity out of the steamed-up windows. Bowen parked by the CSI vans, and they climbed out.

'Looks like they're going that way,' he said. Zipping up her jacket, Sara followed him across the car park.

The woods were a public leisure area. A large sign at the entrance showed several waymarked walking routes of varying lengths. Sara and Bowen followed two SOCOs into the woods. Within a few yards, they had deviated from the main path on to a much less well-used one. It opened out on to an area of heathland, with scrubby grass and random patches of heather and bracken. The paths across the heath were less defined, skirting around a rabbit warren and a couple of sunken pits. About twenty yards on to the heath, Sara could see the CSI team had set up their white tent. The area was already cordoned off with blue-and-white official tape. A uniformed officer stood at the entrance with his clipboard, signing people in and out of the crime scene. They showed their warrant cards and joined Dr Taylor, who was already suited up and waiting for them.

'Didn't think you'd be long,' he said. Once they had pulled on protective suits, he lifted the flap of the tent. 'Don't touch anything.'

'As if.' Bowen ducked inside. Sara followed with a shrug. The tent hid a small hollow covered in dead bracken. The summer fronds had shrivelled back with the onset of autumn, creating an area of dense undergrowth.

'DI Edwards?' Taylor let down the flap of the tent.

'He was down near Bungay,' said Sara. 'He'll be here as soon as he can. What have we got?'

'Mark's done the first round of photos.' Taylor indicated another white-suited man, holding an expensive camera. 'If we're all ready, I'll have a quick look.'

The pathologist stepped beside what looked like a plastic shroud lying in the middle of the hollow. The scrubby undergrowth did a poor job of hiding the body, but it was a dark brown colour, which must have made it hard to spot until daylight.

'Our dog walker, one Mr Laurence Brown, and his lovely retriever, Goldy, found our parcel on their morning walk.'

'Where is he?' Bowen asked.

'He's rather shocked. Denny took him to the café to keep warm and get him a cuppa. Mr Brown said it was quiet when he arrived, the café only just opening. They came along here as they usually did, but the dog dived into the undergrowth and wouldn't come when called. When he realised what it might be, he rang 999.'

Taylor stooped and delicately cut open the head end of the package, revealing a young man's face. The body was on its back, eyes closed, light brown hair matted with damp. As he worked gently along, the photographer followed him, snapping pictures of the new evidence. Using a scalpel, Taylor slit the tape that held the parcel together.

'Looks like a groundsheet of some sort,' he said. When he reached the foot end, he stood up, and they all surveyed the young man. He was nearly naked except for a pair of stained and grubby blue boxer shorts. The legs were bent at the knee, drooping to one side, his neck twisted the same way. His hair was matted with blood from an injury to the skull. Taylor stood back for the positioning shots to be taken. 'His hands and ankles are taped as if someone was trying to lay him out properly. Then he got scrunched up for some reason.'

'During transport?' suggested Sara.

'Maybe,' Taylor said.

'Time of death?'

'Sometime last night, before midnight probably. Rigor has fully set in, so at least twelve hours.'

'Age?'

'Teenager. Hard to be specific until I get him indoors.'

'Why did they lay him out like that?' Bowen asked. 'Did the killer know or like him?'

'Whoa, we don't know what happened to him yet.' Taylor frowned. 'Let's not get ahead of ourselves.'

Bowen looked at Taylor, then grinned. 'Lover's tiff, you thinking?'

'He's very young.' Taylor surveyed the body with a compassionate shake of the head. 'Who knows, in this place and dressed like that.'

Bowen shrugged, then glanced at Sara. 'I'll explain as we go back.'

'I think a cuppa and a chat with our valiant dog walker seems in order,' said Sara. 'I'll update DI Edwards. Let us know when you have any more results.'

'Of course.' Taylor bent over the young man's body to begin his search. Sara took this to be a dismissal and signalled to Bowen to leave. Outside the tent, they stripped their protective suits and dumped them in the plastic bag provided.

'What's special about here, then?' Sara asked as they headed back to the car park. 'It's miles from anywhere, isn't it?'

'Exactly.' Bowen gestured at the main road. 'Nice, quiet A-road, not much traffic. Easy to access the car park, quick to leave. Fakenham is about four miles that way, Norwich about twenty-five the other. Nothing much in between except Holt, and you saw how far away that was. By day, it's a respectable walking spot. The café is popular with delivery drivers and pensioners on a trip out. By night, it's an easy place to bring your clients.'

'What sort of clients?'

'The sort that Vice would be interested in.' The wind cut across the bleak heath. Bowen dug his hands into his pockets to keep them warm. Sara turned up her collar. 'There's no lighting at night.'

'So toms bring their clients here?'

'Both genders. Not just girls.' They had reached the car park, and suddenly the place looked more sinister to Sara. Bowen continued. 'It's a handy exchange point for the dealers, too. The roads from here to King's Lynn and the motorway at Cambridge are quiet. Drugs put teams in here now and again, but they haven't caught anyone yet. It's too easy to send out a warning these days, the place gets abandoned in an instant.'

'So prostitutes and drug dealers? Are we talking local networks?'

A car swung hastily into the entrance and drew up next to theirs. DI Edwards and a rather grey-looking DC Noble got out. Sara smiled inwardly, knowing that Edwards's driving could take a bit of getting accustomed to. The DI marched towards them.

'Possibly,' said Bowen. 'I suspect this will end up being either a boy prostitute, or a county line killing.'

CHAPTER 6

Callum hadn't been in assembly. Nor had he dragged his arse into the period where Sophie was teaching his English group. It wasn't going so well. Trying to explain why they should be interested in Jane Austen was a task that this morning left her feeling defeated. Here was a group of lads who would never read a book voluntarily again once they had left school, and a set of girls whose highest ambitions were to pass for eighteen in a nightclub. The group were not being disruptive, though they were especially silent when she asked them a question that might require an answer. Some had bowed heads and fiddling fingers, checking their mobiles under the desk. One or two gazed out of the windows. She was irrelevant to them, Sophie felt, and her enthusiasm from earlier deserted her.

'No Callum today?' Sophie had asked as she'd entered the classroom at the beginning of the period.

'No, miss.' One of the lads had smirked. 'You need him?'

Sophie hadn't replied. Instead, she'd taken the pile of scruffy essays from her bag and given them to the nice girl on the front row, Andrea Green. 'Hand these back, please. They were rather good this time — well done, everyone.'

Thirty minutes later, she knew that this compliment had bought her about ten minutes of their attention and then she'd lost them. It was the last lesson before lunch, and the smell from the canteen was drifting down the corridors.

'Look.' She dropped her copy of *Pride and Prejudice* on the desk with a thump. 'I know you think that this has little relevance to your own lives.'

Even the largest of the loutish lads at the back of the room looked up at this.

'I know what you think of it, of having to be here and do these lessons, but here's the reality of the thing. If you don't get maths and English at GCSE, no one will take you on a course or give you an apprenticeship when you are sixteen. Whether you want to train in mechanics—' she looked at a couple of the reclining boys — 'or as a hairdresser—' a couple of girls with too much make-up giggled at this — 'or even go to university—' this to Andrea Green in the front row — 'you need to pass this GCSE. So wise up and do some of the stuff to put in your folders. That way, the exam mark will be balanced by the continuous assessment mark. Just don't copy it all off the internet: I can tell.'

The bell rang, and the pupils stuffed their folders and books into their bags. They shouldn't have done this without her permission, but she felt too strung out to object. They surged out of the door and stampeded towards the canteen.

'Please, Miss Bailey.'

'Yes, Andrea?'

The girl fiddled with the zip on her bag. She was small for the age group, smartly turned-out, and her work was usually the best in class.

'Your essay was great,' said Sophie. 'You got an A-star, is there a problem?'

'Not with my essay, miss.'

'Is it about the exams? I'd advise you to keep your CA work at home, so no one else can see or take it.'

'Yes, miss. I do that already.'

'What is it, then?'

'It's Callum, miss. You asked about him.'

'Do you know Callum out of school? Is he not well?'

'We live on Lyndford Road . . .' Andrea hesitated. Sophie waited. 'Callum lives at Lyndford Lodge. It's at the end of our road.'

Sophie racked her jittery brain for the significance of this, then realised. Lyndford Lodge was a private young person's care home. Callum lived in a care home and had no family to look after him. Why hadn't she realised before?

'I'm sorry, miss.' Andrea turned her head to check the corridor, then leaned forward. 'They let them come and go at all hours. I see him from my bedroom window when I'm doing my homework.'

'Callum?'

'Yes, miss. Most evenings. He has a bike. With no lights.'

'You think he might have had an accident?'

'I don't know,' said Andrea. 'I like Callum, even if he is a bit bosky.'

Sophie didn't know what this word meant in teen parlance, even though she was only twenty-four. She ignored it.

'I don't think they'd notice if he was there or not,' Andrea concluded.

'Thank you, Andrea.' Sophie smiled. 'I take your point. I'll see if I can get someone to check up on him. I appreciate you coming forward.'

The girl escaped to the lunch queue. Sophie went to the noisy staffroom. Leaving her work bags on a chair, she hurried into the toilet with her handbag. She checked the other three stalls were empty and locked herself in the end cubicle. She had to be careful — there were lots of staff around now — but most of them would either be in lunch or were already in the staffroom eating their sandwiches. Even so, she could be disturbed at any moment. She opened the leather pouch, carefully balanced the coke wrap on top of the cupboard, took the plastic tube and hurriedly snorted the contents. Leaning against the wall, she listened to the sound of the school outside, waiting for her head to stop swimming.

There was nothing left for tonight or tomorrow morning. Even if Sophie contacted Gary, there was no guarantee he would reply or come to see her. Sinking on to the toilet seat, she tapped a text into her mobile and sent it to him. Then she packed the pouch and the phone back into her handbag. This was an emergency.

Sophie knew she ought to speak to Miss Mitchell, the social worker, about her concern for Callum. If he lived at Lyndford Lodge, he would surely be on her list. But she wanted to speak to him first, to get what she needed. He'd probably just skipped school for a day. Reporting him missing would cause trouble for him and a lack of supplies for her.

Her head recovered and, feeling determined once more, Sophie returned to the staffroom. She had a free period after lunch, so she pulled on her coat and signed herself out in the book at Geoff's window. It might be contrary to school policy to do this personally, but Lyndford Road was only a short walk away.

*

CHAPTER 7

The smoothness of the car ride made Danni feel sick. It sped along the outside lane, the driver flashing his lights at cars in front of him to intimidate them.

She wasn't used to travelling in cars. Her family had been too poor and too large to own one, so Danni had become used to riding the buses and the Tube system alone. Catholic and proud, her father had never agreed with birth control, and Danni was the eldest of seven children. From an early age, she had developed acute observation skills, a keen sense of self-preservation and the wit to understand things not spoken aloud. When puberty arrived, her father had turned his attention away from her exhausted mother to his eldest daughter. His first attempt to touch Danni up had been his last. A private chat with the school social worker had brought the required result — a prison sentence for her father, a foster placement for her.

London hit a button to wind down the window a couple of inches. 'You better not throw up in here.' Danni realised she must be looking green. The fresh air helped.

For the first time in years, Danni felt out of control. Normally she called the shots, like using the social worker to escape home. She'd slept with the nineteen-year-old son of her last foster family to gauge her preferences. He'd been delighted; Danni had quickly found him boring. She controlled Johnny with the promise of favours only occasionally allowed. Now Danni was under someone else's control, and it was making her panic. She drew in a couple of deep breaths to calm herself, silently cursing Johnny for being an idiot.

Glancing at Lisa London, Danni doubted her usual weapon of choice, sex, would help her now. She'd never done it with a woman, though she had no objection to trying. The truth was that London was too powerful and Danni too far below her in the food chain. If London liked ladies, her partner would be a famous actress or model.

What the hell does she want with me? Danni wondered. *How can I regain some control?*

The car fought through the traffic at Hanger Lane, swung right past Ealing Common and into a posh area of old-fashioned, tall terraced houses with pretty front gardens. Danni was utterly lost. She didn't know this area at all, and would normally have hesitated to visit a place as grand as this. They drew up at a detached house behind high walls and a large double gate. The driver pressed a remote on the dashboard, the gates swung open and they were inside before Danni could get her breath back. The house stood in the middle of a neatly trimmed garden. Two wings stretched out evenly on either side of a glass entrance area with windows that reached from the floor to the roofline.

Striker leaped out as the car halted, opened the door for London and offered his hand to help her out. London smiled and accepted. It was her due, it seemed. Striker reached into the back seat, and dragged Danni on to the gravel. She stumbled as he thumped the bag into her chest. He yanked her upright by the collar of her parka, and they followed in London's wake.

A middle-aged woman approached the door from inside the house, holding it open for the party as if London were a member of the royal family. She took London's coat.

London checked her reflection in a long mirror. 'All well, Mrs Strong?'

'Indeed it is.' The middle-aged woman glanced at Danni with a raised eyebrow.

London answered the unasked question. 'This is Danni. She can have the spare bedroom for tonight. She'll need cleaning up. So will her clothes, I expect. Tea, when you have a moment.' Then she turned on her elegantly booted heel and vanished through a doorway.

'Upstairs,' Mrs Strong said briskly to Striker. He pulled Danni up the open-plan staircase that wound in an elongated spiral to the first floor, and they followed the woman along a carpeted corridor. Mrs Strong opened a white-painted door. Striker pushed Danni in and shut the door behind the two women.

The room was immaculate. Cream carpet, beige wallpaper with a trellis-and-flower pattern, a single bed with a white duvet piled high with pillows and beige cushions. It looked like a princess's room to Danni, the sort of thing she saw in the soppy films she watched when Johnny was out dealing.

Mrs Strong opened another door and pointed. 'This is the en suite. You need to have a shower. You're filthy. Give me your clothes.' Danni handed over the bag, which Mrs Strong held at arm's length. 'Those as well.'

'What?' Did she mean the things she was wearing? Danni wondered.

'Don't be stupid,' sneered Mrs Strong. 'I wouldn't be much of a housekeeper if there weren't fresh things ready for you when you came out.'

She pushed Danni into the bathroom, pulling the door shut for privacy. Looking rapidly around, Danni opened the window and stared down. It was a long drop to the ground, and there was no useful pipework or climbing plants. It was still daylight, but it would soon be evening. Perhaps she could get out tonight. She climbed on to the toilet seat and leaned out, as the door opened again.

'You'll hurt yourself jumping out of there,' said the housekeeper. 'The outer wall is electrified, by the way, and the gate's always locked. You can't get out. Just be a good girl and take a shower.'

This time, Mrs Strong stood in the doorway while Danni stripped off her clothes. She wasn't ashamed because she knew her figure was good. All her men told her so. She resisted the temptation to have tattoos or endless piercings, recognising that they gave the wrong impression. Danni looked smugly at Mrs Strong, daring her to criticise her naked form. The woman's look was impassive as she picked up the abandoned clothes and turned to leave, taking the holdall with her.

'There's toiletries and a hairdryer in here,' she said. 'Be ready in thirty minutes or Miss London's patience may run out, and you don't want to be on the receiving end of that, believe me.'

Danni watched as the housekeeper went out of the bedroom. She could see Striker lounging against the wall opposite, arms folded, a scowl on his face. Mrs Strong pulled the door shut, and Danni heard a key turn.

CHAPTER 8

Inside the café, the windows and walls ran with condensation. Sara saw that it was unexpectedly busy. The lorry drivers all seemed to be male, primarily middle-aged or older and tucking into heart-stopping fry-ups with oversized mugs of tea. Several sets of pensioners, mostly female, occupied other tables, gossiping over coffee and cakes. There was a general buzz of conversation, and curious eyes followed Sara and Edwards as they walked to a table near the counter that seemed to have an invisible barrier around it. No one else sat near it.

An older man and a uniformed officer sat there in silence. Their mugs were empty. The man's golden retriever sat under the table, chin snuggled in her owner's lap, offering canine comfort. As Edwards and Sara approached, the officer stood up, clearly relieved to see them.

'This is Mr Laurence Brown,' the officer said.

'And I take it this is Goldy,' said Edwards. Mr Brown looked up. 'Get us a cuppa, would you? Mr Brown, would you like another?'

The man nodded. Sara muttered their order to the officer, who headed to the counter.

'Quite a shock for you,' said Edwards. The dog looked up with baleful eyes but didn't move. 'And now you've had a long wait.'

'I don't mind.' Brown gestured to the officer ordering the tea. 'PC Denny has been keeping me company, and it's not like I have anything else to do.'

'Shall we go outside? It would be more private.' Edwards led Mr Brown and Goldy out through the curious pensioners to a picnic table that stood on a sheltered, grassy area behind the café. They settled on the wobbly benches. Goldy pushed under the table and laid her chin on Mr Brown's lap again.

'No one expecting you at home, then?' asked Edwards. Sara was surprised at the sympathy he showed.

'No, not for a while now.' Brown took a tissue from his coat pocket and wiped his nose.

'Take it slowly.'

The officer returned with mugs of hot tea and a selection of treats. Edwards thanked him and sent him off. Brown selected a wrapped mince pie, opened it and pulled off the pastry lid, which he passed under the table to the dog. Goldy took it gently and chewed for a few seconds before swallowing and putting her head back in the same spot.

'Are you local, Mr Brown?' Edwards dunked his Crunchie in his tea. 'Do you walk here a lot?'

'Not really. I live in Hellesdon. But we come out here sometimes for a change of scenery. It gets boring otherwise.'

'In your car?'

'Yes.' He pointed to a small navy-blue Mini. Sara wondered how he managed with such a large dog in it. 'There's only the two of us. Goldy gets the back seat.' He frowned for a moment. 'She has one of those thingies, you know, to keep her safe.'

'Dog seat belt harness?' Sara suggested.

'Yes, that's it. She doesn't mind it at all. Sometimes we stay local, sometimes we go to the coast or here. Gets me out of the house.'

'And when you got here?' Edwards asked.

'Same as always. I put Goldy on the lead until we're out of the car park, to be safe. Once we're on the path, I let her off.'

At the mention of her name, the dog shuffled her position. Brown fed her another piece of mince pie. Sara opened the flapjack bar that the two men had ignored, watching with some fascination as Edwards dunked his Crunchie again, wondering why it didn't melt away and make the tea taste peculiar.

'Weather isn't very nice today,' she said.

'I didn't check.' Brown patted his padded raincoat. 'We don't mind a bit of rain. Usually means it's quieter for us. Goldy's very friendly, but sometimes other dogs are not so well behaved.'

Goldy's tail swept on the floor. Sara assumed it was a wag of confirmation. 'She seems very fond of you.'

'All we've got is each other. Goldy doesn't understand that my wife isn't coming back.'

Edwards cleared his throat to bring the attention back to himself. 'You went into the woods as soon as you arrived?'

'Yes. We turned down the side path — Goldy prefers the heath,' said Brown. 'You've been down to see?'

Sara and Edwards both nodded.

'She likes to put up the birds or startle the rabbits. They are retrievers, after all. It's what they are bred to do, search for game to flush or bring it back. Normally she comes as soon as I call.'

'Not this time?'

'She wouldn't come back to me. I didn't understand it.' Brown shuddered. 'I climbed through the rough stuff and down into that little pit. Then I saw she was worrying the tarpaulin.'

'Had she moved it much?' Edwards asked.

'I don't think so. It would be too heavy for her. She didn't like me putting the lead on, wouldn't leave it be. I had to shout at her to make her stop.' Brown's eyes filled with tears. 'I never shout at her. Ever.'

'She was shocked enough to move away?' Sara asked. The man nodded.

'At first, I thought it was just some wrapping from the fields, you know, the sort of stuff they put around the silage. Those big black bales. It blows about sometimes, especially in the winter.'

Sara often wondered what the giant rolls of black plastic dotted around fields and farms were. She'd have to look up silage.

'Then I looked at it.' Brown gulped down a mouthful of tea and blew his nose before he could continue. 'I touched the edge, and it felt like an arm, at the elbow. I know you're not supposed to interfere with a crime scene, so I rang for you lot.'

Thank goodness, Sara thought. *Otherwise, he might have opened it, and then God knows what might have happened.*

'That was a good choice, Mr Brown,' said Edwards.

'Is it . . .' the man's voice dropped to a barely audible whisper, 'murder?'

'Far too early to tell. It's a young man, and whatever has happened, someone will be missing him. Thank you for everything you've done. My DS here will take your details, then you and Goldy can get off home.'

Edwards finished his tea and stood up. Sara noticed there were chocolate marks around his mouth and patted her cheeks pointedly. The DI wiped at them with a paper napkin, then headed out to his car, where Bowen and Noble were waiting. Sara took Mr Brown's details.

'As you touched the wrapping,' Sara explained, 'I'm afraid we will need to take a DNA swab, just in case. Can someone pop round to your home later to do that? They can take your official statement at the same time.'

Brown agreed.

'We also need to keep this from the press or social media for the moment.'

'For the family.' Brown nodded and stood up. 'I understand.'

'Do you need any other help for now?'

He shook his head and patted his side to bring the dog out from under the table. Sara followed the forlorn-looking pair back to their vehicle. She could see several faces peering out of the café windows at them. This was quickly going to be public knowledge with all those curious café customers watching the CSI circus. They needed to identify this young man urgently.

CHAPTER 9

Lyndford Lodge was a large, detached Victorian house with a big, unkempt garden. It stood at the very top of Lyndford Road, where the cul-de-sac had a turning circle. It may have once been a rectory, or a rich man's house. A cracked plastic sign, which leaned drunkenly into the hedge, stated that this was a private young person's care home. Sophie's heart sank.

Cuts to regional budgets had left the local council unable to fund enough places in their own children's care homes, and a number of these privately run units had sprung up around Norfolk. They had a dire reputation. No one would dare to confirm it officially, but the young people placed in these units were usually the youngsters that no one wanted to take responsibility for or help.

Sophie walked across the weed-blighted gravel and rang the doorbell. It took several more rings before she heard someone inside trying to unlock the door. A tall young man in a baggy tracksuit, no more than eighteen years old, eventually opened it.

'Are you in charge here?' Sophie asked in her best school-teacher's voice.

The young man grinned and shook his head. 'That would be Matt.'

'Who's Matt?'

'He's the housefather. He'll be in the kitchen. We don't normally use this door, so he won't have heard you.'

'I'm one of Callum Young's teachers, from the Academy.'

'And?' The young man shrugged his indifference.

'He's not been in school today.'

She racked her brains to remember if this was unusual, whether Callum was often missing, but couldn't dredge up the information. On bad days, Sophie could barely distinguish one class from another. Once, short on wraps, she had caught herself teaching *Animal Farm* to the wrong year group. The pupils had said nothing, as she was showing them a DVD of the cartoon version. They'd just sat back and let her, laughing at her as they left and Sophie had realised her mistake, watching them pack their copies of *Wuthering Heights* into their bags.

'I wondered if he was all right? Could I speak to Matt?'

The young man looked behind him in the corridor as a door slammed.

'Who's that?' A man approached from the back of the house. He might have been about thirty-five, Sophie guessed. His blonde hair was ruffled, three or four days of stubble covered his chin, and his eyes were the lightest blue she'd ever seen. He wore jeans and a warm shirt with a check pattern that Sophie recognised from the central aisle at Lidl.

'Some teacher, looking for Callum.'

'That's OK. I'll take it from here.' The young man turned away.

'Are you Matt?' Sophie asked.

'Yes, Matt Morgan, I'm the housefather here. What's this about?'

'Callum Young? He's a resident here, isn't he?'

The man nodded. 'What's he supposed to have done this time?'

'Nothing, so far as I am aware,' Sophie assured him. 'I was worried because he wasn't in class today.'

'That makes a change.' Matt frowned. 'Why do you want him?'

'I was concerned for him.' Sophie stumbled over her words. She could hardly say that Callum was her preferred supplier.

'His bike's not here,' said Matt. 'I assumed he'd gone to school.'

'Do you think he might have got knocked off or something?'

'I hope not.' Matt stood aside. 'You'd better come in.'

Sophie followed Matt through the hall. She passed a lounge with a TV, where a couple of lads were sprawled on a sofa watching something too young for them. One door with frosted glass bore the legend 'Office' on a silvered plate stuck up with electrical tape. Another door showed what must have once been a pleasant dining room with an old glass conservatory at the back. It contained a couple of table-tennis tables. The kitchen was sizeable, with a large wooden table in the middle, a random selection of chairs around it. A catering-sized cooker stood against one wall, but Sophie was unsurprised to see cartons from the various takeaways in the high street strewn across every surface.

Matt was filling the kettle. 'Fancy a coffee?' Sophie nodded. 'Sorry about the mess. Our housemother walked out a couple of weeks ago, and they haven't found a replacement yet.' He pointed at all the takeaway debris. 'I'm not much of a cook, and there's ten lads plus myself.'

'You take care of ten lads on your own?' Sophie asked.

'We had a cleaner come in,' said Matt. He found a couple of mugs and ran them under the tap. 'She left two months ago. The accountant said we'd have to wait for the next budget year for her to be replaced and that we should do it ourselves. You can guess the rest.'

'How on earth do you keep tabs on them all?'

'To be honest, I can't.' Matt made their drinks using a fresh milk carton he pulled from a carrier bag. Then he led her to the office, opening the door with his foot. She sat on one side of the desk while Matt climbed around a folded camp bed to his chair. A sleeping bag and pillow lay on top, with a washbag and towel balanced on top of them, like the tiers of a cake. A holdall of clothes stood by the wall.

'Do you sleep here?'

'No, I have my own room. So? Callum?'

'I was just worried about him.' Her fingers were beginning to twitch. She put the mug on the desk and held one hand firmly with the other to keep them still.

'Your admin lady usually calls if one of mine doesn't turn up,' said Matt. He looked casually at her hands. 'Never had a teacher here before.'

'I would have asked the social worker, but she'd left for the day. So I thought I'd pop round to see if he was OK.'

'Does the school allow that sort of thing?' Matt looked at her with suspicion. 'I would have thought it was against their protection policies.'

'It's just a casual visit,' stuttered Sophie. 'Nothing official.'

'How is he getting on at school?'

The sudden change of subject made Sophie shuffle uncomfortably in her seat. She took a mouthful of coffee before answering. 'He does all right for me. I can't speak for the other subjects.'

'What do you teach?'

'English. Literature, mostly.'

'It's the one thing that singles him out here. He likes to read. I think there's always hope if they like to read.'

Sophie nodded and silently wondered how long it was since she'd read a book for simple pleasure. Any book. Matt watched her, then seemed to make some decision.

'Well, drink up.' Matt pointed to her cooling coffee. 'Then, if you'll come with me, we'll check his bedroom. I'm not supposed to go in there alone. If he's not there, I'll have to start ringing round the hospitals.'

Matt unlocked a key cupboard and selected a key numbered '5'. Sophie followed him up the stairs. The bedrooms were on two floors.

Heading along the first-floor corridor, Matt said, 'I keep an emergency key for each bedroom. But it's a private space. Only the cleaner would normally go in if invited. Of course, that hasn't been happening recently, so I apologise in advance for the state of the room. You know what teenagers can be like.'

He unlocked the door and swung it wide. The curtains were closed, and the room was gloomy. Matt turned on the light, walked to the window and opened the curtains. Contrary to Matt's warning, the room was tidy. The bed had been made, Callum's school uniform was hanging up in the wardrobe, and a few dirty clothes waited in a basket to be washed. A plastic tub filled with bike tools stood next to the bedside table, where a pile of library books showed a taste for fantasy fiction. In fact, it looked like the room of a model resident, except for the desk by the wall.

A reading lamp lit the surface of the desk. A notebook lay open, a pen holding down pages, which showed columns of figures and carefully written notes. To the left of the book, a box lined in purple velvet stood open, a pair of old-fashioned miniature scales nestling in the fabric. To the right, a row of at least forty wraps lay carefully regimented. Sophie recognised them immediately. Matt crossed to the desk and looked over the items.

'Fuck,' he said.

CHAPTER 10

Danni had obediently taken her shower, washed her hair and even cleaned her teeth. Her stomach rumbled — it must have been after her lunchtime. To her surprise, Mrs Strong had put out a fashionable-looking grey tracksuit, pale lemon T-shirt and clean underwear. They were a decent fit, too, Danni realised as she pulled them on. Danni was a slim size ten, and short at five foot two. The sort of clothes she could afford often swamped her. A pair of lightweight towelling slippers stood waiting, the kind with thin fabric soles that would make them difficult to use outside. She was finishing with the hairdryer when she saw in the mirror the bedroom door open.

'Good girl.' Mrs Strong looked Danni over, then nodded her approval. 'You'll do. Come on.'

Danni followed the housekeeper along the landing. She had never been inside a house like this in her life. Paintings hung on every wall. Side tables held giant vases of flowers and antique statues. The carpet was deep and soft, a pleasure to walk on. The walls and carpet were cream or white, but there wasn't a mark or trace of dirt anywhere. They went down the stairs to the hallway, which was so large, Danni suspected that her flat could easily fit inside it.

Striker was seated on a chair near the door, his arms folded. He watched them without comment as Mrs Strong knocked at a door and waited. A voice invited them in.

The room was filled with 1930s art deco furniture and lamps. Lisa London sat on a wide brown leather sofa, and a glass coffee table stood in front of her. A tray with a striking yellow-and-black china tea service rested on it. She was leafing through a large Filofax, which bulged with paper notes stuffed between the pages. London glanced up at Danni, then pointed a manicured finger at an armchair opposite.

'Sit.'

'Would you like some fresh tea, madam?' asked Mrs Strong.

'Thank you, and a brew for the girl.'

Mrs Strong collected the tray and left them alone. London continued to look at her notes and ignored Danni. Unsure what to do, Danni sat tentatively on the armchair, her feet planted firmly in case she had to rise in a hurry. For some reason, it felt clumsy to sit that way. Something about the room, the wealth it displayed, suggested to Danni that she ought to be more elegant — although the only thing she knew about being graceful came from watching period dramas on the television. One thing daytime television had given her was a good knowledge of antiques, and she knew art deco when she saw it. There was a collection of Clarice Cliff pottery in a tall display cabinet. They were such sunny items that despite herself, Danni smiled.

'Something funny?' asked London.

'Oh, n-no,' Danni stammered. She pointed cautiously to the case. 'I just saw those. I've never seen any for real.'

'You know what they are?'

Danni nodded, her tongue stuck to the roof of her mouth. 'Well?'

'Clarice Cliff. The auctioneer's friend.' Danni looked down at her lap. 'Not worth as much now as they were five years ago, but still popular.'

London snorted with laughter. 'You can have a closer look if you like. No touching.'

Danni went over to the cabinet and gazed at the collection until Mrs Strong returned with the tea tray. She heard the housekeeper leave and London move to stand behind her.

'Do you know the patterns?' she asked.

Danni named the various designs: '"Red Autumn", "Bizarre", "Crocus", "Appliqué".' She faltered at a tall teapot, with sugar bowl and jug.

London filled in the detail. 'That's called "Ravel". It's very rare.'

They returned to their seats. London's striking tea service had been refreshed with new contents, while Danni's tea was in a cheap mug. She spooned in sugar, aware that the other woman was watching her closely.

'You learned that from watching TV?'

Danni nodded.

'Seems you might have a brain on board, after all. Unlike Johnny-boy.'

Danni waited, silently agreeing about Johnny, while London poured her own tea with a ritual-like grace. When she was finally satisfied, London leaned back on the sofa and looked at Danni again. 'You are going to do something for me. Take some items on a train trip.'

Danni flinched. She had heard about girls like herself being used as mules, transporting packets of high-value drugs between dealers. Sometimes they didn't come back. Thank God she wasn't on her period. Suddenly her mug of tea seemed to be burning her hand.

'You are going to a place called Norwich,' continued London. 'Heard of it?'

Danni shrugged. 'Sort of.'

'Never mind. It's not that far. Striker will take you to Liverpool Street in the morning. You will carry three packages. Mrs Strong will bring them to you.'

Danni's mind was racing. This was going to be her life from now on, and it wasn't even her fault. It was stupid Johnny's fault. But why would London bother with her like this if Danni was just a mule? Surely that was dealt with further down the chain?

'When you reach Norwich, someone will meet you. They will take you to a safe house, where you will hand over the goods.' London paused to sip her tea and stared hard at Danni. 'You will also take a message. Someone will come to you to collect this message. If you do this well, if you use these brains you appear to have, then I might find better uses for you than being a courier. Do you understand?'

'Yes, Miss London.'

'For fuck's sake.' London sighed. 'No names. Don't be so stupid. How old are you?'

'Twenty-five,' lied Danni.

'Then concentrate, and you may get to your next birthday. If you get it wrong, Striker will find you and deal with you. Is everything clear?'

Danni nodded. London called for Mrs Strong, who had evidently been waiting outside the door. Danni gingerly carried her mug of tea with her, as the housekeeper took her back upstairs to the bedroom. Once there, Danni saw that a remote control had appeared on the table near a television. A plate of sandwiches stood with it.

'Amuse yourself,' said Mrs Strong. 'I'll be back later with your evening meal and the necessary items. Don't touch, steal or break anything.'

Then she left, closing the door shut behind her. The key turned in the lock once more.

CHAPTER 11

The team regrouped at the office. Aggie made sure the coffee pot was full and the cake tin standing ready. Sara had taken a picture of the dead boy's face, which she fed into the computer and printed off. Bowen was cleaning the whiteboard of all traces of their current outstanding jobs, while Noble was stacking old files on a spare desk. DI Edwards pulled the still-damp picture of the boy out of the printer and pinned it up.

'Right, let's get cracking,' he said. 'What can we work out so far?'

'Teenager,' said Bowen. He settled behind his desk and bit into a piece of Aggie's cake. 'Died sometime last night. He's got that bash on the head.'

'Likely circumstances?'

'Cottaging?'

'Do people still do that?' asked Sara. It seemed such an old-fashioned term to her.

'They do at that place.' Bowen nodded. 'Has a reputation for it. Pretty young lad like that, I wouldn't be surprised.'

'Other suggestions?'

'He might not have been killed there at all,' said Sara. 'He was only wearing underpants. Even the toms keep their clothes on when they're working in car parks like that.'

'True,' Edwards agreed. 'It's not good weather for naked outdoor sex, so killed elsewhere and dumped? Wrapping him up would suggest that.'

'Sir?' The team turned to look at DC Noble. His face was bright red. Sara felt sorry for him, but if the subject matter was embarrassing him, he was going to have to toughen up. Edwards nodded to him. 'Would he be on the database? If he's selling sex for cash, he might have a record.'

'You never know. We'll have to wait for the DNA or fingerprints to identify him that way. Good.'

Noble ducked his head in embarrassment at Edwards's approval, which made Sara wonder if he was developing a man crush on his new boss.

'Aggie, check the mispers,' Edwards continued. 'If he's from a nice home, they will already have notified us. Mike, see if by some miracle the CCTV cameras are working up there. Sara, you can organise someone to take our dog walker's elimination sample. Ian, make a list of the burglaries we were looking at, just in case we have time to go back to them later.'

Bowen picked up the phone to harass the district council CCTV team, while Sara went to the stores and signed out a DNA test kit for Mr Brown. By the time she returned, Aggie was pointing excitedly at her computer screen.

'This might be interesting,' she called. 'New report, which the drugs team have picked up already. Teenage boy missing from a care home in Marlham. Housefather rang in to say he'd gone missing, and when they had opened his bedroom, there were wraps of coke on his desk.'

'Bingo! Money on it,' said Edwards. 'Right. Mike, you take Ian and sort out this DNA sample and witness statement. Sara, you're with me, and bring that picture.'

They took the same journey they had taken during the murder investigation in August. Round the bypass, out through Wroxham and on to Marlham. This time, Edwards drove into the town. They skirted the small high street and around the back of a large church until they found the right residential road. It was a long cul-de-sac, with detached and semi-detached houses on either side. One of those 1970s speculative developments that seemed to be a feature of small towns and villages, it had little charm but was respectable and quiet. The care home stood at the top of the road, behind an unkempt hedge. They knew they'd reached the right place, as three police cars were parked in the drive and a SOCO van on the road outside.

'Drugs always come mob-handed,' said Edwards. He parked the car, and they headed for the house.

'Who's in charge here?' he asked the uniformed officer on the exclusion tape, as he flipped open his warrant card.

'DI Powell, sir,' said the officer. He pointed to the front door, and they headed inside.

'That's a shame,' muttered Edwards to Sara. 'Powell can be a bit difficult. I'd hoped it would be Ellie.' He opened his mouth as if to speak, then stopped.

'Sir?'

'How did you describe Mike once?

'Unreconstructed?' Sara remembered her first day on the team vividly. 'A dinosaur?'

'Yeah, well, Powell is one of those.'

DI Powell stood in the hallway of the home, directing his team's efforts. The stairway was blocked off with more exclusion tape. Sara could hear low voices upstairs. Through an open door, she could see a group of young men hovering in what seemed to be a lounge of some sort. Another door was closed, voices murmuring behind it. In the doorway to a third room, a man stood with his arms folded watching the proceedings with obvious displeasure. Edwards and Powell exchanged curt greetings.

'What brings you here?' asked Powell.

'The same thing as you, I suspect,' replied Edwards. 'Just from a different angle. What have you got so far?'

'SOCOs are checking out the boy's room.' Powell gestured to the stairs. 'We're taking initial statements from all the residents about what they know. Had to wait for a social worker to turn up before we could start that.'

'Are the boys all under eighteen?'

'Apart from one and the staff.' Powell glanced at the man with the folded arms with barely concealed contempt.

'The missing boy?'

Powell checked his notepad. 'Callum Young. Been here for about twelve months. But if you ask me, the place is a bloody hotbed.'

'Of what in particular?'

'Just about anything.' Powell's tone was smug.

'Has the young man been found?'

'No,' said Powell. 'Not seen since last night. Why?'

'We may know where he is. Who's the housefather?'

The man standing in the doorway unfolded his arms and moved forward. 'That's me. Matt Morgan. And I'll say the same to you as I've told him.' He jabbed a finger in the direction of DI Powell. 'You can look in the boy's bedroom and his workshop. You can use the homework room for interviews. But I do not give you permission to look anywhere else. No other common or resident's room. None.'

Edwards moved closer to introduce himself and Sara quietly. 'We're a different team to DI Powell. Can we speak in private?'

'Will it take long?' asked Matt. He looked towards the closed door. 'I'm not happy about leaving the lads without my support with all this going on.'

'I think it would be better in private,' said Edwards. Matt led them with a show of reluctance into his office, closed the door behind them, and climbed round to his own side of the desk.

'What do you want to accuse them all of now?' Matt stood with his arms folded. 'They're all on the at-risk spectrum in some way or other, and your colleagues only seem interested in their assumed drug-dealing cartel. I can't begin to explain how much damage that's causing.'

'We're here about the missing young man, Callum Young. Do you think you can identify him from a picture?'

'You actually want to help find him? That would make an interesting change.'

'I'm sorry to advise you that this morning a body of a young man was discovered, near Fakenham.' The DI turned to Sara, who took out the picture. 'This photo is of the young man in question and is, therefore, post-mortem.'

Edwards lay the photo on the office desk and waited until Matt picked it up, before continuing. 'We don't wish to upset you any further. These pictures can be difficult. What do you think?'

Matt stood rigidly. Only his eyes moved as he scanned the boy's face. Sara saw tears begin to form until he shook his head and let out a huge sigh. 'Yes, that's Callum. Poor soul.'

'Thank you, Mr Morgan,' said Sara. 'It must be very distressing for you.'

'Call me Matt.' He suddenly sat in his chair, as if all the air had gone out of his body. 'I let him down. I do my best for them. All of them. But there are ten boys, and I'm pretty much on my own at the moment.'

'I'm sure you do everything you can,' said Edwards. 'You say they are all at risk in some way?'

'Absent parents, abusive families, damaging care homes, lack of supervision, no boundaries.' Matt reeled off the list as if he was used to reciting it, without expecting there to be any sympathy at the end of it. 'Budget cuts, lack of staff, bunking off school, getting into the wrong company.'

'Can you tell us about Callum specifically?'

'Of course.' Matt gestured to the other chairs in the room. Edwards and Sara sat, while he got up to climb round the folded camp bed. Sara saw that there was a large holdall in another corner, clothes bulging out of the top. Matt pulled a file from the cabinet and returned to his seat.

'Callum Young.' He opened the thick green folder. 'Aged fifteen. He has been in care since he was seven. Father unknown, mother was an addict. Callum spent several years in and out of foster or care homes, in between bouts of living with his mum when she was clean. Unfortunately, it was always temporary, she would relapse, and Callum would go back into care. She died when he was eleven, and then he came permanently into care. Not much hope of adoption. Wrong age, already starting to have attitude. After he had been moved around and got himself excluded from a couple of schools, the council homes got fed up of him. That's when they get shipped out to us — the hopeless cases. Then I have to try and give them some hope. Here, have a look.'

Matt pushed the green folder across the desk to Sara.

'When did you notice him missing?' asked Edwards.

'He had his tea as usual last night. I thought he'd gone to his room. We're not supposed to go into their rooms without permission. It's to safeguard their privacy. He didn't show for breakfast, which isn't unusual. I knocked on his door, got no reply. Then I had to go out.'

'Where to?'

'Group staff meeting in Norwich,' said Matt. 'When I got back, there was this teacher from the high school looking for him. I was surprised she was here — they don't usually bother either.'

'Can you give me her name and address?' asked Sara.

'Sophie Bailey. You'd have to ask the school for her address.'

'Did she give a reason why she came?'

'Just said she was worried he'd missed her class. Anyway, we opened the room together, so we had witnesses in case Callum complained. You know the score. We found the stuff on his desk, his bed was cold and, when I checked, his bike was missing as well.'

'Bike?'

'Yeah, it was his prized possession. An off-road Boardman. He worked at a Saturday job for months to raise the money for a second-hand one. He adored it. Often went out in the evenings on it, and I didn't see any harm in that.'

'And it's definitely missing?'

'Yes, I'm sure. He was very particular about locking it up. The chains are still there in the workshop out in the back yard, but the bike isn't.'

'I don't suppose you have a picture of the bike, do you? We need to know where it's got to.'

'I should have one in the kitchen. This way.'

Two of the resident young men were sitting at the table. Matt shooed them out, saying he'd be with them in a few minutes. A large corkboard occupied one of the walls. There were the usual notices and certificates pinned up on one half, but the other half was covered in photos. At the top of this side someone, presumably Matt, had pinned a little sign saying, *'Congratulations on all your achievements.'*

'I started this a few months back,' said Matt. 'Trying to give them something to be proud of, whatever that might be. School test passes, apprenticeships, days out, relative visits. Anything that might help. Callum was so proud of that bike.'

Matt unpinned a snap, which he handed to Sara. Their young victim stood holding a bike. It had a silver frame, dark handlebars, chunky tyres and a racing-style saddle. The word 'Boardman' was flashed on the downtube, blocky black letters standing out on the silver.

'May we take this?' Sara asked.

'Of course.' Matt nodded as he wrapped his arms around his chest as though he was trying to comfort himself. 'Anything to help. I'll show you where he kept it.'

They followed him into a yard. There were a couple of old brick outhouses and a grassed area, with some mini football nets. Matt fished out a key from his pocket and unlocked the smaller of the two buildings. It was tiny, with barely enough room for the small metal workbench that stood along one wall and the space to stand in front of it. There was a rack of tools above the bench, each item neatly put away in a designated space. A pair of strong chains with locks dangled, one from each leg of the table.

'This was his space, to be honest. I might borrow the odd tool, but it was Callum's workshop. He used it to do stuff to his bike and to help the other lads with their cars or mopeds and whatnot. He was clever with his hands. I hoped he might train to be a bike or car mechanic.' He shook his head again.

He really cares for these kids, Sara thought. She admired him for it.

'Thank you for all your help, Matt,' said Edwards. 'I think we should leave this now, and let's get the SOCOs in to have a look. You never know what they might find that could help us.'

As they headed back to the kitchen, one of the teenage residents came bounding out of the back door, his face full of glee.

'Is it true, Matt? Has Callum really been murdered?'

CHAPTER 12

The rest of the school day had passed without incident. Sophie wasn't due to run the after-school remedial reading group until tomorrow, so she managed to get away not long after the kids. Opening the door to her flat, she realised that the air stank of rotting food and dirty clothes and her cheeks burned with shame. Callum's bedroom at Lyndford Lodge was much tidier than this place. She used the little energy she had to tidy up, put on a load of washing and make a short shopping list. There wasn't much furniture, and all of it was second-hand. Her father would be appalled if he saw the state of the place.

Raising her chin with determination, she grabbed a couple of bags and set off down the small high street, checking out the charity shop windows. Several of them offered duvet covers with pillowcases or wraps and throws. It wouldn't take much to make the flat feel more homely. Looking up and down the street for pupils, Sophie went into the shop next to the post office, hoping no one had noticed her. She selected a worn but pretty set of bed linen, a couple of embroidered cushions and a granny-square crocheted blanket in bright colours, and paid the volunteer at the till. Stuffing them into her bag, Sophie made her way to the supermarket to shop for food. She needed to eat more and take less charlie.

Her burst of positivity began to fade as she walked back to the flat. Once inside, it vanished. Sophie dropped her bags of shopping on the floor. She sat on the rickety sofa and slumped on the dirt-stained cushions. In seconds she was sound asleep.

It was completely dark when the doorbell to the flat buzzed insistently. Sitting up with a start and glancing at her mobile, she saw it was after 6 p.m. She went to her front door and pressed the intercom.

'Who is it?' Her head was swimming, and her neck was aching from lying in a stupid position on the sofa.

'Police, Miss Bailey.' It was a female voice. Sophie felt a moment of panic. 'May we come in?'

'What for?' Sophie asked. Then she realised that teachers shouldn't have anything to hide, didn't need to be suspicious. They were pillars of the community, supposedly. 'Sorry. You woke me up, and I'm not quite with it. Yes, of course, come in.'

Sophie buzzed the lock release and quickly carried her shopping bags through to the kitchen. When she opened the front door, two police officers stood waiting.

There was no mistaking what they were, even without their uniforms. The woman was so tall that Sophie gaped for a moment. She didn't consider herself to be at all racist but was nonetheless a little surprised. In her experience, there were hardly any officers who weren't white, either here or at home in Sussex. *Teachers should be on board with diversity,* Sophie reminded herself, pulling her mouth shut. The woman frowned, and Sophie knew she had been caught out. The second officer was a middle-aged man. He was hanging back, allowing the woman to do the talking.

'Miss Sophie Bailey?'

'Yes?'

'I'm DS Hirst, and this is DI Edwards.' The woman gestured to the man behind her. They both showed their warrant cards. 'Do you mind if we come in?'

'Not at all.' Sophie held open the door, and the pair walked into the living room. She saw the man glance at the woman in surprise. Perhaps it wasn't the kind of place they were expecting a teacher to live. She felt the need to defend herself. 'I've not been here long. It's my first place since I left uni. Please sit down.'

DS Hirst sat on the sofa. The DI stood at the window, leaning on the ledge, his back to the street. Sophie hadn't drawn the curtains and now realised that he would be visible to everyone who walked past.

'We've come about Callum Young,' said DS Hirst. 'We understand you were at Lyndford Lodge today when the housefather discovered he was missing.'

'Yes, that's right.' Sophie couldn't help letting out a sigh of relief. She sniffed several times, before reaching for a tissue from the box on the table.

DS Hirst looked surprised. 'What made you go up to the Lodge? It's not the usual practice, is it?'

'No, I suppose not. I was worried because he usually makes my class.' Sophie felt on safer ground discussing her students. 'When we checked his room, it looked as if he hadn't been there all night.'

'What made you think that?' asked the DI.

'He'd done some homework for my class. It was lying on his bed, next to his school rucksack. I suppose I thought that he'd done that last night.'

'You like the lad?'

'He can be a handful. Bit cocky, I suppose. Other than that, he's all right.'

The DS looked at the DI and then back to Sophie. 'I'm sorry to tell you, Miss Bailey, but we believe we have found Callum, and it's not good news.'

Sophie's mobile beeped. She picked it up to turn it off. Glancing at the screen, she saw a text from Gary.

Why is there a pig in your flat?

The knowledge that Gary was outside, watching them, made Sophie's panic return. Her voice shook as she apologised for the interruption. 'I just need to deal with this.'

She sent a text to Gary — *About a pupil. Don't come in.* — then apologised again and asked, 'What news?'

'Early this morning, the body of a young man was found near Fakenham,' DS Hirst explained. 'We have good reason to believe it to be Callum Young.'

'Dead?' Sophie's eyes widened. 'How?'

'We're waiting for the post-mortem results.'

'Why Fakenham?'

'Did you know much about Callum?' the DI asked. 'Did he have any reason to be out there?'

'I didn't know him that well.'

'Then what made you go looking for him?'

Sophie fought for words that wouldn't incriminate her or reveal her real need to find Callum. 'Look, kids round here don't have much ambition. It's not like a city school.'

'I still don't understand.'

'Most of them don't want to carry on in education. They don't value it. Can't wait to leave. For the most part, they don't believe in themselves, and only a few will work hard. If someone shows an interest in my subject, they stand out to me. I was surprised when he missed the one lesson I knew he enjoyed. I hadn't realised where he lived, and once I knew that I was even more concerned. Kids like Callum have it much worse than those with some family support.'

Sophie's phone pinged again. *Get rid of them.*

'I'm not sure how much more I can help you,' she said. Gary was getting impatient, and she was going to need some gear.

'If you wouldn't mind, we'll need a statement about opening the room,' said the DS. 'I can arrange for someone to come and do that here, or you could pop into Wroxham Police Station to do it.'

'I could go there later in the week.' Sophie stood up. Her legs wobbled beneath her. 'If that's OK?'

'That would be fine,' said the DI. 'Thanks for your time.'

Sophie thought the DS seemed reluctant to leave but still rose to follow her boss. As they left the flat, she shut the door and sent Gary a text.

Wait. They're going. You coming in?

She drew the living room curtains, checking that the officers left the block and headed to their car. There was no sign of Gary, and she wondered where he was hiding. She slumped on to the sofa and waited. Minutes passed. Suddenly her bell rang again.

CHAPTER 13

It was late when Sara headed home. She called in at the fish and chip restaurant by the green a couple of minutes from her flat. If a chippie could be fashionable, the clever couple who ran this one had managed to create the most hipster chippie in the universe. Sara joined the takeaway queue that stretched down the street outside, grateful for her warm coat. She was hungry and checked out the extensive menu on the blackboards behind the counter, settling on simple cod and chips. She was climbing to her top-floor home when the door to the flat below opened.

'Bring me any?' asked Chris.

'Sorry, no. I thought you'd be rehearsing.'

'No. I died in a fight last night. Shall I come up and make you a cuppa?'

'You actually have a free evening?' Sara realised that her tone sounded sarcastic and dialled it back. 'Some company would be nice, and I might let you have a chip or two.'

She didn't bother with a plate, eating her supper directly from the packet while Chris fussed in her kitchen. She wasn't surprised to see him bring in a tray with a selection of cakes from his café, along with the mugs.

'I'm going to be the size of a house,' said Sara.

'Let me help you with that, then.' Chris pointed to the chips and selected a handful. 'Good day? Or boring?'

'Neither,' replied Sara. 'Dog walker found a young man's body this morning. Murdered, probably. We traced him to an academy in Marlham. Poor bugger lived in one of those private young people's homes. So not boring. But not good either.'

'That's not far from Happisburgh,' said Chris. 'I think I know Marlham. Has one of those big holiday boatyards.'

'What I don't get is why the body ended up out near Fakenham.'

'That must be at least twenty miles.'

'Indeed. Speaking of Happisburgh—' Sara got up and brought the envelope she had received from her solicitor — 'they have finally got probate on my dad's cottage.'

She pulled out the letter and handed it to Chris, then sat down next to him.

'You feeling OK about that?'

'Not sure.'

'Do you think that you'll move out there?' Chris sounded wary.

'I don't know,' said Sara. 'I haven't decided.'

'It's quite a distance. Difficult to commute, I'd say.'

'Maybe.'

'It would be much better to sell it and stay in the city, surely?'

Sara looked at his face, it was rigid with no emotions showing. *Better for who?* she thought. 'I'm going to have to go up there sometime soon and decide what I'm going to do.'

'I'll come with you,' offered Chris. 'If you want me to.'

'I think I'd like that. Maybe at the weekend, if you don't have a rehearsal.'

'Nope. My next one is Monday evening. We could go on Sunday. Max is due to cover the coffee shop for me.'

'That would be great, if I get Sunday off.' Sara chose a piece of cake and settled back to enjoy a few minutes of peace.

'I'm free Saturday evening as well. How about we have a pre-Christmas meal? It might be my last chance until the new year. The café will be busy.'

'That sounds a nice idea. You choose the place.' Time was going to be precious for both of them over the next few weeks. The television didn't hold her interest and, brushing cake crumbs from her blouse, she gazed out of the French windows. A glow shone up from the seasonal decorations in the street below, gently alternating colours.

The rhythm of life in Norfolk was very different from London, and it all seemed so much more personal when the team were only dealing with one or two of these serious enquiries a year. Sometimes she missed the bustle of the capital. She thought of London at Christmas, feeling a pang of nostalgia. The largest shops would be competing with gorgeous window displays and her favourite Regent Street lights, the giant angels, swinging above the traffic.

They did their best here. The council did a nice line in tasteful decorations strung in the trees and a tunnel of lights that drew admiring shoppers into the city centre. A raft of independent shops gave their windows a glittering makeover, the restaurants displayed party menus and the Theatre Royal advertised its pantomime on bus stops and billboards. Moving to the countryside would be even quieter, so was it the best thing for her to do?

Sara only realised that her mind had drifted when her mobile rang, and the sound made her jump. To her surprise, the screen said the caller was Javed, her stepfather. She pulled herself off the sofa to answer it. As they exchanged greetings, Sara let herself out on to the small balcony. Through the window, she could see Chris take the tray back to the kitchen.

'How are things with you?' asked Javed.

'Good, thanks. We've just had a big case come in this morning. It's going to be busy for a while.'

'That's a shame.'

'Why?'

'Could you come down for a day or two?'

'I hadn't any plans. Was there a reason you wanted me to visit?'

'Your mum,' said Javed. 'She misses you.'

'How would I know? She hasn't spoken to me for months.' Not since Sara had tried to persuade Tegan to attend the funeral and they'd had another fierce argument.

'You haven't rung her either.'

'I got the impression it wouldn't be welcome.'

'Well, she needs you right now, even if she doesn't say so.'

'What do you mean? Javed?' There was silence at the other end of the phone. Sara could hear her stepfather breathing. 'Does she know you've called me?'

'No,' he admitted. 'She would be angry if she found out. But it's important. You ought to come and see her.'

'Why? Something's wrong. Is Mum ill?'

'Not sure.' Javed's voice wobbled in the way that Sara knew it did when he was crying. 'She found a lump. In her breast.'

CHAPTER 14

Mrs Strong roused her early. It was dark outside, and Danni felt muzzy through lack of sleep. The parcels she was going to deliver were in a tiny pink backpack that Mrs Strong had brought the previous evening. It was the sort of bag you could buy in any of the cheap shops on Oxford Street.

'You hide them where you like,' the housekeeper had said. She'd shown Danni three packages, had picked up the slimmest one. 'This one's a fanny pack. Stick it up you if you want.'

As Danni sat on the edge of the bed, the bag lay on the floor next to her feet. She knew that if she got caught with the packets of coke on her, then London would deny all knowledge or connection and it would be Danni that got done for dealing. Her holdall had been returned, and the clothes inside were washed and ironed.

'You've got fifteen minutes,' said Mrs Strong. She put a mug of tea and a croissant on the dressing table, locking the door again as she left.

Danni had a five-minute shower and pulled on her clothes. Swigging the tea to force down the food, she looked at the slim packet. The other two were square and chunky. There was no way she could push them in her orifices, though she could strap them under her clothes. Except what difference would that make? It didn't matter if they were in the bag or strapped to her waist with the electrical tape Mrs Strong had given her. Taking another mouthful of tea, she tried to think of the best way to protect herself if the police showed any interest.

In her favour was the fact that she was young, white and female. Factors that made her less likely to be an automatic suspect. If she felt threatened, she could dump the handbag or throw it out of the train window. If she got to her destination without any gear at all, things would go badly for her. It was better to split the difference. She went to the bathroom and pulled down her trousers and knickers.

The fanny pack slipped up her like an overlarge tampon. Unlike the small ones she used for her real periods, this lay heavily against the wall of her vagina. She was conscious of it inside her as she moved experimentally around the bathroom. It felt like the beginnings of awful period pains. Danni opened the bathroom cabinet door and helped herself to a packet of paracetamol, gulping down a couple with the last of her tea to try and mask the ache. There were some small packets of tissues and the few scraps of make-up on the shelf. With lightning speed, she flashed eyeshadow over her lids and mascara on to her lashes. Then she stuffed the tissues, the pills and the make-up into the pink bag on top of the other two packs, trying to cover them up.

Doesn't Norwich have a university? Danni thought. Her best cover was if she looked normal, like a student perhaps. Pulling on her pink parka, she checked her look in the dressing mirror as Mrs Strong returned.

'This way.'

Danni followed the housekeeper downstairs to the lounge. Lamps glowed on side tables, giving the room a warm atmosphere. Lisa London was wearing a pair of silk pyjamas, with a hand-embroidered dressing gown. Her hair and make-up were just as immaculate as the previous afternoon. Her early morning casual outfit looked as elegant and expensive as her clothes from yesterday. Danni was envious of London's taste and budget. She clearly enjoyed the best things in life, something Danni would like to experience for herself someday. London checked Danni over and nodded her approval. Then she held out an envelope.

'This is the message,' said London. 'You do not tell anyone that you have this. You do not hand it to anyone except a young man called Gary. He looks like this.'

London motioned Danni forward and held up her state-of-the-art iPhone. Danni looked at the photo and tried to commit the face to memory. She took the envelope and put it into the pink backpack.

'Got that?'

'Yes.'

'You better have,' said London. 'Here.'

Mrs Strong appeared at Danni's side with a cheap mobile, which Danni knew would be a burner phone. She took it and put it into the backpack as well.

London moved so close that Danni could feel her breath on her face. She grabbed Danni by the wrist, forcing her hand up to chest level. Danni flinched. London smiled. Her manicured nails raised welts on Danni's skin.

'If you try to contact Johnny-boy on it, I will know. If you try to run away with the gear, I will find you. If you're a good girl, I will reward you.'

'I understand.'

London pushed a small purse into Danni's hand. 'For the journey. Treat yourself.'

London stepped back. Picking up the backpack, Mrs Strong hustled Danni into the hall and out of the front door. Striker was waiting, with her holdall in his hand. A little way down the street, a black cab's engine was idling.

They left through a small door on the electronic gates. 'Get in it,' he instructed. Danni climbed inside, and Striker followed. 'Liverpool Street.'

There wasn't much traffic about, and they soon reached the Westway. She took out the mobile and checked the time. 6 a.m. She opened the purse. It contained a small wedge of five- and ten-pound notes. Under the money was another small present. A small round object, about the size of a hazelnut, wrapped in crumpled silver foil. Danni didn't doubt that this was a nugget of crack, left there to tempt her and see what she would do with it. Well, she wasn't going to fall for that. She promised herself to get rid of it at the first opportunity.

A glance at Striker confirmed that he was silently watching her every move. Danni looked out of the window. Clutching the pink bag to her chest, Danni pulled herself into the corner, as far away from the large man as she could manage, and waited out the journey.

CHAPTER 15

Sara was lucky, and she knew it. Chris was a caring and supportive man, but she couldn't help feeling that he was becoming too possessive. She wasn't used to that from a boyfriend. Sara was still enjoying the freedom of having her own space that she had gained in moving up to Norfolk.

She showered and took Chris a mug of tea before she left for work. Plonking it down on the cabinet next to him, he rolled over and grumbled a little.

'It's always an early call when we have an important case,' said Sara.

'You going to be all right?'

'I think so.' She nodded. 'Javed said they haven't been to the doctors' yet, so I can't do anything for Mum until they go tomorrow.'

'I guess so.' Chris swung out of bed to sit up and pull her into his arms. 'Take care, you.'

'You too.'

As she drove to work, Sara tried to pull together her thoughts about their young victim. His life had been complicated, moving in and out of foster homes or living with a mother who kept returning to her habit. The housefather seemed to be a decent man trying to do his best for the youngsters in his care. At least Callum would have had some chance of stability there. But the drugs in his room seemed a betrayal of Matt's trust and encouragement. Why would he have done that?

The entire team gathered for morning orders.

'First on the agenda is finding the missing bike,' said DI Edwards. 'Aggie?'

'Silver Boardman, off-roader.' Aggie pinned a catalogue picture of the model on the incident board. Sara remembered that her son was a keen racing cyclist, so she knew about this kind of equipment. 'Expensive, even second-hand. In the high-end market for amateur weekend users, so the boy knew what he was doing when he saved up for it.'

'Could he have ridden out to Fakenham?'

'Oh yes, if he was keen. Even from Marlham.'

'Not without clothes on, though,' said Bowen. They smiled a little at that. 'Pathologist's report today?'

'Dr Taylor promised it by mid-morning,' said Edwards. 'Mike, I want you to go to the home with Ian and interview the lads there. Get the SOCOs to go over that little workshop, if they haven't already. Did you get that elimination swab?'

'Yes. I went yesterday afternoon. It's down with the lab,' said Noble. 'It was all a bit sad, actually.'

'How so?'

'His wife died a couple of years ago.' The young DC looked at the floor, not meeting the gazes turned towards him. 'There was this little shrine to her on the sideboard. You know, photos and flowers and a candle. The dog followed him everywhere, wouldn't let him out of sight.'

His face gives him away, Sara thought, watching him with a mixture of compassion and amusement. *He'll have to learn to hide his feelings better. I wonder how he'll cope at the home?*

'Aggie, I want you to start on the CCTV footage in Marlham. Start after school finished. Mike, did you get anything from the council for the car park?'

Bowen shook his head.

'I can chase them again,' Aggie promised, giving Bowen a wink.

'Check on the main road too. It's the A148, for God's sake, there should be cameras somewhere, and we have a rough time frame. Sara, we'll get out to the school. See if his mates there have any idea. We're going to have company, by the way.'

'Sir?' asked Sara.

'Drugs squad are involved as well,' said Edwards. He grinned. 'Luckily, we have a liaison officer from their team.'

'Ellie?' asked Bowen.

'Yes, DS James is being assigned to us for the duration of the investigation.'

The team dispersed to their various tasks. Sara collected Ellie from the Drugs squad office as they went to the car park. She looked more mannish than Sara was used to when they went out drinking. Her blonde hair was scrapped to the back of her head in a tight ponytail. Her clothes were all black; a pair of cargo pants with multiple pockets and a loose black waterproof jacket that disguised her figure. There was no mistaking that she was a police officer, it looked so much like uniform. Even her fingernails were trimmed really short.

'Glad to have you back with us,' she said. Ellie grimaced. 'Not good for you?'

'Yes, it's good to be back.' Ellie's voice sounded tight.

'But?'

'I wish he'd picked someone else, I suppose. Feel like I'm going round in circles.'

Ellie filled them in on the other team's findings as they drove to Marlham. Unsurprisingly, none of the youngsters at the home would admit to knowing that Callum had drugs in his room.

'We think he was dealing,' said Ellie. 'The wraps had all been perfectly weighed out, and he had a notebook that he kept his accounts in.'

'No names in it, I bet,' said Edwards.

'Of course not. Callum seems to have been doing this for at least six months. The dates in the ledger go back to the spring.

If his maths is good, and there's no reason to suspect the figures aren't correct, then he'd made a tidy packet. We haven't found either the cash or any bank or savings account details so far.'

'What about forensics?'

'There are traces of coke around his room. Some in his school bag, and on the homework file on the bed.'

'He was dealing at school?'

'Entirely possible.'

'What homework?' asked Sara.

'English literature,' said Ellie. 'Looked like he kept that one up to date.'

'Just that one?'

'We didn't find any others that looked as neat.'

'His teacher said Callum liked her class,' said Edwards. 'What did you think of her? Miss Bailey?'

'She seemed nervous to me, sir,' admitted Sara. 'I couldn't help but wonder what those texts were that she thought were so important. She suddenly seemed keen to get rid of us once they arrived.'

'Could be anything,' said Ellie. 'Maybe she's having an affair or something.'

'Perhaps. Who knows?' Edwards asked. 'Let's keep it in mind.'

The Academy was on the road behind Marlham's large church. Parents were dropping their kids off outside, some walking with buggies or younger children on foot, others in cars that lined the road on both sides, making it difficult to move. Pupils were streaming in the front gates as Edwards managed to park their car in a visitor space. The brick-built facade was imposing. Faux pillars, painted in white, flanked the entrance, and a large window stretched up to the roof-line on the second storey. A pair of panelled, heavy-looking wooden doors stood propped open. The architecture had a 1950s feel, which reminded Sara of her high school in London.

They followed the flow of pupils inside to a reception hatch. An older-looking man in a boiler suit was leaning on the ledge inside. Edwards flipped his warrant card.

'We've been expecting you,' the man said. 'I'm Geoff, the caretaker. Mr Hanson said you'd be here. If you could sign the visitors' book.'

The three dutifully signed themselves in, while the caretaker made out passes for them. 'Can't be too careful these days,' he said. 'I'll take you straight to the headmaster's office.'

CHAPTER 16

Sophie was having a good morning until the school secretary came into class and told her to go to the head's office immediately. This command caused a whispering around the Year Nines, which she tried to silence.

'Who's going to take the class?' Sophie asked.

The secretary shrugged. 'I'll send a prefect along.'

'Thank you.' Sophie turned to the pupils. 'Get on with reading your poems. If I hear one peep out of you, I'll set double homework.'

It was a hollow threat, and they all knew it. Half of these kids didn't do the required homework in the first place, so extra work was unlikely ever to be completed. They had the wit to stay quiet until Sophie got to the end of the corridor, then she heard the room erupt with noisy chatter. As she turned the corner, she passed the poor prefect who was going to try and contain the noise.

Her good mood had stemmed from last night's excesses with Gary. He was a handsome man, with short dark hair and a winning smile. Smartly dressed and well turned-out, he gave out an aura of being trustworthy. But Sophie knew that he couldn't be trusted. He was a dealer and not a very clever one at that. With her teacher's eye for intellect, she knew very well that Gary wasn't the sharpest knife in the box. She liked him, though love would be too strong a word. What Sophie liked most about Gary were the hits that he brought her, usually for free. Not only did he bring the gear she craved, but hippy-trippy stuff that made her feel amazing. Last night had been a case in point.

Gary had been suspicious and difficult about the detectives' visit.

'What do you mean "missing"?' he'd asked, his tone sharp. 'What boy?'

For some reason, Sophie had hesitated to tell Gary the full story. 'Some kid in Year Eleven. Run away, I suppose. It happens at that age.'

'Who?'

'A quiet lad from one of the villages.'

Her lie hadn't convinced Gary, she had been able to tell. He'd badgered her for the boy's name.

'I'm not allowed to talk about it.'

'Want some of this?' Gary had dangled a plastic bag full of wraps high in the air, laughing when she had been unable to reach it. Suddenly his face had soured. 'What's this bloody boy called?'

'Why do you want to know?' Sophie had countered. 'What's it to you?'

'Never mind,' Gary had snapped. Then he'd produced another bag with tablets in it. 'Shall we?'

Why did I lie about that? Sophie had wondered as they'd got stoned together. It had felt necessary. Perhaps she'd wanted to keep the two parts of her habit separate from each other.

She'd left Gary in bed when she'd come to school early this morning. There was a stack of new wraps, which she'd divided between her secret emergency stash at school and her handbag. She'd felt on top of the world, until this summons.

Sophie knew it wouldn't take much for her world to unravel. A neighbour might casually mention seeing Gary leaving her flat. Or a parent might have seen her giving money to Callum in the churchyard, and reported her. She suspected that Gary would already be on the police's radar. He was usually cautious when he came to see her, but once he got stoned, anything could happen, and his behaviour could be erratic at best.

She feared being called to the head's office as much now as when she was a pupil herself. With a racing heart, she knocked at the office door and went in as soon as the headmaster called. Her agitation increased when she saw the two detectives who had called on her last night sitting in the visitors' chairs. There was a third woman who was introduced as another police officer. To her horror, this one was from the Drugs squad. Sophie felt the colour rise up her neck.

'Miss Bailey,' said Mr Hanson. 'Thank you for coming along.'

'How can I help?'

'I understand that you have already spoken to the police in connection with this sad business with Callum Young.'

'Yes, Mr Hanson,' said Sophie. Relief flooded through her.

'You went to Lyndford Lodge yesterday?'

'Yes. I was worried when Callum didn't show up for my class, so I popped up in my lunch hour. Mr Morgan, the housefather, and I opened his room together.'

'I commend your sense of duty,' said Mr Hanson. Sophie couldn't be sure if he was being sarcastic or if he meant it as a compliment. 'Even if your actions went against school policy.'

'We wondered if you could help a little more,' said DS Hirst. 'Are there any pupils who might be friends with Callum, or who might have seen Callum after school the other evening?'

'One of the girls spoke to me about him. Andrea Green. Apart from that, he tends to hang around with Steven Lister at break time.'

'Can we speak to them?' asked the DS.

'You'll need a child protection officer with you,' said Mr Hanson.

'How old are these pupils?' The DI cut in.

'I'd have to check, but fifteen or sixteen,' said Sophie. 'They're all in Year Eleven.'

'Or a social worker, at least.' Mr Hanson wasn't going to let this one go. 'It ought to be their parents, of course.'

'It's Thursday,' said Sophie. 'Miss Mitchell, our attached social worker, will be here. If it's urgent.'

'A murder enquiry is usually considered urgent,' said the DI, he sounded impatient. 'Just a few simple questions about Callum's movements. He had a bike, and we need to trace it.'

'It's tricky,' said Mr Hanson. 'Besides, don't you think having all these people in the room with one teenager is a bit over the top?'

'DS Hirst can go along with your social worker if that's acceptable.'

'Oh, very well. But only a couple of questions. If you want any more, you'll have to go to their homes.'

'Fine,' said the DI. 'Perhaps you can furnish us with their home addresses, while DS Hirst speaks to them.'

Sophie found herself dismissed. The mid-morning break bell rang as she reached the classroom. The prefect fled through the door as she opened it, rolling his eyes at her. Sophie didn't bother to wonder why. The pupils buffeted around her, escaping with their bags, already eating whatever unhealthy snack they preferred that day.

She knew she was flying close to the wind. She had a dealer in her bed and one of her pupils had been supplying her with hits. Now she was involved in a murder investigation. It was stupid. Sophie needed to get her head around the implications of all this, and she needed caffeine for that. Grabbing her work bag, she escaped towards the staffroom.

CHAPTER 17

When they arrived at Liverpool Street, Striker allowed Danni to buy a frothy coffee so long as she brought him one too. He stood outside the coffee shop, keeping an eye on the concourse while she ordered. Danni watched his back as she waited for the drinks. Adding a small cake to the bag for herself on the journey, she returned meekly to Striker.

'I need the toilet,' she said. 'There's one over there.'

They walked along to a set of stairs that led underneath the street level of the station. Striker dropped her holdall on the floor and grabbed the bag with the drinks. He opened his jacket front just enough to reveal the bulge of his knife in the inside pocket.

'Three minutes,' he said. 'Then I come looking for you.'

Danni knew this was no idle threat. Striker was perfectly capable of marching into the ladies' toilets and kicking down the doors to the stalls until he found her. She nodded and trotted down the stairs.

The toilets smelled sour, as public toilets often do, though there weren't many customers this early. Danni walked as far down the double row of cubicles as she could go, selecting one at the end next to the wall. She locked it, hung the backpack on the door and fished out the purse. Extracting the silver foil nugget, she put it on the lid of the sanitary towel bin and closed it. It made a whirring noise, and then there was a click. She used the toilet and flushed it, before checking the bin a second time to ensure the crack had gone inside. Hitching on the backpack, Danni hurried out to the sinks, where she washed her hands more thoroughly than usual.

Striker grunted as she reappeared at the top of the stairs. 'Platform ten.'

Danni took the bag with the coffee and her holdall, then checked the huge overhead boards showing the departures. The 7.30 a.m. to Norwich, calling at Chelmsford, Colchester, Manningtree, Ipswich, Stowmarket and Diss. She'd never been to any of these places. The only time she had ever left London had been on a weekend outing to a hostel in Clacton that a foster family had arranged for her. The sea had fascinated Danni. Sometimes, she would secretly find a video online and listen to the sound of waves on a shore somewhere that she was unlikely ever to visit.

She followed Striker to the gate, where he produced a one-way ticket for her. With one hand, he held her by the arm, squeezing so hard that she could feel his fingers adding bruises to the flesh where London's nails had left her skin raw. With the other hand, he patted his jacket pocket. He snarled instructions into her ear, his voice low and his breath smelling of coffee. 'You'll be met in Norwich. If you get off and try to run, Johnny-boy will die, and then I will find you. Do as Miss London says if you want to survive.'

He lowered her arm and planted a kiss on her cheek as if he was some family member seeing her off on a trip. As he released his grip, Danni turned away, trying not to spill the drink, or drop her ticket or holdall. A hand on her back shoved her towards the platform.

With a glance back to the barrier where Striker stood watching her, she climbed inside the train and worked her way along until she found an empty seat next to a window. The train moved, slowly at first, and then with gathering speed, through Stratford to the suburbs. A couple of announcements crackled on the intercom, but she couldn't catch what was said. It didn't matter anyway.

Mile by mile, she watched in fascination as the countryside unfolded next to the track. They crossed a frighteningly wide river, stopped in small stations that seemed miles from anywhere. Her insides ached again, irritated by the fanny pack. She took two more of the painkillers with the dregs of the cold coffee.

Eventually, the guard announced that they were reaching Norwich. The train clattered over an old metal bridge and eased into the station. Danni followed the few remaining passengers out of the carriage. There was only one way off the platform. Deliberately waiting until she was at the end of the queue, she ambled out. The station had a high-covered waiting area, with coffee kiosks and shops. A large clock told her it was nearly 9.30 a.m.

She glanced around, unsure of what to do. There were several groups of people on the concourse — railway workers in uniform, office staff in smart clothes with briefcases, a family laden with suitcases. A transport police officer stood idly chatting with a woman behind the information desk. She edged away from him. More than ten anxious minutes passed before a man approached her.

'Danni!' he called, as if he had known her all his life. 'Great to see you. Come on. My car's in the front car park.'

She followed the man without a word. He kept chattering, talking nonsense about how glad they were to see her. The man was small, middle-aged and overweight. His voice gave off a hint of nervous desperation, and when they got outside, she understood why.

Mr Chatty led her to a small car, where a second man sat in the passenger seat. As she climbed into the back, Danni saw that this man had tattoos winding up both hands under the cuffs of his sleeves. His head was shaved, and bulged out of his shirt collar on top of muscles that made him look as if he had no neck at all. More inked patterns snaked from under his shirt and round the back of his collar.

I wouldn't want to be on the wrong side of him, she thought. She fastened her seat belt, but the muscled man didn't acknowledge her. Mr Chatty got in and started the car. With a frightened glance over his shoulder at Danni, he reversed out of the parking space.

The traffic seemed surprisingly heavy, as they worked their way along a road next to a river. On the far side of the water, a large church building dominated the skyline. A cathedral, Danni assumed, like the one in Westminster. The little car negotiated a series of traffic lights before turning out of the city and into a run-down housing estate. The place was a mixture of houses and small blocks of flats, and it reminded Danni of where she lived with Johnny.

Mr Chatty led the way up some stairs and along a corridor. Stopping at a front door, he looked at the other man, then unlocked it.

A push sent Danni stumbling over the doorstep. She fell on to the wooden floor beyond, the breath whooshing out of her lungs. Mr Chatty flew past her. He careered into the wall by the kitchen door and banged his head. He moaned as he slumped on to his knees, holding his face. Blood dripped between his fingers. The door slammed behind them, and Danni felt a small, cold, hard object push against her neck. It had to be a gun.

'Up, bitch,' said Muscleman. 'Give me the goods, or you'll both regret it.'

CHAPTER 18

It hadn't escaped Sara's notice that the young teacher, Sophie Bailey, had been worried at the sight of them in the head's office. It was the way she had tugged at the edge of her blouse, how the red rash of adrenaline had risen up her neck. Sara followed the social worker to a spare classroom, weaving her way between the hordes of pupils changing classes. Miss Mitchell dumped her, returning after a few minutes with cups of coffee and a smartly dressed teenage girl who she introduced as Andrea Green.

They sat down, while Sara helped herself to a drink. 'Tell the police officer what you told Miss Bailey.'

'About what?'

It wasn't quite the helpful start that Sara wanted. She smiled at the girl, who returned a hard stare. 'It's nothing to worry about. Has Miss Mitchell explained why we're here?'

'Callum?'

'Yes, it's about Callum. Do you know what's happening?'

'The head is calling a special assembly after the break,' the social worker interrupted. 'To tell the whole school the sad news.'

Sara glared at the woman, then returned her focus to the pupil. 'Andrea, can you tell me if you're friends with Callum?'

'Sort of,' Andrea answered with a dismissive half-nod.

'Do you see him out of school at all?'

'Sometimes. Callum usually goes out, though.'

'Can you be more specific than that?'

'He has this bike,' said Andrea. 'Very proud of it. Loves to go riding.'

'Did you see him on Tuesday evening?'

'Yeah, I think I probably did.'

'Which way did he go?'

'Always goes the same way. Down the cycle track to the showroom, then out towards Walton. Don't know after that.'

'Do you know what's happening?' asked Sara, her voice soft.

'Callum's missing, isn't he? It's all over the school.'

'I'm sorry, Andrea. Callum has passed away.'

Andrea held Sara's gaze for a few seconds, as if she were willing her to retract her words. Then the tears began to fall. 'I really liked him.'

Miss Mitchell gathered the girl up with a gentle word. 'Come on, pet, let's go to the meditation room. I'll find Steven Lister for you, Detective.'

Things have changed a lot since I was at school, Sara thought as the pair walked away. *Meditation room, indeed. All we had was a sin-bin.*

For once, Sara had a signal on her mobile, which was a blessing this distance from the city. She located the road for Lyndford Lodge. It wasn't far from there to the showroom that Andrea had mentioned, which, according to the map, sold agricultural machinery. The B-road it stood on ran as straight as a die towards the coast. To either side of it was a network of those tiny back lanes that ran everywhere in Norfolk, like the veins of the county. It even passed a turning for Happisburgh, where her cottage inheritance was, before reaching the coast at a village called Walton and turning west towards the various small seaside resorts that the county was famous for. There wouldn't be any traffic cameras on roads like that, but there were several villages to choose from as possible destinations.

Miss Mitchell reappeared with a lanky youth, who made it clear he didn't want to be there. He threw himself casually on to a chair, crossed his legs and folded his arms. He tried to form a superior smile, which looked more like a sneer. 'Yeah? What you want?'

Miss Mitchell sighed. 'This is Steven Lister. If anyone could be said to be a friend of Callum Young, then it's you, isn't it, Steven?'

'So what?'

'Thank you for agreeing to see me,' said Sara.

'No choice, have I?'

'All we're trying to do at this stage is to find Callum's bike.'

'Bloody thing,' said Steven. 'Always banging on about it.'

'I understand that he worked hard to buy it,' said Sara.

The annoying Miss Mitchell interrupted again. 'Steven and Callum had a Saturday job together, didn't you?'

'For a bit.' Steven conceded the point.

'Where was this?' asked Sara.

'Local garage, just off the high street.'

'Not anymore?'

'Nah,' said Steven. 'I got bored with it. Just ended up valeting cars. Callum did the good stuff.'

'You know Callum's missing?'

'Of course.' Steven's tone made it clear he knew everything and thought Sara was behind the news.

'As I said, his bike is missing too. We think if we can find it, then we might be able to trace his movements on Tuesday evening.'

'Good luck.'

'It's crucial. Did you see Callum or speak to him on Tuesday after school at all?'

'Nah.'

'Steven, do you know what's happened to Callum?'

'Bet he's run away.'

'Why would he do that?'

'Said he would, one day. That place he lives, not great, is it?'

'I imagine it's challenging,' said Sara. 'He spoke to you about his plans?'

'Not really.' The youth uncrossed his legs and widened them. Sara knew it was a challenge, that she'd better not glance at his crotch or the boy would make a fuss.

She fixed his eyes with her own. 'I think you're missing a special assembly at the moment, Steven.'

'Hate assembly, waste of time.'

'I can tell you what Mr Hanson is telling all your fellow pupils at the moment. Callum Young has been found dead.'

Steven sat bolt upright. His eyes skittered out of the window and back to Sara. 'Bloody hell. He really has been murdered?'

'We don't know yet. We need to find his bike, to trace his movements. Can you help us or not?'

Steven's foot tapped on the floor. He chewed his lip for a moment. 'All right. We were supposed to be playing football that night, but he never showed up. Went to see that weirdo mate of his, I assumed.'

'What mate?'

'I don't know.' Steven's voice grew louder. Miss Mitchell stood up to intervene, but Sara waved her away.

'Steven,' said Sara, 'this could be important. What mate? Where did this mate live?'

'I don't know,' wailed Steven. 'I really don't know. In one of the villages, but he didn't tell me which one. Said he was an older man, with money.'

CHAPTER 19

The team left the school and drove up to Lyndford Lodge, to see how Noble and Bowen were getting on. Matt Morgan was hovering in the kitchen, supplying drinks to favoured people who were still working in the building. In the back yard, a SOCO team were busy in the workshop that Callum had created from the small outbuilding. Through the kitchen window, Sara could see piles of tools and bike parts laid out in the yard. Matt poured the teas, and they sat at the kitchen table until Bowen appeared, with Noble trotting at his heels.

'We've spoken to four of the residents,' said Bowen.

'The rest are at school or college,' confirmed Matt. He handed over the mugs, then went back to the sink to fill the kettle again.

'When will they be back?' asked Edwards. Sara glanced at a clock on the wall. It was just after midday. 'A couple of them finish school at three. The rest have to get here from their colleges in North Walsham or Norwich, so it may be nearly five for them.'

'Can my officers see them today?'

'Sure. If you want to wait, that's OK with me.'

'How have you got on so far?' Edwards asked Bowen.

'Fine,' said Bowen. 'To be honest, I don't think the ones we've spoken to knew what Callum was up to.'

'He liked his privacy,' said Matt. 'Didn't do the whole "hanging out" thing in the common rooms like the others. He wasn't a socialiser.'

'Not a good mixer?' Edwards asked.

'Callum just liked his own space. Perhaps he'd never had much privacy before coming here. Didn't like the others going in his room, either.' Matt sighed. 'Anyway, now I know why he preferred to be in his room or the workshop.'

'Did he go out on his bike a lot?' Sara asked.

'Yes, he loved that. I thought it was a good thing to encourage. Kept him fit, got him out in the fresh air. Besides, he helped with mending stuff when anyone needed it. Even tried to fix the lawnmower when it packed up.'

'He had a real talent for mechanics?'

'Yes, that's why I hoped he would have a decent future. Once he started at that garage back in the summer, he seemed to have found his niche.'

There was a sound of wood being ripped apart. Matt watched out of the window with a frown. 'I wish they would take more care. Callum worked so hard to get that workshop together.'

Presumably, the SOCOs were also still searching in Callum's bedroom. Sara could hear footsteps overhead, which then descended the stairs. When the door opened, it was DI Powell.

He looked around the team at the kitchen table and shook his head. 'Got nothing better to do?'

DI Edwards pursed his lips. 'Murder is the primary crime,' he said. 'We get precedence, as you know.'

'And you get this evidence by sitting and drinking tea?' Powell smirked.

Edwards stood up. 'We get it by interviewing suspects and collecting information.'

Now there was metallic banging from the workshop. Matt turned away from the window and glared at DI Powell.

'Is all this necessary?' he demanded. 'You're destroying that young man's hard work.'

'He's not likely to know, is he?'

Matt puffed out his cheeks. 'You have no bloody shame.'

'We need to find out where the rest of the drugs are,' said Powell.

'There are no more drugs,' yelled Matt. 'How many times do I have to say this? My lads are good lads.' He marched out of the back door and headed to the workshop. 'Can't you be more careful?'

Powell hurried past Edwards to the back door.

'Ever a man of the people, aren't you?' Edwards said. 'If you treated people with some respect, you might find you get some back in return.'

'Bloody hell, he's trying to get in the workshop.' Powell stamped outside. They heard both men's voices rising. Edwards and Sara followed. Matt and DI Powell were almost nose to nose, the argument spiralling.

'We need to search the workshop thoroughly,' said Powell loudly.

'That doesn't mean you have to trash the place.' Matt's voice was even louder.

'DI Powell, a word, if you please.' Edwards spoke just loud enough to be heard. Powell swung to face him, as Edwards reached the pair. 'Have some professional decorum, man.'

Powell huffed but stepped away. Edwards had seniority. Sara hovered near the back door, glancing at the window, where Bowen stood smiling and enjoying watching the fuss. Noble's shocked face loomed behind Bowen like a ghost.

'Whatever we are looking for,' said Edwards, 'we shouldn't be making assumptions about what's going on. This isn't your standard drugs bust, DI Powell.'

'Sir?' One of the suited SOCOs came out of the work-shop door. 'I think you should both come and see this.'

Powell crowded Edwards in the doorway. Matt stayed where he was, looking unsure. Sara beckoned out the two DCs with a flick of her head.

'Are you sure?' she heard Powell ask. 'How much?'

Sara peered over Edwards's head, while he bent over the workshop floor. Underneath the workbench, there was a small hole, lined with a plastic box. A carefully cut section of floorboards, which must have formed a lid, lay on the bench. The SOCO had opened a blue metal cash box.

'It fits neatly into the hole,' said the SOCO. He pointed to a wad of notes that had been counted out into piles on the bench. 'All of this was inside it.'

'Are you sure you counted it correctly?' DI Edwards asked.

'We've both done it, came up with the same answer.' The second SOCO nodded in confirmation. 'Four thousand, three hundred and seventy pounds exactly.'

CHAPTER 20

'That's a lot of cash.' DI Edwards shook his head.

'Matt Morgan seemed stunned,' Sara said. She settled into the passenger seat.

Ellie was speaking on her mobile as she got into the back. They were heading back to the city in response to a call from Dr Taylor, who had let them know he was ready with his preliminary report.

'Where did he get that much from? Not his Saturday job, that's for sure,' said Edwards.

'Not from his dealing, either.' Ellie had finished her call and leaned forward between the front seats. 'That's what I was checking. The sums in his account book only add up to three and a half thousand. Not bad for six months' small-scale dealing, but not enough for our tin.'

'Therefore, he had another source. Do you think he stole it?'

'Or did he get it from this older man that Steven Lister mentioned?' Sara asked.

'An older man with money,' said Edwards. 'That's not much to go on, is it?'

'Having money doesn't necessarily mean they are rich,' said Sara. 'Just means they have enough to impress a teenager.

Aggie's checking with that showroom, to see if they have CCTV cameras. At least it might give us a direction of travel.'

DI Edwards had already asked for officers to search the fields and ditches beside the coast road for the missing bike.

'That friend of his seemed very on edge,' added Sara. 'Why would that be? Have the pair of them been up to something?'

'If Callum was dealing, was Steven Lister a client?' asked Ellie.

'Or a fellow dealer?' suggested Edwards. 'I think we might need a proper word with him soon, but let's find this damn bike first.'

They parked in the visitors' bays and went on to the mortuary by the staff entrance.

Dr Taylor was waiting for them. 'I managed to get him straightened out.' He was perched on a stool at his workstation at the far end of the mortuary. 'He's been dead long enough for the rigor mortis to begin to recede.'

'I take it there was nothing that would identify him directly?' asked Edwards.

Dr Taylor shook his head. 'I've done DNA swabs, and sent them away.'

'His housefather identified him from a photo. He's willing to come in to do the formal ID.'

'Let me know when,' said Taylor. He swung round on the stool to face them. 'Forensics have taken away the material he was wrapped in, but I'd hazard a strong guess that it was a groundsheet. The sort you might use for camping trips.'

'The binding?'

'Household gaffer tape. Black. I don't know how much luck they will have in getting any other DNA from either item, especially as I think he was there all night. Plus, both the dog and its owner touched the wrapping, so there will be plenty to confuse the evidence.'

'Time of death?'

'Tuesday evening. Between 8 p.m. and midnight.'

'Cause of death?'

'Come and see,' said Taylor.

The young victim lay on the examination table, a white sheet drawn up to his chest for modesty. The Y-shaped stitching indicated that the pathologist had finished with the body, and had sewn the vital organs back inside the cavity. The mobile workstation with its stainless-steel bowls was parked near the sink, cleaned and pristine, ready for the next job. Callum's face looked young and innocent. His physique was muscular, though still not fully developed. His blonde hair flopped to one side of his head. On the other, there was a large gash. The matted hair had been moved aside, so it looked as if he had been partly scalped.

Taylor pointed to the damage on the skull. 'This blow to the head was the culprit. There's trauma around the impact site, as well as the missing scalp tissue.'

'Inflicted how?' asked DI Edwards.

'Two possibilities. He could have been attacked with a large blunt weapon of some kind, or he could have fallen and caught his head on something very hard.'

'Is one more likely than the other?'

'At the moment, I can't be sure either way.'

'Could it have been an accident?' asked Sara.

'It's possible,' agreed Dr Taylor. 'But it would have been very unlucky. To inflict sufficient damage to do this, you would have to either fall from a height or at speed. It's more commonly a fatality in car accidents, where seat belts have failed, for example. I think it's more likely to have been done deliberately. It's the angle of the blow, you see.'

He held his hands above Callum's head, making a slicing motion across the scalped area.

'The damage is consistent with a blow from above. If someone hit him, then they were taller than him and powerful. The object would have been quite heavy and possibly sharp, such as an iron. Alternatively, he could have fallen and caught his head as he descended. I think he had been fighting.'

'Why's that? Defence injuries?'

'No.' Taylor drew down the sheet to reveal one of Callum's hands. 'There are abrasions on the back of his hands like he'd been in a fist fight. In addition, there's a bruise under his lower chin, and one on his cheek. Classic boxing blows, in fact, only without any gloves. It's feasible that he was involved in a fight and a punch threw him down sideways with sufficient momentum. Then he caught his head on a hard, blunt object. Say, a concrete gatepost or large flint.'

'Poor bugger,' said Edwards. Sara looked at him in surprise. 'Looks like he might have picked a fight with the wrong person.'

'Fighting over what?' asked Ellie.

'Good question,' replied Taylor. 'Do you know much about his background?

'In care since he was young,' Sara answered. 'Been at Lyndford Lodge for the last couple of years. It's not much of a life, is it?'

'Probably not.' Taylor sounded guarded. 'What about his personal preferences?'

'You mean, was he a user?' asked Ellie.

'I don't think he was,' said Taylor. 'I've sent off for a blood tox screen. No, I meant as a person.'

'He was young and probably lonely,' said Sara. 'Twice a victim in some senses.'

'He's young, I give you that. I'm not sure about the lonely. Have you got his birth certificate yet?'

'Aggie's doing that,' said Edwards. 'Why? What else?'

'Young Callum here had sex not long before he died. Anal sex. He's not damaged, so it must have been consensual. The signs are quite clear.'

'Can you swab it?'

'Done, gone for DNA testing.' Taylor stood back from the table and shoved his hands in his lab coat pockets. 'My question is, was he sixteen or not?'

CHAPTER 21

Muscleman dragged Danni upright, and the gun slid without loss of pressure into the small of her back. Mr Chatty was sitting crumpled on the floor, his head in his hands, blood trickling down the side of his face.

'Goods,' demanded Muscleman.

Danni opened the backpack and handed over the two packets.

'Where's the other one?'

'I need the toilet for that,' said Danni.

'In there,' he said. He pushed Danni forwards. She climbed over Mr Chatty, who was in front of the toilet door. The room had no windows, and it hadn't been designed with lingering or escape in mind. Danni pulled the last package out by a corner of wrapping. It cut into her as she removed it. It was a relief to have rid of it. After using the toilet, she wiped away the blood from the cuts, then rinsed the plastic covering of the package briefly under the tap.

When she opened the door, Mr Chatty had moved and was fussing around in the kitchen making cups of tea. Through a row of large windows, Danni could see a small balcony outside, where a cat sat among pot plants on a metal table, staring in at the window. She dropped the last package on the table, then slumped into one of the kitchen chairs.

Muscleman was leaning against the window ledge, arms folded. The gun was visible in a holster under his armpit. She grabbed her backpack and pulled it on to her lap to check the contents. To her relief, she saw that the purse and envelope were still there. She'd kept the mobile in her trouser pocket.

Mr Chatty's flat turned out to be a maisonette.

'Let's go upstairs,' said Mr Chatty. He balanced three cups of tea in his pudgy hands as he led the way to a second floor. Muscleman followed, carrying the three parcels. Upstairs there was a small square landing. Danni could see two bedrooms with their doors open, a third door was closed, and a fourth led to a large living room. One end had a television, comfortable chairs and a coffee table. The other end was a study area, with a large desk, a state-of-the-art computer and floor-to-ceiling bookcases. Mr Chatty set the cups down and pointed to a chair. 'You can have that one.'

He went back out on to the landing. Danni heard a door close. Muscleman sat down, watching her. She put the backpack next to her chair, settling back to drink the tea. Muscleman never took his eyes off her. His face was impassive, almost frozen, his gaze locked solid. Worst of all, he never seemed to blink. She shuffled uncomfortably in her seat.

Eventually, he spoke. 'How long you got?'

'I don't understand,' she said.

'You'll get more instructions and move on. When?'

'I don't know. They told me someone would meet me at the station.' Danni wasn't going to risk mentioning the packet for Gary, whoever he was.

'You can make yourself useful while you're here.' He tapped the packets. 'Customers will come, you'll take the money.'

Mr Chatty returned, having washed the blood from his face and fixed a plaster to the cut on his forehead. He was carrying a set of digital scales, the sort of thing Danni saw in laboratories on the television. He dumped a quantity of small clear plastic bags on the table next to the scales. With a noisy slurp of his tea, he settled on to the sofa.

Taking a tiny metal spoon, he weighed out the powder, placing a set amount into one of the little plastic bags, sealing it, then moving on to the next with a practised economy and speed. Specks of powder landed on his fingers as he worked. With a glance at Muscleman, Mr Chatty licked the dust from his skin. 'Waste not, want not,' he intoned. He giggled in a high-pitched way that sounded as though he were becoming hysterical. 'How much? How much do I get this time, Tony?'

'Shut the fuck up,' Muscleman snarled.

Mr Chatty dropped his head submissively, the laughter draining from his face, and returned to his weighing. When he had finished, he counted the bags. 'Two hundred and eleven.'

'Bring the book,' said Muscleman. Mr Chatty went to his desk, opened a drawer and pulled one out. 'I'll take fifty for now. You can have the eleven. Sell the rest at thirty quid a bag. She can help.' Muscleman pointed at Danni, who flinched away from his hand.

Mr Chatty wrote in the book, then carefully counted out fifty bags, put them into a larger bag and gave it to Muscleman. The stuff went into his jacket pocket, next to the gun in its holster.

He stood up with a grunt. 'Keep a record,' he said. 'I'll check when I come back.' He went downstairs, followed by Mr Chatty, who clucked behind him like a hen fussing around to drive a fox from the coop. Danni listened as the front door slammed. There was a long silence.

Finally, she heard Mr Chatty climb the stairs.

'You hungry?'

'Yes, a bit.'

'Come downstairs, then,' said Mr Chatty. She followed him to the kitchen. 'Soup and a sandwich?'

'Yes, fine. Thank you.'

Mr Chatty moved about the kitchen getting the food ready. He kept up a stream of conversation about nothing in particular as he did it. 'Do you like cats?'

'Don't know.'

'Meet my baby, then,' he said. Opening the door to the balcony, he let the pretty grey cat inside. It leaped up on to the work surface, and Mr Chatty stroked her fondly. 'Lovely girl. Did you miss your daddy? Stay out of that nasty man's way.'

He dished out some cat biscuits for it, then put a sandwich on a plate for Danni. He poured out the warmed soup, brought the bowls to the table, then sat down opposite her. They ate for a few moments in silence, the cat winding itself around his legs.

'You really called Danni?' he asked.

'Yes,' she said. 'That's my real name. What's yours?'

'Tony doesn't like names.'

'I gathered.' Mr Chatty's naivety amused Danni. She knew that the tattooed man was also known as Tony, but in her mind he would always be Muscleman. 'What's yours?'

'Nick.'

Danni looked around at the smartly kept kitchen, thought about the rows of books and the expensive computer upstairs. 'How did you get into all this, Nick? You're not a dealer, are you?'

'I wasn't,' said Nick. He looked down with the appearance of shame, hiding his eyes from her. 'I'm a writer, really.'

'Wow!' Danni was genuinely impressed. 'What do you write?'

'Plays. Television stuff.'

'What the hell got you into all this?'

'Bad luck,' he said. 'It isn't a long story. It's a simple one.' Nick gazed at her, his eyes beginning to mist with tears of self-pity. He seemed about to speak when there was a loud knock at the front door. His face flooded with panic. 'You get that when I tell you.'

He raced upstairs. Danni could hear him slamming drawers and running across the landing. She stood in the hallway until he leaned over the railing and called, 'Ready.'

She opened the door.

CHAPTER 22

With a newfound sense of determination, Sophie managed to get through the rest of the school day without another hit. It was one of her extra duties to take the after-school remedial reading group on Thursday evenings, a task that she still thoroughly enjoyed doing. It horrified her that some of the Year Eights and Nines still had difficulties reading, not to mention struggling to write.

Over the last few weeks, they had spent their hour taking it in turns to read their way through *The Lion, the Witch and the Wardrobe*. Some of the pupils still followed the text with a finger. But to her delight, they had taken to both the exercise and the content of the book.

'Good work,' she told them. They gathered up their stuff, and Sophie left with the pupils to head home.

The road outside her flat led to the supermarket car park. A steady flow of shoppers' cars and the street lamps kept the dark skies at bay. Sophie walked quickly to keep out the chill. Once inside, she checked for Gary. There was no trace of him in the bedroom, though he'd made the bed, which was something she rarely bothered to do. The kitchen had also been cleaned. She scanned outside again as she drew the living-room curtains for any sign of him, without success. He was unreliable both as a dealer and as a boyfriend.

Is Gary really my boyfriend? Sophie wondered. *Does he think of me as his girlfriend?*

He turned up when he liked, usually with some gear he wanted to try out. Sure, they had sex — though to be honest, it wasn't good sex. More a satisfaction of a basic animal need. They had little in common if you discounted the hits. A friend had introduced them to each other, during one of those long, lazy days of summer. Gary was new to the area, they'd said, and looking to make new friends. He had seemed like manna from heaven at first.

Turning on her television, she tried to ignore the call of the wraps of coke in her handbag. It preyed on her self-pity. The local news had just begun. As Sophie watched two familiar faces appeared. It was the two detectives and they were standing outside the police HQ, making an appeal.

'We are keen to find the young man's bike,' said DI Edwards.

'He was proud of it,' added the DS. 'We know he went out on it during Tuesday evening. If anyone in the area has seen it or something like it, they should contact us urgently.'

The DI gave out a description of the model, while a catalogue picture of it showed on the screen. 'It may have been abandoned or dumped. It could be in a ditch, outhouse or unused building. If you live in the area and have a building like that, please can you check it for us? If you walk your dog, or ramble or cycle, keep a look out on the verges, in ditches or scrubland.'

The reporter went on to give out a contact number and reiterate the call for help.

The news programme began a different story. Sophie stood without moving, remembering the bike. Out of school, Callum always seemed to be either on it or stood propping it up. As if he couldn't bear to be parted from it. When he had sold her wraps in the churchyard, he'd been leaning on it, one hand caressing the bars. He always slid the wraps out of his jacket and stuffed her cash into a pocket of his jeans. Then he would flick his leg over the saddle and vanish in seconds.

The memory followed her into the kitchen. Her hands were shaking as she ripped the top off a pre-prepared bag of rice and put it in the microwave. She chopped cold cooked chicken to add to the rice, working slowly. Her fingers kept drumming uncontrollably on the work surface. It wasn't because of tiredness or hunger. Sophie recognised this moment all too well, and it had defeated her so often before. Throwing the knife on to the chopping board, she rinsed her shaking fingers under the tap and went to the bedroom.

Gary may have made the bed, but on the side she slept a weed pipe lay near an overflowing ashtray. At some point it had been kicked over on the carpet, leaving a trail of dirt. A sticky shot glass lay on its side on the carpet, a grubby stain spreading underneath it. Her clothes lay scattered and unwashed. The room smelled like an untended kennel.

Dogs live better than this, Sophie thought.

She opened the window a fraction to let in some air, then pulled anxiously at her clothes until she managed to remove them. Her skin was beginning to itch. She scratched at her arms, breasts and thighs with broken nails until she raised welts. Sweat was running down her face.

'I won't give in,' she snarled. She grabbed a rarely used pair of whimsical pyjamas from a drawer. She pulled them on and stuffed her feet into a pair of pink crocs. 'No more.'

Back in the kitchen, she tipped the hot rice into a bowl and threw the chopped chicken on top. Taking a fork, she perched nervously on the edge of her sofa and began to eat the bland food. Each mouthful tasted like sawdust. Sophie had to force herself to chew and swallow. About halfway through her meal, she gave up, banged the bowl on the table and let the fork clatter out of her hand.

'Half a wrap.' Sophie knew she was bargaining with herself. 'Just half. That's the way to cut down.'

She opened a wrap and poured half the powder on to the glass top of the coffee table. Using the edge of her hand, she scraped it into a rough line, then kneeled on the carpet to snort it up.

Slipping back on to the sofa, she waited for the world to stop spinning. The drug raced around her system, bringing back the sensation of being able to do anything. A smile grew on her lips. Yes, now she could deal with anything and anyone. Even whoever was ringing at the door. It would be Gary, of course.

Sophie crossed to the access buzzer and opened the outside door without bothering to check who was there. A few seconds later, the knock she was expecting came. With a grin, she flung open the door. The shock stopped her from moving or speaking.

It was Matt Morgan, the housefather from the care home.

'Sorry to be a bother, can I talk to you?' he asked. His eyes widened as he took in her sparkly unicorn pyjamas. He glanced over Sophie's shoulder and saw the obvious signs on the coffee table.

He frowned. 'I think I'd better come in, don't you?'

CHAPTER 23

The team gathered for the early morning briefing. Aggie had tracked down a birth certificate for Callum Young. Edwards was gazing at the incident board, where a variety of maps, pictures and photos were pinned.

'He was only fifteen,' said Aggie. She produced the birth certificate and gave it to Edwards. 'His birthday is in March.'

'Confirms the details in the Lyndford Lodge files,' he said.

'Which means he had sex underage,' said Bowen.

The gruff tone he used for such statements used to fool Sara into thinking that he didn't care. Now she knew it meant he was putting a lid on his emotions.

'Consensual sex,' she said. 'Could be one of the others at the home. Or what about that friend of his from school — Steven Lister. Is that what he was hiding?'

'Kids experimenting? Might be true,' agreed Bowen. Sara watched him relax back into his chair, the tension in his shoulders easing away. 'It's just the reputation of those woods makes you wonder.'

'The DNA results should help,' said Edwards. 'We ought to visit Lister at home today and have another word. What else, Aggie?'

'The agricultural showroom sent me some CCTV files,' she said. 'The best view is across the customer parking area at the front, where it catches the road outside. Someone is using the cycle path about 4 p.m., which might be our victim. You can have a look yourselves. The cyclist turned down the lane opposite and headed out towards Lessing Common.'

'Which would confirm what Andrea Green told me,' said Sara.

'The council came back to me about the café car park,' said Bowen. 'Most of the CCTV cameras at Stiffkey Woods are broken. The guy told me that they keep replacing them, but they get trashed again regularly, and they assume it's deliberate. However, there is one in the trees behind the café, which was recording. There is a surprising amount of activity in the evening. It's not very clear, so I've sent it down to IT for a digital clean-up.'

'Let us know when it's back,' said Edwards. 'How did you get on at Lyndford Lodge?'

'We talked to all the other boys,' replied Bowen. He shrugged and looked at Noble for support. 'To be honest, I think they're getting fed up with us. Drugs gave them a hard time, and they were getting defensive, wouldn't you say?'

'Yeah,' agreed Noble. 'Aggressive with it.'

'Are you saying we're heavy-handed?' Ellie asked. She sounded offended.

'I'm saying someone gave them a roasting.' Bowen turned to her. 'Now they're closing ranks on us, to protect themselves and Callum.'

'If one of them is dealing, they all will be,' retorted Ellie.

'You don't know that,' snapped Bowen. 'Innocent until proven guilty, in case your team have forgotten that.'

'For fuck's sake. You know how it goes in these places.'

'No, I don't. You don't either.'

'DI Powell does know. I'll go with his opinion.'

The phone in Edwards's office rang. He went to answer it, leaving the two bristling at each other.

Aggie went to fetch water for the coffee machine, as Noble dropped his head in embarrassment. Sara looked on in surprise as Bowen stamped back to his desk and Ellie flung herself on to a spare chair. *What on earth is going on between those two?* she wondered.

'Coats, everyone,' called Edwards from his office. 'Think we've found Callum's bike.'

* * *

Ellie travelled with Edwards and Sara back out to Marlham, making it clear that she wasn't prepared to travel with Bowen. As they approached the small town, they took a turning off the main road that Sara hadn't seen before. It cut across the corner and came out near the agricultural equipment showroom.

'That's where I think Callum went on his bike,' said Edwards. He pointed to a small lane on the right opposite the showroom. A few yards further on they turned down another narrow lane on the left.

They passed a farm and half a dozen cottages. Their car bounced over the unevenly patched surface, and they rounded a sharp bend before a small wooded area enveloped them. On either side of the lane, two vehicles were parked in the passing places. One was a police car. The other belonged to North Norfolk District Council. Four men stood by the police car, two in uniform, two in overalls and hi-vis jackets. Blue-and-white exclusion tape was already wound between the trees on one side of the lane. Edwards parked behind the small council lorry, which had high wire sides. The logo said that it belonged to the Waste Disposal department. Bowen drew up behind them within seconds.

'Morning, sir,' said the older of the two officers. 'Think these gentlemen may have found what you were looking for. I can show you when you're ready.'

'Sounds promising,' said Edwards. 'What have you got?'

'Up in the trees, over there.' One of the council workers pointed through the thicket. 'A silver bike and a bin bag.'

'Bin bag?' asked Sara.

'Yeah, just the one. Normally, if it's rubbish, there would be lots of them.'

'Take a statement, DS Hirst,' said Edwards. He strode off through the trees with the other officer, and Ellie closely behind. Bowen and Noble waited as Sara took the men's details.

'Why are you here today?' Sara asked.

'Got a report of fly-tipping.' The man turned and pointed beyond their truck. She glimpsed a pile of old car tyres and nodded for the man to carry on.

'I saw you on the television last night,' said his mate. 'You said about this area. I said to Sid, we should have a look around while we're here. Marlham being so close.'

'So we did. And there it was. Says "Boardman" on the bike, like you said. I thought it might be what you're after.'

'We didn't touch it, did we?' Sid continued. 'Rang up and your lot came straight out.'

'Well, thank you both,' said Sara. 'We'll be in touch for a formal statement. Otherwise, I think you can go now.'

'Mind if we pick that lot up?' Sid pointed to the fly-tipped pile. 'It's why we came in the first place.'

'Not at all,' confirmed Sara.

The two men went back to their truck and began to heave the tyres over the wire guards into the back.

'Bet they can't wait to get back into the depot. Heroes for a day.'

Sara, Bowen and Noble tramped through the under-growth, following a vague path among the leaf mould and fallen branches. The bin bag was hidden behind a tree, stuffed down into a gap between the roots and taped shut with gaffer tape. Sara took her mobile and snapped positioning photos, then, wearing latex gloves, she tried to pick open the tape gently. It wouldn't move, and as she attempted to pull it away from the black plastic, it ripped a small hole.

'Bugger it,' she muttered and put her finger into the tear to lift back the plastic. The bag contained clothes.

They walked over to where Edwards was crouched by a silver bike frame, tangled in old brambles and dead ferns. The wheels had been removed, and the chain was jammed around the rear gear mechanism.

Ellie was hovering next to Edwards. 'I've taken photos, sir,' she said. 'That water bottle doesn't look right. Can we take it out?'

Edwards put one gloved hand on the frame to steady it and pulled the bottle out of its steel cage. He stood up, turning it over in his hands. The normal plastic top was missing, which would have made it difficult to take a drink from the neck. His fingers found a catch and the bottle split down its length. One half levered up on two tiny hinges to form a lid.

'What the hell?' Edwards muttered. 'Bowen, are SOCOs on their way?'

'Yes, sir,' said Bowen. 'Called them a few minutes ago.'

'Stick this thing in an evidence bag.'

Noble fished a bag from his coat pocket and held it open.

'Right, take it steady,' said Edwards. 'Try not to disturb too much, but let's see if we can find the wheels for this thing.'

They walked through more undergrowth. 'Is it Callum's bike?' Sara asked.

'It will have to be checked, of course. But who else could it belong to?'

'Why take the wheels out?'

The copse was small, reaching no more than fifty yards back from the road to the edge of a ploughed field. A shout from Noble brought the rest of the team to his position, next to a ditch separating the copse from the field.

The water in it ran swiftly, full of recent rain. The banks were covered in dead grass and weeds, which had been trampled flat. Down the side of the bank nearest to them, under the water and masked by the winter reeds, lay a pair of chrome bike wheels.

CHAPTER 24

There had been a steady flow of customers visiting Nick's front door until late the previous evening. Word had spread, and at one point, an expensive black car had pulled up outside. A couple of well-dressed twenty-something men had come up to buy twenty packets, not flinching at handing over 600 pounds in cash.

'Having a party,' said one. His tone sounded more Belgravia than Norwich. Nick had shrugged and put the money in the desk drawer with the rest. It all got written down in the book.

'Don't know why I bother,' he commented. Placing the book on top of the cash, he added the remaining little bags and locked the desk drawer. 'I'm not sure Tony can read — he can bloody well count, though. That's enough for today. Don't answer the door anymore.'

They ordered a pizza, watched television and Nick got through a couple more of the little packets. His mood swung from morose to eager and back to tearful as each hit took hold, then wore off. At eleven he sent Danni to bed in the sparsely furnished second bedroom.

To her surprise, she drifted off to sleep, and overslept as well.

The next morning, she selected some clean clothes from her holdall, washed her face and stole the use of Nick's toothbrush. The television was chatting to itself on one side of the living room. Nick sat in front of the computer at the study end. He swivelled in his chair as Danni came in, peering at her through bleary-looking eyes.

'Oh, hello,' he said. 'Get yourself some breakfast if you want anything.'

'You got up early?' Danni asked.

'No. Up all night. The muse struck.' On the computer screen, Danni could see some document in a weird-looking format, cursor blinking. Nick turned back, ensuring he saved it carefully before powering down. 'I guess Tony will be here soon.'

It was later than she had first thought, Danni realised after she had put the kettle on. The kitchen clock said 11.15. Even at home with Johnny, they were usually up before this. It briefly crossed her mind that Nick might have put something to make her sleep in that last cup of tea the previous night. But she didn't see why he would bother. Working her way through the cupboards, Danni found mugs, a bowl and cereal. She heaped coffee into the mugs and helped herself to some cornflakes.

'Coffee?' she called upstairs.

'OK, thanks,' shouted Nick.

She was spooning up cereal when he joined her at the kitchen table. He had a wodge of cash and the book. With a calculator, he began to add up the figures in the ledger. He pushed the money across the table to Danni. 'Count this lot for me.'

This was something she did with Johnny and knew the routine. Dividing the notes into ten, twenty and fifty-pound piles, then turning each note to face the same way, Danni counted it all out.

'Two thousand, two hundred and fifty quid.'

'Agreed,' replied Nick. They packed the money into a plastic bag. 'That's some good-quality shit you brought.'

'Is it?' asked Danni. 'I don't use it myself.'

'Good idea,' said Nick, smiling ruefully.

'How did you get into all this, then? You were going to tell me last night when we got interrupted.'

Nick sipped his coffee and launched into his story, as though he couldn't wait to finally share it with someone. There were long hours on film sets. Sitting up all night to do rewrites. Posh actors who used coke to keep their eyes bright and memories sharp on late-night shoots. Worst of all, a sense of not belonging and a need to feel that he was one of the gang.

'I'm just a working-class boy. The rest of them are private-school-educated, even the women these days.' Then a failing career, desperation, begging for work. Nick barely stopped for breath.

Danni had very little idea what he was talking about, but it seemed to her that he had squandered a good career and bright future. She also knew that charlie could do that to anyone. That was why she always resisted Johnny's offers of *Just try this, you'll like it.*

Nick finally ran down, like one of those mechanical toys she saw on the antiques programmes. The silence was punctuated by a thumping at the front door.

'Here we go again,' Danni said. Leaving Nick sitting at the table, she went to open it.

Two men stood outside. The one banging on the door looked in his mid-twenties. Tall, with smartly cut brown hair and fashionable clothes, Danni recognised him from the picture on Lisa London's mobile. An older man hovered behind him. Smaller, with stooped shoulders and greying, greasy hair, he dropped his gaze as soon as Danni looked at him. His clothes looked dirty and worn. The warm jacket he pulled shut around his chest had food stains down the front.

The young man pushed past Danni and went straight to the kitchen. 'Nick? Where you at?'

The older man followed, stepping warily past the door and hovering in the tiny hall. 'You the one that's been sent?'

'Sorry?' Danni closed the door and looked at the man.

'He'll want what you got.' The older man pushed Danni into the kitchen.

The young man was holding the bag of cash high in the air with a grin. 'Look at this, Les. Bonus time.'

'Don't,' said Nick. He reached up at the bag.

With a laugh, the young man dangled it too high for Nick to reach. 'Come on, then.' He dangled the bag even higher, like someone playing with a kitten, teasing Nick, who climbed on to a kitchen chair. This time he allowed Nick to grab the bag of money and turned to Danni. 'You got something for me, don't you?'

Danni felt Les prod her. She looked at the man, who nodded. 'What were you given? Give it to Gary.'

'I'll fetch it,' she said. The pink backpack was in the spare bedroom. As she reached the top of the stairs, the mobile buzzed in her pocket. It was a text message.

Give the boy the envelope. The sender's number was withheld.

Bloody hell, can someone see me? Danni wondered. She carried the bag to the kitchen, pulled out the envelope and handed it over to Gary. He grabbed it with delight, tearing at the seal. He scattered the contents on the kitchen table and turned them rapidly over, one at a time.

'What's this?' asked Gary. 'Why do I need this lot? I asked for fucking money.'

Danni could see a passport, some travel tickets and some foreign currency.

'I don't want this shit.' He swept the stuff on to the floor. Les dropped down and gathered it all up again.

Gary grabbed Danni. He swung her around and pinned her against the door to the balcony. 'Money. Where's my money? You fucking stole it, didn't you?'

Danni tried to speak, to deny it, but Gary was shaking her by the shoulders. Her head was spinning. She could hear Nick saying something. The sound was far away. Her head clattered against the glass in the kitchen door, and stars flashed in front of her eyes.

There was another thumping sound. Through unfocused eyes, she glimpsed Muscleman striding into the kitchen behind Gary, hands raised.

She began to vomit.

CHAPTER 25

The SOCO team leader was as surprised as the rest of them. There was a second hiding place on the bike. A small metal bike pump had also been split in half, the guts removed, and the lid lifted on tiny hinges.

'It's very clever work,' he said. There was admiration in his voice. 'Assuming the boy did this himself, he was good with his hands. No one would think twice if he was carrying these items. You wouldn't leave them on the bike in case they got stolen. You'd bring them inside the house with you.'

'Drugs,' said Ellie. No one contradicted her. 'You could get several packets in each compartment, coke or pills. Whatever was hot on the market.'

'We'll test it and look for traces.'

'Bloody clever, though,' said Bowen. 'Think he did it himself?'

'It's possible.' The DI pointed at the trees surrounding them. 'We're going to need a full fingertip search of this area. Shame there have been so many vehicles along the lane. Check the mud anyway.'

'It's going to take a couple of days,' said the SOCO. 'Let's hope the weather holds.'

They all knew that if someone had dumped the bike on the same night as Callum's body, then too much time had passed. The team drove back into the town.

Marlham High Street was a mixture of charity shops and small local businesses, including an independent butchers' shop and a hardware store. Two cafés stood at opposite ends of the street. The first, at the end near the Norfolk Broads boatyard, had scrubbed pine tables with tiny vases of fresh flowers. The menu promised paninis and homemade cakes. The second, at the other end near the post office, had wipeable oilcloths on old metal-legged tables, and a heart-stopping menu of big breakfasts, burgers or sausages and chips with everything. They joined the local workers in the latter.

'We'll start with the garage. Did you find out which one it was?'

'Is there more than one?' Sara asked.

There were four, the woman who brought their lunches confirmed. One only sold second-hand cars. Another was a small business in a bunch of sheds behind the high street on the old station site, which specialised in classic cars. The final two were opposite the school. Of these two, one was a specialist tyre-fitting depot and the other was a general garage and MOT testing station.

'Mike, I want you, Ian and Ellie to check the ones near the school and the car dealer,' said Edwards. 'We'll try the classic car place. Eat up.'

They paid for their lunches and went back on to the high street. Splitting into two teams, Sara and the DI headed for the old station site, which was made up of three identical units, two with their doors open. At the first unit, a man was loading boxes of pet food into a delivery van. The garage was in the second unit. It belonged to a middle-aged man, dressed in grimy red overalls. He was trying to work something loose under a car bonnet and swearing loudly when Edwards and Sara walked in through the open garage doors. They introduced themselves.

'Dan Wade,' the man said. He stretched up, dropped his spanner on the floor with a thump, and rubbed his greasy hands down his front. Sara was grateful he didn't offer to shake hands. 'What do you want?'

'We're trying to find out about a young man from the town,' explained Edwards. 'Name of Callum Young.'

'Callum?' The man sounded wary. 'He's not this murder victim you wouldn't name yesterday, is he?'

'I'm afraid he is,' said Sara. 'We believe he may have worked here?'

'Yes, he's been with me for a while,' said Wade. He looked at the picture Edwards held out to confirm it. 'That's him. Poor sod.'

'And his friend, Steven Lister?'

'Lister only stayed a few Saturdays,' said Wade. 'Didn't take to it. But Callum did. He paid attention and seemed to enjoy it. I thought he might come to me on an apprenticeship when he left school.'

'Was Callum with you for long?'

'Started in July on work experience. I offered him some hours after that, and he came in on Saturdays. Weekdays during the holidays.'

'You paid him?'

'Of course.' Wade sounded offended. 'What do you take me for?'

'May I ask how much?'

Edwards put the grease-covered photo back in his pocket without comment and looked carefully around the garage.

'Twenty quid a day. What has that got to do with anything?'

Sara pointed to cutting and welding units in the corner of the workshop. 'Did you let him use all the equipment?'

'You won't catch me out like that,' Wade said. His voice was taking on an angry tone. 'He was too young to use stuff like that. I never allowed him to.'

'Well, thank you for your time,' said Edwards. 'If we need any more information, we'll give you a call.'

Wade grunted in reply, picked up the spanner and ducked back under the car bonnet. Edwards and Sara walked back to the high street until they were sufficiently far away.

'Everyone seems to think that Callum bought the bike with proceeds of his Saturday job,' said Sara. 'Not on twenty quid a day, he didn't. It might be part of the extra cash in the workshop, surely that wouldn't account for the whole amount.'

'Let's try Steven Lister next,' said Edwards. 'Your thoughts so far?'

They walked past the school and turned into a new-build estate. Sara checked her notepad. 'Lister's house is that way, sir. Aggie reckons the bike would cost at least five hundred pounds second-hand, probably more. And what about all those tools in the workshop? They'd cost a fair bit.'

'I think it's a fair assumption he was using that bike to collect and deliver drugs locally,' said Edwards. 'But how did he afford it in the first place? Which came first, the bike or the money?'

'Or the drugs, sir,' said Sara.

'He was dealing before he got the bike, you think?'

'It's possible. We don't know who was supplying Callum. What if they were already doing it and this just made it easier?'

'It would need to be someone local.'

'Someone at Lyndford Lodge, or school perhaps.'

'Or someone he worked with,' said Edwards. 'Did you notice anything odd about that garage? Compared to the building next door?'

'No, sir. I take it you did?'

'All three units are the same size on the outside.'

'They certainly seemed to be.'

'Didn't you think Wade's place felt smaller than the pet food place? On the inside, I mean.'

'It's possible. There was an office along the back wall and a place for customers to sit.'

'What was beyond that? The back wall?'

'I think so, sir.'

'I'd like a good look around that garage. Bet we'll need a search warrant before Mr Wade lets us.'

CHAPTER 26

DI Edwards and Sara found Steven Lister's home in the corner of a cul-de-sac on the new-build estate. The place still had that sense of being a showcase rather than lived-in homes. Front lawns were manicured, tasteful Christmas decorations hung in the windows, rubbish bins were hidden discreetly in wooden cabinets. A polite knock at the door brought a smartly dressed, forty-something woman to answer it. Steven's mother looked shocked when they showed their warrant cards. Although Edwards stood in front, she stared at Sara with barely concealed curiosity. After a moment's consideration, she showed them into the immaculate front room, waiting to ensure they had wiped their feet on the mat in the porch first.

'Why do you want to speak to my son?' she asked.

'It's about his friend Callum Young,' said Edwards.

Mrs Lister scowled. 'The dead boy? Steven had nothing to do with him. He lived in that home.'

'We understand that they worked together at the garage,' said Sara.

'Only for a few days,' said Mrs Lister. 'Part of a school initiative to get work experience. That man treated them as free labour. It was dreadful. I told him he didn't have to go back. My Steven will be going to Cambridge, not grubbing about in a run-down garage.'

The living room was carefully laid out, in the best Scandi-modern taste. An artificial Christmas tree stood in one corner, sparsely decorated with expensive glass ornaments and artificial candles in individual holders. A single complex wreath of greenery lay along the mantelshelf above a gas fire that imitated an expensive log burner.

'We need to ask him about several things that have come up in our investigation,' said Edwards. 'He knew Callum at school and may be able to help us.'

'What sort of things?' Mrs Lister sounded suspicious. 'My Steven's a good boy.'

Edwards exchanged a glance with Sara. 'A parent should be present while we speak with him.'

Mrs Lister drew herself up and squared her shoulders. 'In that case, I'm going to call my husband.'

'By all means,' said Sara. Mrs Lister glared at her. 'Is he at work?'

'Of course. He can be here in a few minutes, providing he doesn't have a client.'

'A client?'

'He's a solicitor.' Mrs Lister sounded triumphant. 'You'd better wait in your car while I call him.'

She shooed them out of the house, closing the door firmly behind them. They had left their car in a car park on the far side of the high street. They walked back, then drove round in it to the estate. School must have finished for the day. They wove through crowds of pupils and around streams of cars pulling up indiscriminately to collect children. It must have taken them at least fifteen minutes, and now a car stood in the drive. The sound of raised male voices came from inside when they knocked at the front door.

Mr Lister let them in. After checking their warrant cards, he pointed along the hallway to the kitchen. 'This way.'

It was as immaculate as the living room. The only untidy item was Steven. His uniform looked dishevelled, his rucksack slung next to a cabinet, books spilling across the floor. He sat on a high stool behind the cooking island, face red with embarrassment, hands clasped rigidly together. His mother was pretending to prepare vegetables at the other end of the unit, a small, sharp knife in her hand.

'You wished to speak to Steven?' Mr Lister's tone was neutral and efficient, his body language protective as he sat on a stool next to his son.

Sara felt Edwards bristle, which was a bad sign. She spoke before Edwards could begin. 'Steven was kind enough to help me yesterday at school.'

'You interviewed my son in school?' Mr Lister sounded offended. 'You had no right to do that.'

'It's a murder investigation,' said Edwards sharply. 'A neutral third party was there.'

Mr Lister turned to Steven, who shrugged in reply. 'School social worker.'

Mrs Lister dropped her knife with a clatter. 'Social worker?'

'Someone to represent the school and Steven,' said Sara. She hoped her tone was soothing. 'We needed to find Callum's bike. It was urgent. A member of staff said that Steven and Callum were friendly, so we hoped he could help us.'

'And could he?'

'Steven kindly confirmed how important the bike was,' said Sara. 'It was found this morning.'

'Where?' asked Steven. His hands clenched harder, and his knuckles turned white.

'In a wood, just outside the town,' replied Edwards. Steven's face drained white. 'Steven, how old are you?'

'He's sixteen,' Mr Lister cut in. 'Why?'

'You don't have to answer these questions, Steven,' snapped Mrs Lister. 'And talk to the organ grinder, not the . . .'

'*Clare!*' bellowed Mr Lister, before his wife could finish the phrase. He tugged at the collar of his shirt. She looked mutinously at Sara, then dropped her gaze.

'Steven,' said Edwards. 'I need to ask you something really personal. Are you sexually active?'

Mrs Lister gasped with indignation. 'How dare you? Steven is still at school.'

'You don't have to answer that,' said Mr Lister.

Steven's head drooped.

'It seems that Callum was,' said Sara.

'Typical,' said Mrs Lister. 'They have no control over those kids up at that place. Run wild in the town, causing trouble. They could be up to anything.'

'Are you suggesting that Steven was having gay relations with this boy?' demanded Mr Lister. 'That's a serious accusation.'

'Indeed, it is,' said Edwards. 'Given that Callum was only fifteen.'

Mrs Lister drew in a sharp breath. Mr Lister's mouth opened and closed like a frantic fish. The atmosphere in the room was rigid.

Steven groaned. 'Not me,' he muttered. 'Never done it. Not with anyone.'

'Steven?' Sara tried to coax the young man to look at her. 'It's OK. We believe you. Have you any idea who he might have been seeing?'

Steven shook his head.

'You were friends, though? You liked him?'

'He was a cocky bugger.'

'Steven, language.'

'Please, Mrs Lister.' Sara looked at her with pursed lips. The woman's lips curled with anger, but she didn't say any more. 'You liked him?'

'He was all right.'

Sara guessed that this was high praise from one posturing adolescent to another.

'Did you do things together? Outside school?'

'Yeah, sometimes. Football and that.'

'Recently?'

'Not so much, since he got that bike.' Steven looked up, folding his arms around himself. 'We were supposed to be playing on Tuesday night, but he never turned up to fetch me, so I didn't go out.'

'Do you know what Callum got up to? On his bike?'

'I told you,' he said, his voice dull. 'I don't know. Some bloke he used to visit. Someone with money.'

'Did he talk about this man?'

'He used to laugh about him. Said he was earning loads of money from him.'

'Earning?' asked Edwards.

'Yes.'

'Did he say how?' asked Sara. 'Perhaps he boasted to you about it?'

Steven shook his head, tightened his arms as if he was trying to stop his own breathing.

'Steven, we know about Callum selling drugs.'

Mrs Lister squealed in horror. Steven shuddered. His father put an arm around his shoulders. 'What are you suggesting? If you want to ask anything else, it ought to be done properly. Steven, don't say any more and I'll get you a lawyer.'

'That's your prerogative, Mr Lister,' said Edwards. 'Steven, this is urgent, we need to find out what happened to Callum. Can I continue?'

Steven's eyes darted between his father and DI Edwards before he nodded.

'Is that what Callum meant about earning?' Edwards asked. 'Was he getting these drugs from this older man?'

'I think so.' Steven's voice wobbled. 'It all started in the summer.'

'When you worked together at the garage?'

'Yes. We were good mates before that. After I left the garage, he started getting cocky. Said he was going to earn his fortune and get away from Marlham. Said he wanted to go to London, that this man would take him there.'

'Why did you leave the garage?' asked Sara.

Steven looked at his mother. 'They used to smoke stuff,' he said.

'Weed?'

'Steven!' Mrs Lister's voice had risen at least two octaves. 'You never.'

'No, I never,' the boy snapped. He jumped up from his stool and slammed his palm on the worktop with a thump. 'They offered it to me, I tried one drag, and it made me feel sick. I never did it again. You don't trust me. Why can't you just leave me alone? Why are you always badgering me?' He rushed from the room, slamming the door behind him.

Mrs Lister sank on to a chair, one hand to her chest, the other twitching in her lap. Tears ran down her face. 'Badger him? I love him.'

CHAPTER 27

Nick and Les picked Danni up and sat her on a kitchen chair. Muscleman had taken Gary on to the balcony outside the kitchen. The young man was breathing heavily, his gaze focused behind Muscleman's head, not meeting his eyes.

'You OK?' Nick whispered in Danni's ear. 'Need anything?'

Danni shook her head. 'No, thanks. Just need to sit still for a minute.'

Nick patted her shoulder and went to the sink, where he ran water and floor cleaner into a bucket. Taking some kitchen roll, he began to clean up.

Her head was thumping. She looked out of the window at Muscleman and Gary. The pair obviously knew each other. She had assumed that Muscleman was in charge of the street gang for the area, given the way he spoke to Nick. That all this was purely business, even the envelope. Now he stood with one hand leaning heavily on Gary's shoulder trying to calm the young man down. It was the sort of gesture a big brother or some other family member might make. It was confusing. Who *was* Gary? Why did he need these documents? What would happen to her now she had delivered them? Whoever Gary was, he obviously had a problem with his temper and Muscleman knew all about it.

'It's OK, Gary,' Muscleman said. 'We can sort this out. We'll call her. We don't need any more trouble now, do we? Let's take it calmly, eh? The girl is just a mule, she wouldn't know what she was carrying.'

Gary sucked air in through his nose, pushing the breath out through his wide-open mouth. It took several goes before Muscleman rewarded Gary by releasing the pressure on his shoulder. Gary circled his shoulders back and forth as if to release the tension.

'OK now?' asked Muscleman.

Gary nodded and, stepping back inside, he looked at Danni.

'Sorry, babe,' he said with a sheepish smile. 'I guess you didn't take the money.' He looked at her appraisingly. 'You're pretty, aren't you?'

Nick had taken the bucket to flush the mess down the toilet. The smell of disinfectant was making Danni feel queasy. She tamped it down, knowing it would be better to keep the peace, and smiled. 'Thanks. You're pretty smart yourself.'

Gary grinned. Les had collected up the documents and currency. He offered them warily to Gary. 'Italy, Gary.' He pointed to the printout. 'Naples. That's nice. I thought it might be Spain. Too obvious, I guess.'

'Family,' said Gary. He turned over the passport, looked at the picture and checked the name, then proffered it for Les to read. 'Family name, look.'

Les picked up the euros and counted them. 'Couple of thousand here. When's the flight?' He took the ticket from Gary's unresisting hand, read it and nodded approvingly. 'That's great. Norwich via Amsterdam. Not until Monday, but you'll be there in plenty of time for Christmas.'

'Doesn't matter. I'm not going, and I need some cash now,' said Gary. His tone sounded defiant and full of bluster. He waved at the wallet of cash on the table. 'That yours?'

Muscleman stood in the doorway, with a resigned look on his face. 'Yeah, that's mine.'

'Well, it's mine now.' Gary snatched up the money. Muscleman grabbed the bag and tugged at it, pulling Gary towards him until they were nose to nose.

'Only if you tell her,' he said. Then he let the bag go and Gary stumbled back a step.

'Sure. Dead easy.' Gary grinned and pointed at Danni. 'Then we gonna go, right? Taking her with us too. For security purposes.'

Pulling out a mobile, Gary went out on to the balcony again to make his call. Muscleman followed him to listen.

'If you insist,' said Les. With a shrug at Danni, he tucked the paperwork and the euros into his coat pocket. 'Get your stuff, girly.'

Danni hurried upstairs to the room where she had slept. She stuffed her few belongings into the holdall, pulled on her parka and picked up the pink backpack. At the moment, she could only see two choices. Refuse to leave with Gary and risk the consequences from Muscleman, who she still assumed was Lisa London's chief commando in Norwich. Or go with Gary and see what happened to her next. Danni didn't fancy crossing Lisa London. The young man should be the softer option.

Back in the kitchen, Les was waiting while Gary spoke loudly into his mobile. 'Ah, don't be like that, sis. I need some cash . . . Yes, yes, I've got all that, but I've got expenses here too . . . Yes, she's here.' Gary looked at Danni. 'Gonna take her back with me . . . I need some company . . . No, I won't, I promise . . . Yeah, Knucklehead is here . . . She wants to speak to you.' Gary passed the phone to Muscleman, who turned away and spoke more softly.

Gary emptied the wallet of cash. 'Says I can have a grand. You count it out for me.'

Nick included the fifty-pound notes in the count, much to Gary's delight. The remnants of the money sat on the table until Muscleman came back inside. He passed the mobile back to Gary. With a sigh, he picked up what was left. He peeled off a couple of hundred, which he gave to Nick, and pushed the rest into his trouser pocket. He looked extremely fed up.

'You ready?' asked Les. Danni nodded, and the four of them left Nick alone.

Despite a growing headache from the collision with the door, once outside, Danni read the house number. As they went downstairs, she made a mental note of the block name and the route to the car park. Les's car was small and silver. Muscleman opened a door and pushed her inside. He watched as they drove off.

After a few minutes, they skirted a large church, pulling up in a queue of cars at traffic lights on one side of it. It looked really old, although it had a newer building attached to it with a bizarre name above the door — *The Narthex*. She wasn't sure how to pronounce that word, but it was distinctive, and she ran it over and over in her head to lodge it in her memory.

They drove through the city, out through some suburbs and on to a busy dual carriageway, frantic with traffic. Once beyond that, they were out into the countryside, and the afternoon closed in on them. It seemed to take them ages, passing through small places with lighting and back into the growing dark again at intervals. Gary fiddled with the radio, settling on Radio One, much to Les's annoyance.

'Bloody noise, that's all that is.'

Gary laughed, patting Les on the shoulder playfully. 'You can't help being a boring old bastard. Good, isn't it?' He turned to look at Danni, who shrank down in her seat, hoping he couldn't see her very well. He laughed again, turning away and joining in with the latest Dua Lipa hit with a reedy vocal.

The line of traffic they were driving in got shorter as commuters reached home and turned into housing estates or side lanes that Danni couldn't see down. Bare hedges crowded in on the vehicle as the roads reduced in width. Finally, they reached a gateway with a sign over it that she couldn't read in the dark. Tiny rechargeable lights marked out a gravel roadway, with static holiday caravans on either side. Most of them looked empty, their curtains open, the rooms inside abandoned. One or two had lights on, and Les pulled up next to one of these.

Gary rolled out of the car, still singing, and unlocked the caravan door. Les came round to Danni, took her bag and guided her towards the van. She stopped for a moment, taking a breath of fresh air to calm the pain in her head. A strong breeze blustered around the empty caravan park. The wind was cold, sharp and salty. She could hear a strange rattling sound, then the breaking of waves. Memories of her childhood flooded her brain.

She turned to Les. 'Are we at the seaside?'

CHAPTER 28

Matt Morgan had not been kind last night. But, Sophie acknowledged, it was in a tough-love kind of way. Matt had barged past her, swept up the remains of the half-packet and flushed it away. Then he'd demanded the other wraps, which he had confiscated. She'd let him do it. His reaction at seeing the stuff had reminded her of the way her father behaved, and experience had taught her that it was easier, in the long run, to allow an angry man to do what he wanted. When he'd finished, Sophie had quietly opened the front door and waited, offering a silent prayer that he wouldn't report her to the school.

'I'll come back tomorrow,' he'd said. Sophie wasn't sure if it had been a threat or a promise.

She'd got through the night, managed with one hit at school and was now back at her flat, skin itching, hands shaking, and the emergency stash from the staff toilet cupboard on her table. She sat on the sofa looking at the wraps and tampons, knowing she had to choose whether to hide them again. Matt knew nothing about this other stash. The door buzzer saved her from having to make a decision.

'Evening,' said Matt. She let him in.

Glancing at the table, he steered her back to the sofa and sat beside her. 'Where did you get this lot from?'

'School,' said Sophie. 'I keep an emergency supply there.'

'But you brought it home with you today?'

Sophie nodded.

'Have you taken any since last night?'

'One. This morning.' Sophie held up her trembling hand.

Matt took her fingers in his large, capable palm. 'Seems to me that you need help.' His mood seemed far more subdued this evening. 'Perhaps I could do that. How long has this been going on?'

'Years,' she said. 'Since I was at uni.'

'Can't be so long, then. How old are you? Twenty-five?'

'Twenty-four,' said Sophie. 'I started when I was doing my finals. It kept me awake, so I could do my revision and get my submissions in on time.'

'After that?'

She turned on him. 'I don't see that this is any of your business. Why did you come here last night, anyway?'

'I was worried about a couple of things,' said Matt. 'One was Callum Young. I had to go to identify him at the hospital today. It wasn't easy, I can tell you.'

Sophie slumped back into the sofa. 'No, I suppose not. I've never seen a body.'

'Me neither. It felt unreal, and more real than anything else, all at the same time.' Matt's mind seemed to focus internally. Sophie wondered if he was seeing the teenager laid out in the mortuary again. 'Poor bugger. He'd been bashed about on the head, you could see it.'

'What was the other reason?'

For a moment, Matt continued to gaze into the distance. Then his focus snapped back to her. 'You. I was worried about you. I still am.'

'That's kind, I guess,' said Sophie. 'You don't know me, why the hell would you care what happened to me?'

'I have to ask you something,' he replied, neatly sidestepping Sophie's question.

'Go on, then.'

'Did Callum supply you?'

'What would you do with that information if I told you?' she asked. 'Tell the police and get me arrested?'

'I could have done that already if I'd wanted to,' he said. Sophie shrugged, and he continued. 'The police are all over the Lodge at the moment. One set are trying to find out what happened to Callum. The other set are trying to prove that my care home is a hotbed of drug dealing. My job is far more on the line than yours at the moment. If there are others involved and it has been going on under my nose, then I'm incompetent and will get sacked. I might get sacked for what Callum did anyway. I need to find out exactly what Callum was doing because I don't think the rest of them are involved.'

'How can you be sure?'

Matt had got up from the sofa and was pacing up and down the room. His hands were gesticulating as he spoke, the pitch of his voice rising as he described his work.

'I can't be,' he said. 'But I believe them. Most of them aren't bad kids, not really. They've just had shit lives, and we're the last place they get to before they're abandoned by the system, thrown on the scrap heap. I'm the only person to stand between them and getting in with the wrong people, followed by prison and God knows what else in the future. There are sod all resources round here — rural kids don't feature on the government's radar. Nice scenery is supposed to cure everything, according to them. And before you say "bleeding-heart liberal" to me, I'm not ashamed of what I'm trying to do. Someone has to make an effort.'

'I wasn't,' said Sophie.

Matt stopped pacing and looked at her.

'Going to call you a bleeding-heart liberal,' she confirmed. 'But why me?'

'You remind me of my sister,' he said. 'When you came to the home the other lunchtime, I didn't believe your story. No one else gives a damn if one of my lads doesn't attend school. There had to be another reason you came to find him.'

'I see,' said Sophie.

'I know the signs,' said Matt. 'This crap claimed my sister a couple of years ago. We got her into a clinic, which helped for a while. Now she's vanished, and we can't find any trace of her.'

'I'm sorry.'

'If you help me with Callum—' he pointed to the wraps on the table — 'then I can help you with that shit.'

'Do you think Callum was doing this on his own?'

'He can't have been, can he?' said Matt. 'Callum must have been getting his supplies from somewhere. I'm just praying it isn't another of my residents. They took away that book from his room. It recorded his sales and now they've found a heap of cash hidden in his bike workshop.'

Sophie sat up in alarm. 'Did the book have names in it?'

'Not that I know of. Would you have been in it, if there were?'

'Probably.'

'Was he supplying you?'

Sophie thought of the brief, half-coded conversations in the dining hall at school, followed the next day by the clandestine meetings in the churchyard. It was insanely stupid. What the hell had she been thinking? Her skin was starting to itch again. She scratched at her arms.

'Yes,' she said. 'OK, yes. Callum was, sometimes.'

Matt sat next to her and gently held her hand to stop her from gouging at herself. 'Who else? Was it one of my lads?'

'No.' Sophie let him keep her hands still. 'I have a boyfriend.'

Matt pulled away from her. 'I'm sorry, I didn't know.'

She took his hand in hers this time, not wanting to lose the human contact. 'That's not why I'm telling you. He's not much of a boyfriend, really. In fact, I don't know that he would describe me as his girlfriend. He's a dealer, I think.'

'You think?'

'He seems to have access to all sorts of stuff.' Sophie frowned as she tried to describe her relationship with Gary. 'I don't know where he gets it from. Brings it here and we try it out. Sometimes we, you know, sleep together afterwards.'

'You're his guinea pig? That's appalling. He could be giving you anything.'

'He's not from around here,' said Sophie, her thoughts tumbling out incoherently. 'But he lives here. Somewhere. I don't know where. When he visits, he leaves me wraps.'

'And when he doesn't visit?'

'I get them from Callum.'

She stopped, feeling deeply embarrassed at the admission. Without questioning it, she had wandered into this situation with Gary. Naive and trusting, only waiting for the next fix, she had allowed him to use her. Then she'd used Callum in return.

'Bloody hell,' said Matt. 'You really are out of your depth, aren't you?'

CHAPTER 29

Sara knew that they hadn't handled the interview with Steven Lister particularly well. At least Mr Lister had prevented Mrs Lister from calling her a monkey. Having lived in Norfolk for several months, Sara had come to see that there was sometimes a disconnect between the liberal city with its two universities and young population, and the more conservative countryside. This wasn't to say it was full of intolerance, only that their thinking could be old-fashioned. She had been on the receiving end of this attitude on their last investigation, and it had made her wary. People didn't stop to think that phrases that had once been commonplace were actually insulting.

The lights were still on in Chris's café, though the door was locked. She knocked, waving at Chris when he looked up from his open-plan kitchen behind the counter.

He locked up again behind her as she came in. 'Coffee?' he asked. 'I've got some Christmas paninis left over if you'd like one?'

'Yes, please,' said Sara. 'To both.'

She took off her coat and settled in a soft chair that was at least partly out of sight from the street. Chris wouldn't want customers thinking he was still open. He soon had two warm sandwiches and frothy coffees on the table for them.

'Busy day?' she asked.

'Very. If it isn't at this time of year, I'll be in trouble. The takings we get now will ease us through the January blues. How about you?'

'Here and there.'

They ate in silence for a few moments.

Sara wiped her fingers with a paper napkin and stretched her arms over her head with a yawn. 'That's better. It's been a difficult day.'

'How come?'

'Interviews could have gone better,' she admitted. 'Edwards is a great boss, but he can barge around sometimes, leaving me to clear up the damage.'

'The gentle touch?' asked Chris. With a smile, he cleared their plates to the kitchen. 'I'm going to be a while. There's still a pile of tidying up to do. Are you off home or would you like to stay here? I'd appreciate the company.'

Sara settled back in her chair to watch him working, his head bobbing up and down as he loaded the dishwasher and stacked clean plates. She knew she ought to be grateful that Chris didn't object to her job and hours. Being in the police made personal relationships difficult. They didn't live in each other's pockets, as the saying went, though their time together was usually pleasant. He was generous in bed too, and she enjoyed their nights together. Whether that added up to love was another matter. Sara wasn't sure she had ever been in love, and sometimes wondered if she didn't understand what it meant. Perhaps she placed too high a premium on her independence. Living in her own flat and making all her own choices was still a new experience.

She thought of her mother. Tegan would have visited the doctors' today, and she wanted to know how she'd got on. After the family row back in the summer, Sara had bought her stepfather a pay-as-you-go mobile. It was their secret — at least it still was as far as Sara knew. It took Javed a while to get used to it. He kept forgetting to charge it and turning it off when he was at home. She had shown him how to put a number lock on it to keep it private, insisting he didn't use a birthdate as the passcode.

She dialled it and left a message. 'Hi Javed, it's me. I just wondered how Mum had got on at the doctors'? Can you call me?'

'Did you like the panini?' Chris leaned on the counter, scribbling notes on a pad. 'Should I do them again?'

'It was lovely,' said Sara.

Chris adjusted the figures on his order form, then looked up at her. 'Feeling better? Want to talk?'

'I'm OK,' she replied. 'It's only the second murder I've had to deal with here. I'm finding it frustrating. We must be missing something. And I guess I'm feeling sorry for this victim.'

'Don't you always?'

'In theory, yes. This youngster has had a terrible life. I guess it feels unjust twice over. He was no saint, got in with some wrong people, I suspect.'

'Who were these "wrong people"?' asked Chris.

'That's the problem.' Sara sighed, rubbing her face with her hands. 'We can't find them.'

Her mobile trilled. Javed's name was on the screen. Sara reached to answer it. Chris waved his order pad and went to the phone in the kitchen to make his call.

'Can't be long,' Javed said as soon as they connected. 'Your mum is in a state. Thought I ought to let you know.'

'It didn't go well, then?' Sara tried to keep her voice calm. 'What did he say?'

'She,' said Javed. 'Nice woman, very kind. Said she didn't like the look of it and wanted Tegan to go to the cancer unit.'

'When?'

'I'm not sure. Said she would send the referral today, and it would only take a few days. I don't understand it all.'

'Me neither,' said Sara. 'Has Mum being going for her mammogram check-ups?'

'I thought she had.' Javed paused. 'Now she tells me, she'd not bothered. Stupid. I'm so angry with her.'

'Are you at home?'

'Tegan wanted me to go out, said she needed some private time. Whatever that is.'

'Don't be too long,' said Sara. 'She doesn't mean it.'

'I know.' Javed sounded resigned. 'I'm just walking around the block.'

'Will you let me know when the appointment comes through?'

'Sure thing. Can you come down?'

'Don't know,' said Sara. 'Keep me posted, yeah?'

Part of her wanted to jump in her car and drive directly to her mum's home. The other part of her recognised with a sinking heart that she still wasn't sure she'd be welcome.

Sara could hear Chris finishing his order to the catering suppliers. He would be ready to leave soon. She still had a few minutes to herself. Flicking on to the café's internet connection, Sara typed in her query. The first hit was the charity Women and Breast Cancer UK.

If you have found this site, it read at the top of the home page, *you or a member of your family has almost certainly found an unexpected lump in the breast.*

CHAPTER 30

Weak sunlight creeped through the curtains. The wind was still as blustery as it had been last night, tapping against the roof and walls like bony fingers. Danni could hear the sea, and her heart pounded with expectation. She'd only seen the sea once before. Perhaps now she would see it again.

Last night had been revealing. The caravan was clean, modern and warm. Les had left them alone after a few minutes, and Danni had stood by the door, not knowing what to do with herself. Gary had proved to be a careful host, offering her the chance for a shower. At her request, he had put her clothes in the washing machine and lent her a dressing gown. He had also apologised about his outburst in Nick's kitchen.

'Don't know what came over me.' He'd looked genuinely apologetic. 'Did I hurt you much?'

'Not really,' she'd said. 'Got a headache, though. If you have any painkillers.'

Gary was no chef, but two pizzas had been warmed up and waiting with a packet of paracetamol when Danni had emerged from the bathroom. They had eaten while watching the television before he'd made his move. Danni had expected it, had decided when she was showering that she wouldn't resist. After all, he wasn't bad-looking, and she didn't want to aggravate him. His lovemaking wasn't great, but it hadn't been forced either. Danni hadn't shocked him by suggesting anything unusual. As with Johnny, her accepting passivity had seemed to be enough. But at least Johnny generally waited until she came before letting himself go.

Danni had spent much of the night thinking about her situation, before finally falling to sleep.

The early morning light had disturbed her. Checking her mobile, she saw that it was before seven o'clock. She was wide awake, and felt the need for a moment of privacy. Danni pulled on the borrowed dressing gown and padded through to the main living area. The kitchen was methodically laid out, so making a drink didn't take long. Making sure that her clothes were tumbling in the drier, she drew the curtains, then snuggled on to the sofa to sip her tea. Clouds raced along, driven into ribbons by the wind. Somehow the sky seemed larger here than in London. She longed to go out to see the sea. Shaking her head at being so fanciful, Danni focused her mind to plan her next move.

They were obviously in a caravan park, the sort that families would use for their summer holidays. The rows of accommodation stretched either side of this caravan and in three more rows opposite. Danni counted as best she could and decided there must be about twenty of them. Most seemed unoccupied, their curtains open, and through the windows opposite Danni could see white plastic patio tables and chairs stacked, waiting for the summer trade to return.

One caravan further down their row had its curtains drawn, which made her wonder if this was where Les lived. She couldn't see the silver car. A fence of wooden panels separated the park from some bungalows across a narrow road. Occasionally little puffs of sand whirled into the air and settled on to the trimmed lawns between each holiday van. They were obviously a long way from Norwich, and Danni needed to get her bearings. Where was the nearest town or shops or café? Anywhere she might be able to order a taxi?

The best way to access information would be through Gary. She could see that he had a really short fuse, especially if others didn't do what he asked or expected of them. On the other hand, he had tried to make it up to her, seeming to be genuinely sorry for losing control. If she pretended that she liked him, Danni reasoned, enjoyed being with him, then she could earn his trust and find out something that would help her situation. Such as, who had he been talking to on the phone yesterday? Presumably 'sis' meant sister — if so, who was she?

Surely it was Lisa London. The woman had sent her with this package for Gary. It would make sense. Danni snorted in amusement as she compared Gary's behaviour to his sister's. Lisa London's chill, calm efficiency didn't suggest that she easily lost control, though they shared that streak of violence. The other question was how long she would have to keep up the charade. When was Gary supposed to be leaving? She didn't believe for a moment that he would disobey the instructions from 'sis'.

Finishing her tea, Danni listened at the bedroom door. Gary still sounded asleep. Last night he had put the papers from Lisa London in a kitchen drawer. She pulled it silently open and took out the items one at a time. The plane tickets had been printed from a home computer. There were two lots, one from Norwich Airport to a place called Schiphol — Amsterdam Airport. That was Holland, wasn't it? The flight was on Monday morning. The other ticket went from Schiphol to the Aeroporto Internazionale di Napoli. Naples, Italy? She folded the sheets and put them back.

The passport was burgundy, with something unpronounceable printed in gold at the top of the cover and '*Passaporto*' on the bottom. The photograph in the passport was of Gary, though the name was different. Danni didn't know how to pronounce any Italian but guessed that 'Giovanni di Maletesti' was his original family name.

A thump from the direction of the bedroom warned her that Gary might be getting up. She put the passport back, closed the drawer, then tugged her clothes from the drier and locked the bathroom door to get changed. When she emerged, the television was blaring, and Gary was making toast for breakfast.

He held up her cup. 'Don't do that,' he said. 'If you've finished with it, put it in the washer. I can't bear the untidiness.'

'Sorry,' she said. 'I'll remember in future. Did you want a drink?'

Everything has to be just so, she thought, watching Gary move around the space. It was one way of keeping control, she supposed. They had their tea and toast sitting on the sofa, Danni choosing carefully to sit close enough to seem unafraid, but not close enough to be invading his personal space. As soon as they had finished, Danni offered to tidy up.

'I'll get a shower,' said Gary.

'Afterwards, can we go to the beach?' asked Danni.

Gary froze. 'How do you know we're at the beach?'

'I can hear the sea over there.' Danni pointed out of the window to the bungalows. 'Oh, please. Can we? I've only ever seen the sea once in all my life.'

'Really?'

'Truly,' she said. 'When I was young, we had a holiday in Clacton. That's the only time I've ever been out of London.'

'That's rough,' said Gary. 'We went abroad on holiday all the time when I was little.'

'How lovely.' Danni stacked the dishwasher and cleaned the kitchen surfaces. 'So, can we? I'd really love that.'

Gary seemed to consider this, twiddling at his T-shirt, looking her up and down. He looked out of the window. 'It's sunny enough, I suppose. It will be cold, though.'

'I don't care about that.'

'I need to visit Les first. That's on the way to the gap. We can get down on to the beach there if the tide is out.'

'Wonderful.' Danni clapped her hands excitedly. 'That will be wonderful.'

CHAPTER 31

There were few people in the building on Saturday morning, apart from Edwards's team and DI Powell's Drugs squad, who were having their team meetings. As Sara passed their office and glanced in the window, she saw that Ellie was sitting on the edge of the group, not taking an active part in the conversation. She was beginning to think that ACC Miller's idea to divide the detective staff into different teams wasn't his best. Having them separated like this seemed to cause conflicts of interest or an unnecessarily competitive atmosphere, rather than enhancing focus. Crime, like life, rarely fitted into boxes as easily as that. In the SCU office, Aggie was busy putting the coffee on, Bowen and Noble sat hunched behind Bowen's computer, and Edwards was on the phone.

'Morning, Sara.' Aggie pointed to a cake tin and smiled. 'Have some tea bread with your coffee. It will set you up for the day nicely.'

Sara helped herself, turning on her computer and going through her mundane morning routine until Edwards came out of his office. He gathered them around the spare desk, where Aggie plonked mugs, milk and the coffee pot.

'We're making some progress,' Edwards said. Aggie poured out each drink as they dug into the cake tin with greedy fingers. 'Firstly, the bike. The only prints seem to belong to Callum, and the wheels were washed clean by the stream. So not much help. I don't know why the person who dumped it bothered to separate them.'

'He probably had to take the wheels out to get it into a car,' said Aggie. 'We have to if we take my son to a race.'

'At least we know it belonged to our victim.'

'And the bag of clothes?' asked Sara.

'No use, they'd been washed and dumped while still wet.'

'What about the bottle?'

'Definite traces of cocaine. Ellie was right. It was how he was transporting the stuff.'

'But we still don't know where from.'

'Exactly. However, Dr Taylor has DNA results from our victim's sexual partner. Let's start with the sex offender register, as he was underage. It doesn't matter if it was consensual or not — it's still rape. What about the CCTV footage?'

'Forensics have returned the enhanced footage from Stiffkey Woods car park,' said Bowen. 'We were looking at the results. Activity seems to peter out by about 11 p.m., apart from one later visitor, who arrived just before midnight.'

He brought up the video on his computer screen and pointed at a small car. 'Looks like a silver Ford Focus, older model. You can see a partial registration number, which indicates a 2009 purchase. We need to ring the DVLA for a list of corresponding cars with owners in this area. It should be having regular MOTs if nothing else.'

'Right, plan of action this morning,' said Edwards. 'You two get this list and let's hit the most likely local owners with a visit. Now we've got the DNA results, Aggie, you can check the police database for matches, and Sara, check ViSOR. Are there any released offenders known to be in the area? I'd better update ACC Miller.'

Sara settled at her computer to start her searches. 'I'm surprised the ACC is in today.' Bowen grunted, and gave a note to Noble who obediently went back to his desk and made a phone call.

Bowen came over to Sara's side and leaned over to speak in a low voice. 'Next door are planning a raid.' He gestured to the Drugs squad office. 'I didn't tell you this, but they're going after Lyndford Lodge first thing tomorrow.'

'Poor buggers,' said Sara. 'It's been days. Surely they would have moved anything that could be evidence long before now. What are they up to?'

'Not sure,' said Bowen. 'DI Powell doesn't like the housefather, Matt Morgan, at the Lodge. Thinks he's deliberately obstructive. Plus, Powell is looking for a promotion, and I suspect he'll take any opportunity he can get.'

The office door opened, and Bowen sauntered over to inspect the cake tin.

'Good morning,' said Ellie. She dropped her bag behind Sara's desk and helped herself to a coffee. Bowen dipped his hand in the cake tin and lifted out the last piece of tea bread. Ellie held Bowen's gaze as he bit into the cake before turning away and heading for Noble's desk.

'What was that all about?' Sara asked when Ellie sat down next to her.

She hunched her shoulders. 'Don't ask me. You know what he's like sometimes. What are we up to today?'

Sara recognised diversionary tactics when she heard them. 'I'm checking the sex offender register.'

Their search brought up two hits for Norfolk, one recently released and living on the Suffolk border, the other a short jail term, long since expired, for a teenage boy who would now be in his late thirties. Neither were in the Marlham area, but most people had cars in Norfolk because public transport in the countryside was either poor or non-existent. Noble had managed to get a list of likely vehicles from a cooperative office manager at the DVLA. Twenty-seven cars matched their partial plate, model and colour.

Edwards looked disappointed with the results when he returned to the office. 'That's a lot of cars to eliminate. Let's find our two ex-offenders first. Mike, you and Ian can have the run down to Chedgrave. Sara, you can come with me to Horsland.'

'What about me, sir?' asked Ellie.

'You can go with Mike unless your own team need you for anything.'

DI Edwards missed the scowl on Ellie's face and Bowen slamming his chair under his desk as the three officers headed out. Sara didn't.

'Don't go in too heavy,' Edwards called after them. 'See if they can account for their time on Tuesday evening. Then we'll move on to the cars.'

The DI drove them further round the bypass than Sara recognised from previous trips, cutting north of the airport. Horsland was a commuter village, with modern housing estates arranged on either side of the straight road that ran through the centre and on towards Holt. There was nothing attractive or romantic about the place, no older buildings on view or pretty village green. It did have a short parade of local shops, which bustled with activity, and a school next to a modern village hall. They turned off the road into one of the estates, parking on the grass verge of the quaintly named Angel Lane.

The house they were looking for was a semi-detached, with a short gravel drive and neatly trimmed garden. An estate car stood near the front door, its doors open as a thirty-something couple tried to wrangle three small children into the back. Edwards spoke to the father, briefly flipped his warrant card and introduced Sara. The man turned white as he acknowledged them and confirmed his name.

'This won't take long,' said Edwards. Sara was conscious that the mother had urgently quietened the children and stood up on the far side of the car to listen. 'It's just a formality. Can you tell me where you were on Tuesday evening?'

'Why does he have to do that?' asked the wife. 'Tom, what is this all about?'

'I was here,' said the man. 'Babysitting.'

'Tom? What's going on?' The wife walked round to join them, holding a toddler firmly by the hand. 'Why do they want to know where you were?'

A hunted look came across the man's face, and Sara's heart sank. His offence had been a teenage indiscretion, committed with a girlfriend of the time, and was many years old. He had paid his debt to society as prescribed by the court. So, if he'd chosen to move on with his life, who could blame him? He obviously didn't know that he could have applied to be removed from the register by now.

'Babysitting?' asked Edwards. 'Tuesday night? What time?'

'Yes,' the wife cut in. 'Tuesday is my choir night. Tom puts the kids to bed for me so that I can go out.'

Edwards turned to look at the wife. 'When do you get back?'

'Practice finishes at ten,' she said.

'And you come straight home?'

'It's only a few minutes' walk from the village hall. Yes, I come straight home? Why?'

'And then?'

'We had supper and went to bed,' said the man. His shoulders had slumped.

'That's fine,' said Edwards. 'Thank you for your cooperation.'

As they headed back to their car, Sara heard the wife begin to question why the police were interested in her husband. When he muttered a shamefaced reply, her voice began to rise. Sara tried to close her ears to the argument. The personal damage their visits could cause sometimes stuck in her craw. It never seemed to bother her boss.

Edwards called Aggie when they settled back in the car.

'There are three cars of possible interest registered within five miles of Marlham,' she said. 'I'll send Sara a text with the names and addresses.'

'Any getting MOTs locally?'

'One of them,' Aggie replied. 'I'll put that at the top of the list. It's in Walton, up at the coast.'

CHAPTER 32

With some reluctance, Sophie had agreed to let Matt help her. After making her something to eat, he had allowed her to keep a wrap and then took the others away with him.

'I'll visit you each evening,' he said. 'Give you a wrap, so that you can come off it slowly. If you have a really bad day, come up to the Lodge and see me for some more.'

Feeling relaxed and back in control after the hit, Sophie had agreed. It was great not to have to face this on her own. She didn't want to think about what she would do next time Gary came to see her.

She had managed some self-care this morning, as she liked to think of it. Cleaning the flat, putting on a load of washing and finally taking a shower with her favourite gels and shampoo. Most people did this kind of thing automatically, Sophie realised, but for her, it was a step forward. By late morning, she was starting to get jittery.

'I need some fresh air,' she murmured. The weather was mild, and watery sunlight peered through long, thin clouds. 'The sea, I'll go to the coast. I need some ozone.'

Hunting through the debris on the coffee table, Sophie unearthed her car keys. She hadn't driven in weeks, as she could walk anywhere she needed to go in the town. The

Nissan Micra had been a graduation gift from her father, to allow her to visit home in Sussex whenever she wanted to. He had presented it to her, saying how proud he was of her. As she unlocked it, Sophie realised that she hadn't spoken to him in weeks. To her relief, the car started, though there wasn't much fuel left, and she briefly queued at the supermarket petrol station.

Sophie didn't know the area very well, but remembered one place at the beach, a few miles away. Following the signs out of Marlham, she drove up a long straight road to a village called Walton. With its wide beaches, caravan parks, café and chippie, it was popular with visitors all year round. She found a space on the seafront to park and walked along the sea wall footpath to check the view below.

The tide was out, leaving a crisp band of beach that would be easier to walk on than the softer sand close to the concrete sea defences. Sophie climbed over the sandy ramp to access the strand and turned along the shoreline. It wasn't crowded, not like the summer when Sophie had come here for picnics with her friends and met Gary for the first time. She felt her mood lift as she set an easy pace. There was an official walkers' trail along the top of the crumbling, sandy cliffs. Sophie decided to walk as far as the next gap on the beach and return along the ramblers' path. She didn't keep track of the time, and the fresh air made her feel good. Matt had taken his young charges into Norwich for the morning, to go Christmas shopping. Something she would have to think about soon. Perhaps she could call her dad and go home for the holiday.

The gap in the cliffs had a concrete access ramp, which came out between a set of old wooden bungalows on one side and a holiday caravan park on the other. About a hundred metres inland on the rough lane was a flint-and-brick barn that had been converted into a café. The sign outside promised food and hot drinks, and she decided to treat herself.

The café was warm, its windows steamy with condensation from the kitchen. Farmhouse-style scrubbed wooden tables jostled against a selection of old-fashioned chairs made comfortable with homemade cushions. Dressers and shelves were covered in vintage china and ornaments, all of which seemed to be for sale. Sophie chose a small table by one of the windows, which ran floor to ceiling across one side of the café, and studied the menu.

'What can I get you?' asked the waitress. The voice was familiar, and Sophie looked up in surprise.

'Andrea? What are you doing here?'

'Saturday job, miss,' said Andrea. She waved her order pad as if to prove it. 'Besides, it's my mum's café.'

'It's very nice,' said Sophie. 'Are all these things for sale as well? I could do with getting some Christmas presents.'

Andrea glanced at the piled shelves. 'Yes, they are. If you go through that way, there's the craft shop. My auntie runs that, she's got some nice stuff.'

Sophie ordered a toasted sandwich and a latte, then, leaving her coat over the back of the chair, she went to explore the little shop. Tables, shelves and display cabinets held everything from shell jewellery to knitting kits, prints of Happisburgh lighthouse and Norfolk lavender soap. She selected several items and took them to the till.

'Your lunch is ready, Miss Bailey,' called Andrea from the doorway.

Sophie smiled in acknowledgement. 'I'm Andrea's English teacher,' she explained as the woman packed her purchases into a paper bag.

With a nod, the woman popped in a couple of extra soap samples. 'Andrea talks about you,' she said. 'Enjoys that class very much. Thank you.'

The sandwich was delicious, the coffee freshly ground and stimulating. The gift from the aunt had been heart-warming. Sophie settled back in her chair to finish her coffee, feeling more human than she had for a long time. Gazing out of the window, she idly watched other people wandering towards the beach. Some came from a car park along the road. Others walked along the footpath that led back to Walton, which ran behind the wooden bungalows. Sophie racked her brains to remember what a friend had told her in the summer. Hadn't this once been an early holiday park, back in the 1950s? If so, the wooden bungalows were still going strong after all these long years, defying the winter storms and dangerous days when the crumbling cliffs eroded in sudden landslips.

They're survivors, like me, she thought.

As she watched, a familiar figure came out of one of the bungalows. Was that Gary? A young woman followed behind him. They turned back to speak to an older man who appeared in the doorway, then slammed the door in their faces. Gary laughed and taking the woman's hand, he led her down the concrete ramp to the beach. Sophie finished her coffee with a gulp. She left some cash on the table to pay Andrea and hurried outside.

What on earth is Gary doing out here? she thought feverishly. *And who is this woman?*

They were walking along like young lovers. Perhaps they were. Panic flooded through Sophie. She didn't want Gary to see her. Somehow she had to get back to her car on the seafront. Pushing her bag of Christmas gifts into her handbag, Sophie pulled the long strap over her shoulders, pulled up the hood on her coat to hide her face and headed along the footpath as quickly as she could.

CHAPTER 33

Walton was just a couple of miles beyond the turning for Happisburgh. The DI and Sara drove past one of those large medieval churches that every village in north Norfolk seemed to have, and as they rounded a sharp bend, the great grey waves of the North Sea rolled towards them. The parapet to the concrete sea defences and a small wall was all that seemed to prevent the water from flooding the road.

They turned away from the beach on a small lane that ran between a caravan park and a private road. The address they were looking for was at the far end of the crescent. Sara checked the back gardens to each property as they drove slowly past. 'They don't all seem to be occupied.'

'Some will probably be holiday lets,' said Edwards.

'It's remote. No street lights, no CCTV? That's not going to help.'

At the back of each bungalow was a fenced-off garden. Most had postboxes and numbers by the back gate. Small communal paths led between alternate homes to the front of the properties. The buildings themselves seemed to be made out of a combination of wooden panels and brick walls.

The house they were looking for was covered with grey exterior paint that had once probably been white. The windows were streaked with salt and sand. There was a shed of sorts in the back garden, and a bizarre rockery, with an old blue rowing boat balanced on top of it and dead-looking plants in the gaps between the flints.

If you left something like that in your garden in London, it would soon vanish, Sara thought. The garden and house both looked dilapidated compared to their neighbours. Rather like her father's cottage, the place could do with some TLC. A red Vauxhall Corsa stood behind the fence, its nose towards the house.

'This is the back,' said Edwards. He pointed to a path between two of the bungalows. 'We might have better luck at the front.'

Edwards led Sara down the nearest cut-through, which opened out on to a large green. The identical bungalows faced one another across the mown grass. Each had a wooden veranda up a couple of steps, leading to the front door. Their target was the second to last at the farthest end of the sweep of properties. The green ran to a cliff edge. Sara could hear the sea pounding below them as she rang the doorbell.

An older man answered the door. Sara estimated he was in his late fifties. His greasy brown hair was receding and going grey around the temples. His skin looked sallow, as if he didn't get out much or had a bad diet. Pulling his glasses on to his nose from the top of his head, he checked their warrant cards, holding the door half-open to lean out and peer closely at the one Edwards held up. They were not invited in.

'Sorry to disturb you,' said Edwards. Sara plastered a friendly smile on her face when the man looked at her. She wasn't sure if he could see her properly, or if he was squinting for some other reason. He pushed his glasses back up on to his head. 'Mr Les Myers?'

'Yes.'

'We're trying to trace a car,' said Edwards. 'A silver Ford Focus. We understand you own a 2009 model?'

'Used to,' said Myers. 'Why?'

'We need to eliminate it from our enquiries.'

'They sent a detective inspector to ask about a second-hand car?' Myers sounded suspicious. Sara moved behind Edwards to try and get a look inside the hallway. The way Myers was deliberately obscuring their view made her wonder if he had something to hide. The man watched her, and pulled the door even closer to his body. 'Sold it.'

'When was this?'

'Last week. Decided to get a newer one.'

'DVLA still have you as the owner,' said Edwards. He reeled off the registration number, and Myers nodded.

'Yeah, that's it. The garage probably hasn't done the paperwork yet.'

'Who did you sell it to?'

Myers hesitated, as if he was calculating whether to cooperate or not. 'Dan Wade. In Marlham.'

'Doesn't he usually do up classic motors?' Edwards sounded surprised.

'Couldn't say. Answered an ad on the internet.'

'Thanks for your time,' said Edwards. They stepped off the veranda, but as Edwards reached the grass, he turned back to look at Myers, who was still clutching the door and watching them. 'Where were you on Tuesday night, Mr Myers?'

The man stiffened. 'Don't have to answer that.'

'That's true. Why would you not want to tell me?'

'Here,' said Myers. 'I was here all night.'

'Can anyone verify that?'

'I don't know, I was watching telly, on my own.'

He slammed the door. Through the frosted glass panel, they could see him draw a door curtain. When they reached their car, Sara checked the back view of the bungalow. She could see Myers watching them through the kitchen window, even though he was standing well back inside the room with the lights turned off.

'You think that was odd?' asked Edwards. He turned the car around and drove out of the private road away from Walton.

'Yes, sir,' said Sara. 'He didn't want to talk to us, did he?'

'No alibi, either. Look, I'll show you something.' The dirt track wound along behind the caravan park until it met a tiny lane. Edwards drove inland, and within half a mile, they had come back to the bigger road that ran through Happisburgh. They turned towards Marlham, and Edwards pulled up outside the first row of cottages. 'Adam's cottage. Your place now.'

'Yes, sir,' she said.

'It would be a bit of a commute, but manageable with the new bypass.'

'Shouldn't we be getting on?' Sara wished he would mind his own business. It was obvious that he was fishing to find out her intentions. After all, her probation period was up in a few weeks.

Edwards shrugged, and they carried on towards Marlham. 'What did you think of Myers?'

'Didn't want us to see inside, did he? I can't help wondering why.'

'Let's speak to Wade and see what he has to say about this car.'

* * *

The place was busy when they pulled up. A young man was rearranging a pile of old tyres at the very back of the garage, while Wade was lifting a sleek classic sports car on an electric ramp. A customer was sitting in the waiting room, watching their arrival with unalloyed interest. Wade didn't look any more pleased to see them than Myers had. Edwards gave him the car details.

'Oh yeah,' said Wade. He wiped his hands on a greasy rag. 'Last week, wasn't it?'

'Have you still got it?'

'Sold it again a couple of days later. Amazing what a quick engine tune and a bit of spit and polish will do.'

'Can you remember when?'

'Not without checking my books. I have a lady who comes in three mornings a week to do my paperwork.'

'Could you check now?' asked Edwards.

Wade shook his head. 'Got a customer waiting.'

'It wasn't a request,' said Edwards. The young man was hovering by the pile of tyres, watching them and openly listening.

Wade shrugged. 'Is it that urgent? Can't you see Tracey on Monday?'

'Mr Wade, this is a murder enquiry.' Edwards was getting angry, which Sara knew was her cue to step in.

'Could I have a look, Mr Wade? Would you mind?'

'Place is a mess,' said Wade. 'If you want to have a go, feel free.'

He walked back underneath the car on the ramp, checking something. The young man came over to join him. With a shrug, Sara led Edwards into the tiny office next to the customer seating area.

It was cold. An electric heater stood near the desk, but it wasn't on. A bright white strip light in the roof gave less illumination than was useful. Boxes of paper were stacked, their contents scattered on the desk and the floor. It looked as if the place had recently been broken into and ransacked. If it had, Wade certainly didn't seem concerned about it. Sara leafed through the piles. There seemed to be no special order or system. Forms for MOTs lay on top of sales invoices and car component catalogues. A computer stood idle, its keyboard littered with items that were, presumably, waiting for Tracey's administrative attention on Monday.

'Any use?' asked Edwards. He had found a classic car magazine and was flicking through the glossy pages. Sara found half a dozen V5C car sales forms and checked each one.

'None of these are for a Ford Focus.' She put the pile back on the desk. 'They go back for months, date-wise.'

Edwards threw the glossy magazine on to the desk. 'Looks like we might have to speak to Tracey, then. Get her details as we go.'

The customer was feigning lack of interest and drinking something sludgy from a paper cup as they went back outside. Sara extracted Tracey's phone number from Wade as they left. The young man watched them silently, his eyes wide and mouth open, until they climbed into the car.

'Damn it,' said Edwards. He drove them down the high street to get out of Wade's view. 'There's something odd going on here, don't you think?'

'Yes, sir, I agree. But what?'

'Call this woman, let's see what she has to say.'

Tracey answered her mobile almost immediately. Sara explained who they were, and without hesitation, she invited them to her house. It was on Lyndford Road. She was waiting at the front door, inviting them into the kitchen and offering cups of tea before Sara had time to draw her breath. Edwards detailed the car they were interested in.

'Can't say I do remember it,' said Tracey.

'It wasn't there the last time you were in the office?'

'I can't be sure. I only do three mornings a week. Keep the office going, you know? But the forms would have been in the files. Couldn't Dan find them for you?'

'Mr Wade was rather busy,' said Sara. 'He allowed me to have a quick look. To be honest, I couldn't really tell what was going on. The place was rather a mess.'

'A mess?' Tracey bristled. 'What do you mean? When I left the office on Thursday lunchtime, the paperwork was up to date, and the office was immaculate.'

CHAPTER 34

Wade's garage was locked and in darkness when they returned. Tracey had a set of keys and let them in. She flicked on the light switch by the door and headed straight to the office. Sara and Edwards could hear her swearing as soon as she opened the door.

'What the hell has been going on? Did you do this?'

Sara joined her in the door. 'Not guilty.'

'Have we been burgled?'

'I don't know,' said Edwards. 'If you have, Wade didn't see fit to mention it.'

'I keep this tidy,' said Tracey. She climbed over the mess on the floor and began to pile the files back on to her desk.

'Can you tell if the paperwork for that Ford Focus is here?' asked Edwards. Tracey shook her head.

'Not without doing some sorting out first. I would make out a file for a new car until Dan's made up his mind what to do with it.'

'In what sense?'

'To be honest, the best money is in the classic car work, but he makes some second-hand sales. Occasionally, he takes a car in part-ex. If it's not worth selling on, then it would go to the auction to sell for parts. Rarely, a vehicle is so poor that he'll strip any parts of value and send it to be cubed.'

'He told us he had already sold it,' said Sara.

'Well, I don't remember it,' said Tracey. She stood with sheaves of paper in her hands, looking bewildered.

'The previous owner was Les Myers,' said Edwards. 'He claimed he'd sold it to Mr Wade last week.'

'Oh well, if it has something to do with Les Myers, that might explain things.' Tracey sounded sarcastic. She sat on her chair with a sigh. 'This is going to take ages.'

'How about we have a cuppa and lend you a hand?' suggested Edwards. 'You can tell us about Dan Wade and Les Myers.'

The drinks from the automatic vending machine were pretty disgusting. They were not surprised when Tracey said she normally brought in a flask. Sara helped her sort the paper into piles, while Edwards settled into the spare office chair to check each set of car documents they pulled out.

'Myers and Wade are friends?' he asked.

'I'm not sure,' said Tracey. She slurped the coffee and shuddered. 'This is muck, isn't it? I'll have to speak to Dan about it.'

'Les Myers?'

'They're mates, I think. Or perhaps you might call them colleagues. I've no idea how they met.'

'Colleagues or friends, you're not sure?'

'Sometimes he does some casual work for Dan,' explained Tracey. 'Myers is usually skint, so he runs into Norwich to get car parts for whatever job we have on, and Dan gives him a few quid for it. Other times, he just hangs around the garage.'

'You don't like him?' asked Edwards.

'Not much,' said Tracey. She was stuffing papers back into storage boxes as she spoke, and now she looked up at Sara. 'I'm glad if he's not around when I'm working. Gives me the creeps, to be honest.'

'Why's that?' Sara stopped sorting the papers she held. 'Does he do or say things you don't like?'

'No, it's not that.' Tracey considered her reply before starting sorting again. 'There's something unpleasant about his manner. Slimy, I'd call him. It was better before he started coming in.'

'Has he been helping Dan for long?'

'For a few months now. I honestly don't know why Dan puts up with him.'

They worked on for a few minutes until the floor reappeared from under the mess, and the place was beginning to look more organised.

Suddenly Tracey angrily threw a pile of papers on to the desk. 'Why is all this stuff here?' she said. 'Some of this goes back years. Look. MOT certificates from before it all went online.'

'You have to keep them?' asked Edwards.

'Seven years, it's part of our accounting requirements. I tend to keep them longer, to protect us during official checks.'

'Don't you normally keep all that in here?'

'Only the current year and the previous year, until it gets audited. Then it goes into the store.'

'What store?' asked Sara.

Tracey pointed out into the garage. 'At the back. We hardly ever go in there. How has this stuff got in here?'

'What's in the store?'

'Just filing cabinets and some of the more expensive car parts. The sort that collectors might want.'

'Sounds interesting,' said Sara. 'Do you have a key?'

'You want to look?'

'Oh, yes please,' said Edwards with a grin. Tracey took her bunch of keys and sorted through them until she found one to fit a padlock. All three of them went out in the garage.

The overhead light wasn't bright, and the wall across the back of the space was in shadow. It was painted in the same colour as all the other walls. Greasy marks, grimy handprints, sprays of discolouration and stains decorated it, like some bizarre abstract painting. Sara stood back and looked hard. The plywood wall stretched from floor to ceiling. Its construction looked amateur, now that she was paying full attention to it. Moving in closer, she realised that the panels must be nailed to a frame behind to keep them upright. Some of the edges looked ragged, where the paint was missing, and fresh wood was showing.

'It's just a store, then?' asked Edwards.

'It is now,' said Tracey. She headed towards one side of the garage as though she was going to walk straight into the wall. 'It wasn't originally.'

'What was it for?'

'When I first joined, it was a spray booth. You know, for respraying cars.'

'Dan doesn't do that now?'

Tracey stopped in the far corner, where Sara could see that there was a small gap between the outer brick wall and the wooden panels. She turned back to look at them. 'Not for a while. We send stuff out now if we need to. Dan said there wasn't enough of a market for it. I asked him to fill in the walls and make a storage space. You got a torch?'

Edwards and Sara followed Tracey down the gap. As they followed her, their bodies blocked out what little light there was. Sara flipped on her mobile's torch. The gap ran to a dead end at the rear brick wall of the building, where there was a wooden door. It looked as though it had once been an interior door for a house, left over when someone had been renovating. A metal hasp had been fitted, with a padlock to keep it secure.

Tracey fiddled with her key. 'Damn it, I was sure it was this one. Can you shine the light on it?'

She tried several more times without success. Then she tried the other small keys on her bunch. None seemed to fit.

'Could Mr Wade have changed the padlock?' asked Sara.

'I would have thought he'd let me know,' replied Tracey.

Before they could turn back to the office, the main door of the garage slammed open, and an angry voice started shouting, 'I don't know what the hell you're doing in here, but I've already called the police.'

CHAPTER 35

'No need for that, Mr Wade,' said Edwards as they emerged from the gap. 'We are the police.'

'What are you doing in here?' Wade said, his face red with anger. 'I haven't given you permission.'

'I let them in,' said Tracey. 'They were only looking for some car details. Where's the harm?'

'I'll deal with you later,' said Wade.

'It's a murder investigation,' she objected. 'That poor young lad who worked here. Surely we should be helping all we can.'

'You shouldn't have let them in,' said Wade. 'You should have asked first.'

'Was a time when you trusted me.' Tracey blushed. She turned sharply and headed for the office.

'Have you changed that padlock, by any chance?' asked Edwards.

'What's that to you? It's my place.'

'We'd just like to look inside at the paperwork, that's all.' Sara could see the back of her boss's neck beginning to colour as his adrenaline rose. She knew they would both be thinking the same thing. Why would Wade want to stop them from seeing in the store? Tracey burst back out of the office, coat fastened, handbag swinging and the set of keys in her hand.

She stormed up to Wade and thrust the keys at him. 'Don't bother dealing with me later. I won't be working for you anymore. You've been treating me like dirt for months now. Ever since that man came here, and I don't want anything else to do with you or him.'

Wade stepped back, a look of shock on his face. He didn't take the keys, so Tracey threw them on the floor and stamped out down the track towards the high street. 'Oh, and by the way,' she called, 'the coffee in that vending machine is muck. No wonder you've been losing all your customers.'

'I'd like you to leave now.' Wade held open the door. 'If you want to look anywhere else, you'll have to get a search warrant.'

Sara followed Edwards outside. The garage door slammed behind them.

'What's he hiding?' she asked. They went back to their car. Edwards put his mobile in the hands-free slot and punched up Bowen's number.

'I don't know,' Edwards said. 'But there's something he doesn't want us to find, that's obvious. Mike? Where have you got to?'

It turned out that Bowen and Noble were on their way back to the office. Their follow-up with the sex offender had been pointless. The man had an alibi.

'You still got Ellie with you?'

'Yes, sir. I need to drop her at the office to collect her car. She has an early start tomorrow.'

There was an unmistakable sarcastic edge to Bowen's tone. Ellie would have heard every word.

What's happening between them? Sara thought. She was nosey enough to wish she knew what it was. It was a failing every detective had.

'Good,' said Edwards. 'Then get out here, both of you. And bring some food and coffees. We'll wait in the car.'

'Will do, boss.'

Edwards snapped the phone shut. 'You got any plans for tonight?'

'Well, I did have. I was going out for a meal with Chris.'

'Chris?'

'Yes, sir,' said Sara. Surely she'd told him this before? 'My boyfriend.'

'Better give him a call, then. We won't get an early finish tonight.'

Inside the garage, they could hear Wade talking loudly on his mobile. If he was warning someone, there was nothing they could do about it. They were on their own for the time being. Edwards parked his car on the high street, opposite the entrance to the old station site buildings. They sat with the interior light on, ensuring that when Wade left, he couldn't fail to notice them. Edwards got busy making calls while Sara watched the garage. Aggie was still loyally at her desk and happy to get on with the paperwork for a search warrant for Wade's premises. Edwards contacted the nearest station in Wroxham and requested a marked car with two uniformed officers to join them outside the garage.

'Let's make our presence felt,' he said. 'I'd like to search Les Myers's place too. Unfortunately, I doubt I have enough to justify it yet, even though he tried to imply that he had only just met Wade. Either way, I don't want Wade taking any evidence out of that place before we get the warrant through.'

Sara got out to call Chris. 'You finished work?'

'Just closing up,' he said. 'Was going to do a quick clean, then get home to wash myself. You on your way?'

'I'm sorry,' she said. 'It looks like I'll be here for some time yet. I doubt I'll be back in time to go out tonight.'

'Oh, I see.' She could hear the disappointment in his voice.

'You know I can't always get away when we have a big case on.'

'Yes, yes, I know. It's just . . .' Chris's voice trailed off.

Sara felt annoyed with him. She'd been looking forward to a night out, just as much as he had. In the background she heard one of his café assistants calling goodnight.

'Hang on.' He must have placed the phone on the counter. Sara heard him go to the café door and lock up. 'Are you sure you can't get away? I've booked a table. With Christmas and rehearsals, I'll be busy every night from now on.'

'I'm sorry, I really don't know what time I'll be back.'

'What about tomorrow?'

Sara cursed silently. She'd forgotten that they had said they might visit her father's cottage on Sunday morning. 'I think I'll have to work. Is that your last day off too?'

'Yeah,' said Chris. 'It's my place, and I have to be here when it's busy. My next day off will be Christmas Day. It would be nice to have a normal date for once.'

'That's hardly fair.'

'What do you mean?'

'I've been free in the evenings for weeks, and you've been rehearsing that damn play.'

'That damn play means a lot to me,' said Chris. His voice was dangerously quiet.

'More than me?'

'You don't understand. I wanted to be a professional actor, but I never got the chance. Doing this play is as close as I can get. Don't make me choose.'

Sara's breath caught with anger. 'And my job's more important to me than a dinner date.'

There was a difficult silence. Sara had been keeping a watch on the garage door. It swung open, and Wade emerged. She tapped on the car window at Edwards. 'I've got to go. I'll try to call you later.'

'Don't bother,' said Chris. 'It will be too late.'

Too late for what? She killed the call without giving a reply.

Wade locked up, before hurrying to his car. Without acknowledging them, he drove away down the high street. He must have known they were there. Sara racked her brain to remember if there was a shredding machine in the office. He'd been inside long enough to get rid of a few documents that way.

The car from the local station turned up first. One of the uniformed officers said he would recognise Wade, being from Marlham himself. Sara gave him Wade's car registration as a backup.

'You make sure that he doesn't come back here in the middle of the night,' said Edwards. 'He can't be allowed to remove anything from the place until we have a search warrant in place. Make yourselves obvious and wait for a replacement when the shift changes. Understand?'

The pair nodded and settled down to wait. The evening closed in. The street lamps flickered on, and the local shops began to lock up. It was another forty-five minutes before Bowen and Noble turned up. They had chips in cones, bags of cakes and coffees all round. They sat in the back of Edwards's car to demolish the food.

'You're on watch tonight,' said Edwards.

'Here?' Bowen was surprised. He pointed to the local car. 'With them?'

'No. I've got another job for you. Wade was calling someone after he sent us out. I suspect that it was Les Myers. I don't know how he fits into this, but I'm sure he does.'

'He lives in Walton,' said Sara.

Bowen groaned. 'Does he have a car? Walton's a remote place to be without one.'

'Yes, he does,' said Edwards. 'Even if he's gone already, we need to keep an eye on his house. Leaving or coming back, I want to know what that man is doing. You can follow us, and we'll show you.'

The two cars made their way out to the private road. Most of the homes were in darkness, but not all. The caravan park on the other side of the lane also looked largely unoccupied, just two of the vans showing lights. The café was closed, its gravel car park empty. Edwards pulled into it, with Bowen behind him. As Sara got out, she could hear the sea hissing beyond the houses, as it washed up and down on the bank of flints and pebbles that gathered against the sea defences at the turn of the tide. The wind was getting up, picking up loose sand and driving it into her face.

Bowen joined her, and they walked quietly along the back of the crescent so Sara could point out which bungalow belonged to Myers. The curtains were drawn, and there were lights on inside, but that didn't mean Myers was still there. The red car hadn't moved.

'We've nothing to stop him with?' asked Bowen.

'Only suspicions,' said Edwards. 'If he comes out, walks, drives or even gets a taxi, follow him. I'll get backup from Powell's team to relieve you later on.'

'You'll be lucky,' said Bowen. 'They're raiding that kids' home first thing tomorrow. Best we stay all night, I suppose.'

With a resigned shrug, he got back inside next to Noble. The young DC had opened the car door and was stretching his lanky legs with a satisfied grunt. They could take it in turns to nap if they needed to, and Sara knew they wouldn't let Edwards down.

'What about us?' Sara asked as she got back into Edwards's car.

'Back to base,' said Edwards as they left the car park. 'Aggie should have the warrant paperwork sorted out. We have to find someone to sign it off. God help us, on a Saturday night.'

CHAPTER 36

It proved easier than she had expected. As Sophie reached the cliff path, she could see that Gary and the young woman had turned east along the beach. All she had to do was retrace her steps the other way, back to Walton seafront, where she had left her car. The back of her neck prickled a warning that she was being watched, but Sophie reached the car without incident. Not even stopping to shake the sand from her boots, Sophie had driven back to Marlham, left the Micra in the residents' car park and hurried to lock herself away in her flat.

The panic slowly subsided until she felt able to turn on the television and settle on the sofa to look at the gifts she had bought. It distracted her long enough to find a notepad and make a list of people she wanted to get Christmas presents for until the familiar itchy skin and cravings disrupted her concentration. It had grown dark as she watched anxiously out of the window for Matt to arrive. Eventually, she saw him walk around the corner from the high street and was waiting at the buzzer when he reached the door to the block.

'Best not let the neighbours see,' he said. Drawing the curtains closed, he brought a wrap out of the inside pocket of his jacket. Sophie barely managed to stop herself from grabbing the folded paper out of his fingers. She held out her hand, and Matt placed it in her palm.

Unwrapping it, she snatched up the old biro casing and snorted the line. The powder was gone in a second, and made Sophie's head spin. She sat on the sofa, wiping her nose on the back of her hand. As the drug coursed through her system, she felt the control and power return. With a shamefaced glance at Matt, she slumped backwards. 'You must think I'm disgusting. Why do you bother with this? With me?'

'I told you,' said Matt. He settled on the sofa next to her. 'You remind me of my sister.'

Sophie shrugged. She still wasn't convinced by his reason. Maybe he was keeping an eye on her because of Callum's death or something. That cut both ways, of course, because she could keep tabs on his actions too.

'How was Norwich?'

'It was a blast, actually,' he said. 'Some of the lads haven't much experience of Christmas. I suggested they buy presents for one another and put them in groups of three, like a sort of Secret Santa. Gave them thirty quid each and met them again at McDonald's a couple of hours later. You should have seen them.'

'Excited?'

'Just a bit. Bags everywhere, some of them were mine. I get them all something from my own money.'

'Was their spending money from you too?'

'You got me!' Matt slapped two hands to his chest as if he'd been shot, and they both laughed. 'I suspect the McDonald's was a big part of the excitement. Tastes like cardboard to me, but they love it.'

'I haven't had one since I was at uni,' said Sophie. Her head and veins were buzzing with energy now, and she stood up, pulling at Matt's reluctant hands. 'Let's have one now.'

'God, no way,' he said. 'Two in one day? Not a chance. Besides, we'd have to drive into Great Yarmouth to get one. How was your day?'

'Went to the beach for a walk.' Sophie released Matt's hands, staggered slightly and giggled. 'Stopped for lunch at a little café. You missed out.'

Her door buzzer prevented Sophie from teasing Matt any further. With a puzzled shrug, she answered the intercom.

'Hey babe, guess what I've got for you.'

'Gary, oh, hi,' she stammered. Her face flushed as she looked at Matt. 'Hold on.'

'Who's that?' Matt looked as if he had already figured it out.

Sophie let go of the button so her visitor couldn't hear. 'Gary.'

'Your erstwhile boyfriend and dealer?'

'That's him. What the fuck do I do now?' The buzzer shrilled insistently. 'How do I turn him away?'

'You don't,' said Matt. He stood up to move out of view of the door. 'Let him in.'

She pressed the lock release, then opened the door to her flat just enough to peer out at Gary crossing the small lobby.

'Sophie, babe!' said Gary. He pushed at the door, expecting her to open it. She resisted him. 'What the hell?'

'I'm busy,' she stammered. 'I've got work to do. Schoolwork.'

'It's Saturday,' said Gary. He looked puzzled. 'You can do it tomorrow.'

'Not if I get wasted,' she said.

Gary pushed harder on the door. 'Let me in, woman.' He pushed his face close to hers in the gap. 'What's the matter with you?'

'I told you,' she said.

Gary threw his weight against the door, kicking at the panel like a petulant toddler. 'You've got someone in there,' he shouted. 'What the fuck?'

Sophie felt Matt's hand cover hers and pull the door open, moving her aside as he did it. Gary staggered past them into the living room, crashed into the coffee table and rolled on to his side. Snarling abuse, he sat up, rubbing his knees.

His face was dark with anger. Sophie slammed the door shut, turning in time to see him scramble up and lunge at Matt.

'Who the fuck are you?' Gary's hands were outstretched, but Matt sidestepped him. Gary bounced off the wall and spun around, chest heaving with anger.

'You'll be Gary, I take it,' said Matt. 'Sophie's told me all about you.'

'She don't know "all about me",' said Gary. He strode forward and aimed a punch at Matt, who moved to one side again. Incensed, Gary tried again, only to find himself evaded a third time. 'Who are you? She didn't mention you.'

He turned on Sophie, who was standing with her back to the door. She flinched as he strode towards her, raising her hands to protect her face.

'Why've you got another man in here?' He slapped at her hands, trying to make her look at him. 'Don't hide from me.'

Matt shot round the coffee table and grabbed Gary from behind, winding his arms around his opponent's chest. He was, by far, the larger of the two, with the toned muscular body of a fit thirty-five-year-old. With little effort, he swung Gary to one side, sending him staggering towards the kitchen. Grabbing the doorframe, Gary turned himself. He slapped his hands against the wall. 'You can't have two men,' he yelled. 'I won't allow it.'

'Shut up,' screamed Sophie. 'I can do what I like.'

'I'm your boyfriend,' Gary insisted. His shook his head from side to side. 'Aren't I?'

'Oh yeah? One rule for me, and another for you?'

'What do you mean? I don't know what you're saying.' Gary's face contorted with the effort of stopping the tears from falling.

'I was at the beach today,' said Sophie. Her tone was bitter and vicious. 'I saw you. With a girl. A teenager. Like a bloody school romance, walking along the sand, hand in hand.'

Gary let out an inarticulate cry that was somewhere between a wounded animal and a howl of frustration. 'She's nicer than you. I have to bring you hits before you'll fuck me.' He pulled a handful of coke wraps out of his coat pocket and threw them at Sophie.

She laughed. 'Well, at least I don't have to take that shit before I can get it up.'

Gary lunged forward. Sophie felt Matt's hands grab her shoulders and push her to one side. Running at her, eyes blinded by tears, Gary collided with Matt's solid body. To Sophie's surprise, Matt wrapped his arms around the raging young man and pulled him into a manly hug.

'Come on, buddy,' said Matt. He dragged Gary to the sofa, pulled him down on to the seat and held him until his anger began to subside. Sophie watched in amazement. Slowly Gary regained control.

'Got some tissues?' Matt asked.

The whole situation is getting very surreal, she thought, as she righted the coffee table and put the box of tissues on it where Matt could reach them. He grabbed some, then gestured at the wraps Gary had thrown at her. 'Pick those up, will you?'

Sophie collected them, putting them reluctantly into Matt's outstretched hand. He stuffed them into his coat pocket. 'What now?'

'I think you should go home, buddy, don't you?' Matt addressed Gary, pushing tissues into his shaking hand. 'How did you get here?'

'Taxi,' mumbled Gary.

'I can take you round to the taxi office if you like.'

Gary blew his nose noisily, dropping the tissues on to the carpet, and nodded in agreement. 'Yeah, great. Thanks.'

Matt led the snivelling Gary to the front door.

'Will you come back?' asked Sophie. The pair went out into the lobby. Matt had one arm over Gary's shoulders. As they reached the outer door, he glanced back at her.

'I don't know,' he said. 'I thought I could help you, that you were a victim like my sister. Now, I'm not so sure. Whatever you saw this morning, there was no need to be cruel.'

CHAPTER 37

It had been a good day. They'd walked on the beach for a couple of hours until the turning tide had driven them back to the caravan park. About 4 p.m., a mobile wagon selling fish and chips had parked on the seafront and Gary had brought them two fish suppers. Afterwards, Danni had declined the wrap of coke that he had offered her.

All the while, Gary had chatted away like he'd known her for years: generalities about being brought up in Soho, how he'd hated school and gone into the family business as soon as he could. The details of what the firm did or his role in it were not forthcoming. Danni figured they didn't need to be. Lisa London ran a drugs racket second to none over a wide turf on some of the worst housing estates in the capital. Presumably, Gary had been involved in some way. He had also obviously done something wrong or was in danger of giving them away. Otherwise, what was he doing exiled up here?

Once she'd declined the wrap, Gary had phoned for a taxi and gone out, leaving Danni locked inside the caravan. She didn't mind because she'd already figured out that there was an exit through one of the big picture windows. Besides, the front door could be opened from the inside because of fire regulations. If she wanted to leave, she could go whenever she chose. This wasn't the right time.

The other question was, why did Gary suddenly need to be sent to Italy? In his urge to talk, Gary revealed that he had been living out here since the summer and was very bored with the situation. He was desperate to get home, to 'get back to work', as he put it. Yet it seemed that his sister suddenly wanted to send him even further away.

Danni put on the dressing gown Gary had lent her. She assumed that she had the evening to herself and intended to relax. After taking a shower, she turned on the television. Shutting out the dark skies, Danni settled back to watch television.

Bugger Johnny, she thought. His mistakes had landed her here, and she didn't feel obliged to carry on paying his debts. It seemed that Lisa London had taken a bit of a shine to her, implied by her trusting Danni to bring this important package to her brother. Allowing herself a moment of excitement, Danni calculated that if she played this right, she might be able to move her own life on, rather than just rescuing her dim-witted boyfriend. Being in control, that was the key, and Gary's sister might be the route.

The rattle of the door handle pulled her back to the present. Danni didn't know where Gary was. The taxi had arrived to pick him up, bibbing its horn from the gateway to the park, and he'd left with a grin and cheerful, 'Bye, see you later'.

The door consisted of two frosted glass panels. Danni could see someone standing outside. The handle rattled again, and the figure raised a hand to knock. She sat silently on the sofa. People left their televisions on to pretend they were in, didn't they?

'Gary, are you in there?'

It was Les. What did he want? Their visit to his house this morning had ended in a row.

'Gary?' called Les.

Danni assumed he would go away if he thought the place was unoccupied. Instead, she heard something jingling, and a key slid into the lock. Les stepped through the open door. He was shocked to see Danni sitting on the sofa.

'Fuck me. I thought it was empty. You gave me a bloody fright.'

'I'm surprised you have a key,' she replied. Curling her legs up on to the sofa, she smiled sweetly at the man. 'Does Gary know you have them?'

'I don't know,' mumbled Les. He stuffed the spare keys into his trousers as he closed the door. 'You keep that bit of information to your bloody self.'

'If you say so. Why are you here, anyway?'

'I wanted to see Gary.'

'Well, duh,' said Danni. 'Why, though? You didn't sound much like friends this morning.'

'Who the hell do you think you are? You've only been here half a day.'

'Lisa sent me to keep an eye on Gary.' Danni watched to see how this lie would sit with Les.

The man's brow furrowed. 'Gary only decided to bring you on a whim.'

Danni suspected this was true, but she was beginning to enjoy the game. 'Gary decided to bring me here after he spoke to his sister.'

It wasn't a lie. It was a bending of the truth. She waited for Les to process this possibility, and to her delight, he seemed to buy it.

'She thinks I haven't been doing a good-enough job, is that it?'

'Someone had to bring those papers. Someone has to make sure he gets on that flight. Can you do it?'

'I've managed so far,' said Les. He sounded offended, looked Danni up and down. 'You're just a kid. What makes you think you can do it if Lisa thinks I can't?'

Danni knew she was on dangerous ground. If Les knew London well enough to complain, or even to check up on her, Danni would be in big trouble. She needed to turn Les into an ally, not an enemy. At least for now.

'I think it's more that two people trying to persuade Gary might be better than just one. Why did you let yourself in?'

'I wanted to know if he kept that paperwork. Thought I might hide it until Monday.'

Danni stood up, pushed past Les and went into the kitchen. She placed the passport and flight details on the counter.

'Money?' asked Les.

She picked up the wad of euros, waggled them and put them back inside the drawer. Les leaned across to the counter to pick it all up.

Danni slapped her hand down on top of them. 'If he notices they're missing, he'll go ballistic. You know how he keeps this place.'

'He has to get on that fucking flight,' said Les.

'I'm not sure he will,' said Danni. She folded up the flight details and put all the items back in the drawer in the same order they had been in before. 'I'll look after it until Monday.'

'You better. I want that boy gone.'

'Well, we'll have to see.'

'See what?'

Les shot round as Danni pushed the kitchen drawer closed under the counter. Neither of them had heard Gary returning. He stood in the doorway, his face blotchy and red with anger.

'What the fuck are you doing here?' he demanded. He strode across the living room, grabbed Les and twisted him against the kitchen worktop. 'How did you get in?'

'She let me in,' said Les.

Danni wasn't having that. 'Bollocks. Les has a key. He let himself in.'

'What key? You have a key to my home?' Gary was shaking Les. The older man's back snapped against the overhanging ridge of the countertop. He cried out in pain.

'Lisa wanted me to have it,' he stuttered. 'In case of accidents.'

'Or to spy on me?'

'Your sister wouldn't do that,' said Danni. She held her hands up to try and pacify Gary. 'Let him go. Please. For me?'

Gary stopped shaking the older man, and whirled away to turn the television off and bury his face in his arm. Danni could see his shoulders heaving, as Les collapsed on to the floor. She stepped over the prone man to gently touch Gary on one shoulder. He shrugged her off and moved away. She tried again. This time he turned towards her, his face bewildered. 'Why is everyone turning on me?'

'I'm not,' said Danni.

'Don't know that, do I? First Sophie, now Les.'

'I'm here,' she said. Who the hell was Sophie? She pointed to Les on the floor. 'I could have got out before he came. There is a fire exit.'

'You stayed for me?'

Danni nodded and smiled. 'I like you.'

Gary looked between Les and Danni, seeming to become even more confused, then resorted to stating the one fact he was certain of. 'I won't go to Italy. I want to go home.'

'Lisa wants you to go,' said Danni. 'It must be for the best.'

'I won't go. I don't care. No one can make me.'

'The police can,' said Les. He had rolled over and was resting on his knees, one hand clutching the small of his back.

'No police,' shouted Gary. He moved to threaten Les again. 'No police. They can't find me. You promised.'

Danni watched in horror as Gary pulled Les up from the floor by the neck until the older man's feet were dangling. Les struggled, gasping and wriggling, gripping Gary's arms at the wrists and trying to break free. She launched herself at Gary, barging into his back, trying to grab at his arms. The surprise made Gary drop his victim, who bounced sideways as his ankles bent on impact. Gary turned on Danni. 'You said you liked me.'

'I do,' she said. 'Don't make it worse by hurting Les. If the police are involved, you need to go to Italy.'

'Shan't. Won't.' Gary sounded as if at any moment, he might stamp his foot like a toddler. 'No one can make me.'

'You should have thought of that,' said Les. Curled up on the carpet, he massaged his neck with both hands. He coughed roughly, as he clambered up with the aid of the kitchen unit. 'Before you thumped that fucking kid and left me to do your dirty work.'

CHAPTER 38

It took some time for Danni to persuade Gary to sit on the sofa. She made Les take the spare armchair, where he sat rubbing at the red marks on his neck. For once in her life, Danni was in charge. Both of these men were under her control, at least for the time being. She appeased them both with strong, sweet tea.

She sat on the sofa next to Gary. 'I don't know what you two are talking about.' Danni held up her hand to stop Les from speaking. The less she knew about what these two had done the better. Safer for her that way. 'It must be serious, though, or Lisa wouldn't want you to leave the country.'

'Won't go,' muttered Gary.

Danni ignored him. 'You say you cleaned up after Gary?' she asked Les.

'Like usual,' he said. Glowering at Gary, he banged his mug on the table angrily. 'It hasn't been worth the price.'

'Price?'

Les ground his jaw for a moment, then addressed Gary. 'You know, don't you?'

'Come on, Les,' said Danni. 'If I'm going to help you both, I need to know what the deal is between you two, don't I?'

'You?' Les laughed. 'Stick to being the mule, babe. It's the least of your worries.'

'He's supposed to help me,' said Gary. He squeezed Danni's hand. 'My sister pays him to do it.'

'Really?'

Both men nodded. Les said, 'They said it was just a babysitting job.'

'Who by?'

'Tony.'

'The man I met at the flat in Norwich?' Danni still thought of him as Muscleman.

'Yeah,' said Les. 'Said he would give me extra for keeping an eye on young Gary here. Needed to get out of London for a while. Got into a spot of bother, didn't you?'

'Lisa said I should get away,' said Gary. He hung his head. 'Said to have a holiday until the heat was off. I was just unlucky. I didn't mean to cause trouble.'

'That's what you said the other night,' snapped Les. He adopted a whining child's tone. '*I didn't mean it. Just an accident.*' The tone changed to contempt. 'You're a twat.'

Danni felt Gary bristle with anger next to her and laid her hand gently on his arm.

'He's been trouble ever since he arrived,' said Les. 'Junkie girlfriends, arguing with local kids. Upset my bloody network, he has. Then this youngster. I did my best, but it's all over the bloody news. Police are everywhere. Came to my house this morning.'

'What?' Danni and Gary said together.

'Looking for my car.' Les twisted his fingers. 'I don't know how they got on to me. Thank God I'd already shipped it off.'

'Hence the red one in your drive?' asked Danni.

'Well, you are a nosey bitch, aren't you?' said Les. 'I got rid of it last night. It was the last of the evidence. Now I think I'm being watched.'

'What? Where?' Gary twisted to look out the window.

'There's a car with two men in it, parked outside the café. Been there since teatime. Making themselves obvious.'

'But you came here,' said Gary. He shot up and made to grab Les's neck again.

The older man raised his arms and yelled. 'Stop it! I'm not stupid. They didn't see me.'

Gary pulled his hands back to his side and glanced at Danni, who asked, 'How?'

'Went across the green to the cliff footpath, and along to the gap between the houses. There's a gate there from this site down to the beach for the kids in the summer.'

'Well, you can't go back there now,' said Danni. She sounded more in control than she felt. 'You'll have to stay here.'

'What are we going to do?' Gary whispered. Les looked at her expectantly, eyes wide, a sarcastic twist to his mouth.

'Nothing for now,' she said. 'We should make it look as normal as possible, for as long as possible. Les can sleep in the spare bedroom tonight.'

Danni had never been at the centre of attention like this before, making decisions and dictating to the men. It was intoxicating.

'If they'd found it, then they would have pulled Les in for questioning. You two stay inside for now, just in case. They wouldn't know me from Eve, so if we need to go out, I can do it. Let me think about the morning. I'll deal with it.'

'Got a drink?' asked Les. Gary nodded and brought a bottle of expensive-looking whiskey from the kitchen. Danni refused any, and the two men started drinking it in large measures. After an hour, the pair of them were becoming sufficiently wobbly for Danni to suggest they all turn in.

She locked up and went into Gary's bedroom. She heard Les muttering as he fell on to the bed next door with a thump. Danni slid into bed next to Gary. He rolled over and pulled her into his arms.

'You stayed for me,' he murmured. He sounded sleepy, and she began to rock him gently. 'You'll look after me. Just like Lisa.'

Danni waited for nearly an hour, listening to the waves and the wind. Finally satisfied that Gary was asleep, and reassured by snores from Les, she slipped out of bed. She padded silently to Gary's clothes. Watching him breathe under the duvet, and searching slowly and gently, she finally found his mobile.

Praying that both men were heavy sleepers, she took the tracksuit from her holdall and went into the living room. The burner mobile Lisa had given her was still there. The bedroom door closed with a loud click. Danni froze, waiting for a reaction. None came. She carried her clothes to the sofa and put them on. Finally, she pushed both mobiles into her pockets, opened the door, paused to make sure no one else was moving, then dropped on to the grass outside.

There wasn't much moonlight, but the sky was clear. Danni walked away from the site entrance and made her way along the back fence until she found the gate Les had used. It was propped open on a tussock of stringy grass. Beyond, a well-trodden path led along the outside of the perimeter fence. When she reached the road, Danni stared at the waiting car. After a few minutes, a tall man with long legs climbed out and walked slowly around the back of the café. He seemed to be alone.

She ran as silently as she could across to the narrow path that ran past one of the bungalows opposite towards the beach. Danni reached the wooden steps that went down the small sandy cliff to the sea defences. More steps climbed over the wooden wall and dropped on to the beach beyond. She turned to check behind her. She was alone.

The beach stretched away either side of her. To her right, the cliff grew higher, so she turned that way. The tide was out, the choppy waves breaking on the sand at least thirty yards away. After struggling for a couple of hundred metres, she found a hollow and settled down with her back to the wooden wall. Holding the two mobiles in front of her, Danni tried Gary's one first. It didn't even have a number lock on it.

She made a small derisive sound in the back of her throat and scrolled through the contacts list. Every number had a nickname or mnemonic. Panic rose in her throat.

At last she found the one labelled 'Sis'. Danni dialled the number. It rang out the first time. Taking a moment to record the digits into her burner mobile, Danni tried again. This time, a voice replied.

'Gary? What the fuck are you doing calling me at this time of night?'

There was no mistaking Lisa London's voice. Danni drew in a breath, mentally crossed her fingers and spoke.

'This isn't Gary. It's me, Danni. I'm sorry it's late, but I thought you ought to know. There's a big problem here.'

CHAPTER 39

Search warrant in hand, Edwards and Sara were waiting in Marlham High Street early the following morning. The rest of the team stood near their vehicles, yawning and blinking as daylight began to tinge the skies. The DI had called Bowen and Noble to join them. Their vigil in the café car park had been pointless — there'd been no movement at Myers's house all night. Sara handed round some coffees.

As a courtesy, Edwards had called Wade on his mobile to say they required access to the premises and would meet him there at 7.30 a.m. At least, he had left a message. Sara wasn't surprised when the team tramped around the corner to the garage to see that Wade was conspicuous by his absence. The two uniformed officers on watch at the garage joined them, confirming that no one had been near the place all night.

Double-checking the time on his mobile, Edwards gave the signal and Bowen deftly swung the door ram against the white wooden garage door. It splintered at the first blow and burst open at the second. Edwards stepped over the bar at the bottom of the gap, shone his torch along the wall and located the light switch. In a matter of moments, the team had managed to open both entrance doors. Sara checked the high street before joining them. No lights had come on in the flats and houses that stood on the next alley. No vehicles were moving. The small town was silent.

Inside, Sara could hear Edwards speaking from the gap next to the storeroom, followed by a metallic crack. Two of the team had headed to the office. She walked down the small gap to join the others outside the storeroom.

'Well done, Mike,' said Edwards. Pulling on nitrile gloves, they filed into the space one after the other. It was lit by a single bulb dangling from a wire in a wooden ceiling. When they put on their torches, this also looked as if it had been looted. Four old-fashioned metal filing cabinets stood by the back wall, where, Sara assumed, Tracey stored the business records. A wooden table had been pulled in front of the cabinets. Piles of boxes had fallen across its top and on to the floor around it. Four sets of metal shelves that may once have stood opposite the filing cabinets seemed to have been dragged at right angles to form a makeshift wall. More boxes of car parts and paperwork had been scattered in the process. Some boxes had opened as they'd fallen, disgorging their contents into the mess. The dirty concrete floor was only visible in patches underneath the chaos.

In their torchlight, beyond the makeshift wall of shelves, they could make out a large shape. Edwards and Bowen pulled aside one of the units and clambered behind to investigate. Sara peered through another set of shelves as the two dragged at an old tarpaulin, pulling it towards the wall to reveal a small silver Ford Focus.

'Gotcha,' said Bowen. Sara shone her torch on the rear number plate. They had found the car they were looking for.

'Don't touch anything,' said Edwards. 'Mike, get a CSI team in here pronto.'

'How the hell did they get it in here?' asked Noble. They gazed at the car and the mess on the floor.

'I think I can guess,' said Sara. 'I noticed this yesterday.' She led them back into the garage, where the outside of the storeroom wall was hidden behind a pile of old tyres, plastic containers and oily rags. Shining her torch at the edge of one of the wooden panels, she pointed at the newly splintered wood.

'I think they took this wall down in a hurry, hid the car inside and nailed it back up.'

'It wouldn't take long with one of those nail guns,' said Bowen.

'I bet they piled this lot in front to make it look like it had been there for ages. That youngster was working over here when we called yesterday, sir.'

'So he was,' said Edwards. He clapped Sara on the shoulder, gave her a broad smile. 'Good work, Detective. We'll have to wait for the CSI team to be sure about everything, but I think you've cracked this case.'

Bowen gave her a friendly punch on the arm before heading outside to call for a CSI team.

'I think we should pay Mr Wade a visit,' said Edwards. Despite their late night, both of them felt energised now. 'You made a note of it?'

Sara flipped open the traditional small black notepad that she used and flicked back a couple of pages. She read out the address, and Edwards punched it into his mobile. It was on the far side of Marlham, on another of the endless 1970s housing estates. It didn't take much to find it. There was a car in the drive, which they parked behind. Edwards strode up to the front door and hammered with his fist.

There was no reply. Edwards hammered again and Sara located a doorbell, which she rang for far too long. A light snapped on in an upstairs bedroom. She rang again, and a woman's voice called out, 'All right, I'm coming.'

A middle-aged woman in a pair of pyjamas and a dressing gown opened the door. 'What's so important?'

'Mrs Wade?' asked Edwards. He offered his warrant card, introduced himself and Sara rapidly. 'Is Mr Wade here?'

'No,' said the woman. She sounded surprised. 'What do you want him for?'

'We need to talk to him urgently about a car at the garage.'

'There's always cars in the garage. What do you mean?'

'Is Mr Wade here?' Edwards's tone was insistent.

'Well, no,' admitted the woman. 'Can it wait until my husband gets back?'

'I doubt it. Where has Mr Wade gone?'

'He had a phone call last night,' explained Mrs Wade. 'From his mother. She's very elderly, you know. Over ninety. Asked him to go round.'

'Where does she live?'

'Great Yarmouth. What is this all about?'

'Can I get her address?' Sara asked.

'I suppose so,' said Mrs Wade. 'The thing is, she must be quite poorly this time.'

Sara tensed, thinking of her own mother heading for the hospital.

Mrs Wade continued, 'Dan called me late to say he wanted to stay with her all night.'

CHAPTER 40

Matt didn't return on Saturday evening. Sophie paced up and down the living room, twitched at the curtains, made food only to throw it in the bin. By 10 p.m. she had to accept that he wasn't going to turn up. Angrily, she realised that she had passed control of her life from Gary to Matt, only to have the pair of them abandon her. As the coke rush subsided, her outlook became even bleaker. Depression gnawed at her. She scratched at her arms until blood ran freely past her wrists and shreds of skin stuck under her fingernails. She curled up on the sofa and sobbed herself to sleep.

The slam of the front door of the flats woke Sophie, as another tenant left early on Sunday morning. She was exhausted. The sleeves of her sweatshirt were stained with blood. When she pulled it over her head, her arms looked like a wild cat had mauled her. Already the desire for a hit was overwhelming her, yesterday's good work lost for ever. Her skin began to itch again.

Uttering a curse that would have shocked her pupils, Sophie limped into the bathroom and turned on the shower. She stepped into the scalding water, the welts on her arms stinging. When she shampooed her hair, it became almost unbearable.

'Serves you right,' she scolded herself. 'Matt was right. It's like *Jekyll and Hyde*. You turn into a monster as soon as you've taken it.'

As Sophie soaped her body with a soft sponge, the itching and cravings subsided enough for her to think more clearly.

'If today's a bad day, I need an extra hit. Even if it's in two halves.' She dried and brushed out her hair. 'Matt didn't mean it. He just got caught up with bloody Gary.'

The warmth of the hairdryer on her scalp was a fleeting comfort, making her feel more human. She picked out clean clothes that would keep her warm, and moved to the kitchen, made a drink and poured cereal into a bowl. All the time, she kept up her monologue.

'He promised he'd help me. Said I was like his sister. Not that he managed to help her, did he? If Gary's gone and Callum is dead, where will I get a hit now? Matt has to help me. I'll ask him nicely. I was out of order last night. That stupid prick Gary deserved it, though.'

As the caffeine seeped into her system, Sophie realised that she had been talking aloud. With a sigh, she knew that she sounded mad, speaking the thoughts of her good self and bad self. Had she ever done this at school? No one had ever commented on it if she had. Or was it because her intake had been drastically and too swiftly cut?

She rubbed ointment into the wounds on her arms and pulled on some boots and a padded coat. It was almost eight o'clock. Surely they would be awake at Lyndford Lodge. She locked the flat, and walked along the path at the back of the supermarket. It came out halfway along the high street, where she skidded to a halt. That pair of detectives she'd spoken to during the week were climbing into a car. It pulled away in a hurry. Anxious not to be seen, Sophie stepped behind the wooden notice board for the Methodist chapel, which was tall enough to conceal her for a few seconds. With relief, she watched the car head off in the opposite direction to the one she needed.

She slid back out from behind the notice board. Another police officer was talking on his mobile, wandering up and down on the pavement. No doubt there would be more. This called for a change of route. Fortunately, her boots had soft, thick soles, which made little noise on the tarmac. Lengthening her stride, Sophie headed across the high street to a cut-through that would take her out of view of the garage. There was a slight rise on the street, but she knew that it wasn't the incline that was making her breathless. It was the worry of what the police were doing at that garage. Surely this must be something to do with Callum's death. Even so, it felt as if a vice were tightening around her. Paranoia gnawed at Sophie as she hurried on. Was this nightmare ever going to end?

Somehow the high street here was managing to survive, although several shops were boarded up with 'To Let' signs, making it look a little run-down. This early on a Sunday morning, it was deserted, and there was no one else in sight. At the junction, Sophie regained her original route well out of view of the police at the garage. She strode on, turning up Lyndford Road before slowing down to catch her breath.

As her pace reduced, arguments played out in her head. How could she persuade Matt to give her the wraps back? They were her property, weren't they? Pulling out her mobile, she debated trying to ring Matt first.

Chaos descended on the quiet street. Tyres squealed as engines powered up the road behind her. Half a dozen cars, some with police markings, others plain saloons, roared up the road. The leading two swung into the drive for Lyndford Lodge. Sophie stepped back in alarm.

Officers piled out of the cars. Some ran around to the back of the Lodge. Two hammered on the front door violently, yelling Matt's name as they did so. Within seconds, two officers in stab-proof outfits and helmets were battering down the door with some ramming device. The door smashed, they raced inside, shouting. Two more officers followed them.

Shouts and screams sounded from inside the Lodge. Sophie stood mesmerised as more officers ran inside. She could hear doors being kicked open, instructions yelled at the occupants. Crossing the road, and peering down the drive from behind the hedge, Sophie watched as the young residents got brought out, some in hastily pulled-on clothes, several with bare feet. Matt was yelling complaints at the police while he tried to reassure his charges.

A small white van pulled up behind the other cars. Two more officers climbed out, then brought out a pair of dogs, whose tails were wagging frantically. As they approached the house, one of the men paused to speak to a plain clothes officer, who looked up in Sophie's direction. The dogs were taken inside.

The officer marched over to her, his warrant card open for her inspection. 'Can I ask what you're doing here, miss?'

Sophie stepped back, unwilling to speak, unable to take her eyes off the madness in the driveway. Before she had time to frame an answer, one of the dogs began to bark repeatedly. There were more scuffles inside. Sophie heard Matt's voice raised. The police officer looked over his shoulder at this new distraction.

'I knew it,' said an older officer in a drab overcoat. He was obviously in charge and sounded triumphant. 'I told you, didn't I?'

Matt was dragged outside, his arms behind his back.

'No surprise here, then,' the officer said. He leered at Matt, who was shaking his head and struggling with the two uniformed officers who held him captive. 'It's always the managers. Child abuse or drug dealing, you buggers are always involved somehow.'

'It's not mine,' shouted Matt. 'I'm telling you, it's not mine.'

The officer standing with Sophie turned to her, a smug smile on his face. 'I think you should be moving along now, miss. You've seen enough.'

'I can't,' she began. The officer spotted the mobile in her hand.

'You haven't been filming this, have you, miss?'

'No, no. Of course not.' Sophie's voice rose in fear.

'Don't want this all on social media in ten minutes, do we?' He held out his hand for the phone. When she didn't hand it over, he tried to grab it, and she let out a small scream.

'What's going on?' shouted the man in front of Matt. 'Who the hell is that?'

Matt looked up to where Sophie was clutching the mobile to her chest, the officer pulling at her arms.

'Stop that,' the senior officer called, and the younger one let go of Sophie.

'She can tell you,' called Matt. 'The stuff is hers. Sophie. Please, tell them the stuff is yours.'

'Well? What's he saying?' the older officer shouted to her.

Sophie looked at Matt. She shook her head. 'I don't know what the hell that man's talking about. I've never seen him before in my life.'

She turned tail and started to march away from the Lodge.

CHAPTER 41

Danni returned to the caravan. Both men were still asleep and didn't seem to have noticed her absence. She pulled off her shoes and snuggled up under the dressing gown on the sofa. She lay for a while, thinking about how she would deal with what they needed the following morning until the sound of the sea lulled her to sleep. It was Gary shouting her name that shocked Danni awake again. It was still dark. Drawing the curtains and checking outside, she headed to Gary's bedroom. Gary had also woken Les — Danni could hear him muttering in the other room. She perched on the bed next to Gary, and crooned, 'It's OK. I'm here.'

'Thought you'd buggered off,' he said. Catching at her hand, he pulled Danni towards him until their faces were close enough to kiss. His grip was vice-like, and she doubted that she could pull away. Momentarily, Danni wondered if he intended to headbutt her in the face. 'Like all the others.'

'I was only in the living room.' Dropping a light kiss on his lips, Danni stroked his cheek with her free hand. 'I needed to think, and I didn't want to disturb you.'

Gary didn't reply. She watched him weighing up whether to trust her or not. He released the pressure on her hand without entirely letting go. 'I missed you.'

'Breakfast?' Danni asked. 'What would you like?'

'I think there are some eggs.'

'Omelette, or boiled eggs?' Danni smiled as Gary let go of her hand and sat up.

'Boiled.' He smiled in return.

'Toast soldiers?'

'Of course.'

Racking her brains, Danni tried to remember how long you were supposed to boil the eggs for, dredging up some memory about it being five minutes. Les emerged, grumbling, from the spare room. Gary moved nimbly around her in the kitchen making cups of tea, his mood opposite to the one he had woken with. She soon had them all sitting down and eating. The eggs had burst a little in the hot water, but at least they weren't raw.

'What are we going to do next, then?' Les demanded.

'We're going to go to Norwich,' said Danni.

The two men looked at her in amazement.

'Your house is being watched, yes?'

'Yes.'

'No,' said Danni. 'Go and look.'

Les shot over to the window, craning to look into the café car park.

'They've gone, haven't they?'

Les nodded and returned to sit in his chair. 'So?'

'Is there anything to connect you and your car to Nick or Tony in Norwich?'

'I go there sometimes to collect gear.'

'What about you?' she asked Gary.

'Never been there before the day I met you.'

'Good,' said Danni. 'Then we should go there. It's got to be safer than here. It won't be long before they realise you've gone missing and I don't want them connecting you to Gary. Not helpful.'

Her voice sounded commanding, which was a surprise even to Danni. She turned to Gary. 'That taxi company you used? Will they be there this morning?'

'Don't know.'

'They would be curious about a group like this going to Norwich early in the morning,' said Les.

'I figured that,' she said. 'We won't be going that early or as a group. There must be other taxi firms as well. Are there any trains here? It would be better to split the journey.'

'North Walsham is the nearest station,' said Les.

'Do you know the times?'

Les laughed. 'I'm not a bloody trainspotter, how would I know?'

'Got a mobile? Check on the internet. And give me your keys.'

'What? Why?'

'Here's what's going to happen.' Danni leaned forward. 'I'm going to your place, by the back route, while your spotter team are missing. I'll bring you a few things in a bag. Make it look like you're still there. You sort out the train times and order two taxis from two different firms.'

'What about me?' asked Gary.

'I'm getting to you, babe. I want you to clear up here and pack your bags.'

'Not going to Italy. I won't go.'

'Just Norwich for today. I want to get you to a safe place before we decide what to do next.'

'We'll be seen on the train,' objected Les.

'Yes, we will,' replied Danni. 'That's why we won't be sitting together or talking to one another. No one knows about Gary or me, anyway.'

'Good for you,' snapped Les.

'Shut up and listen,' Danni snapped back. 'When we get to Norwich, can you find Nick's place without a taxi?'

Les thought about this. 'I think so. It will be quite a walk, though.'

'Good, and the more twisted the route, the better. It will make it more difficult to trace us on the CCTV cameras. We'll follow you at a distance.'

'Bloody hell,' said Les. There was a begrudging admiration in his voice. 'You've really thought about this, haven't you? Quite the scheming little bugger, aren't you? No wonder London sent you here.'

Danni smiled.

'I'll have you know my girlfriend is as smart as a smart thing,' said Gary. He reached out to hug her. 'I knew you'd look after me.'

'Right,' said Danni. Ignoring Gary's claim to boyfriend status, she stood up. She was tempted to clap her hands like a teacher. 'Let's get going. I want you all organised by the time I get back.'

She allowed Les to show her the route out of the back of the site, even though she'd previously found it for herself. The lie about London was still holding Les in line, thank God. Let Gary think she was his girlfriend if it got the desired result. The one thing she wasn't going to admit was that the move to Norwich had been London's idea. London had told her to make up the details for herself. 'And don't fuck it up,' London had said. 'He's my brother, and if the bastards get hold of him, I will make sure you go down with him, either to prison or the grave.'

Danni had no intention of fucking it up, although she understood the risks they were taking. She crossed the green in front of the bungalows, and followed a narrow footpath between two houses to reach the rear of Les's home.

The key Les had given her opened the back door. Danni glanced around the untidy garden to make sure there were no neighbours were watching her. Then, sliding her sleeves over her hands, she unlocked the door and went straight into a narrow galley kitchen.

A radio stood on the window ledge, and the blind was drawn down. Danni pulled on the pair of Marigolds on the side of the sink. Following Les's explanations, she found a rucksack in the bedroom, and shoved clean underwear, shirts and a pair of trousers into it. She grabbed shaving stuff and deodorant from the bathroom, adding a towel from the pile of clean ones stacked on the basket in the corner.

In the living room, the curtains were closed, with the overhead lights turned on. Danni shut off the lights and opened the curtains to let in the morning light. The sky was crowded with scudding grey clouds that looked full of rain. Putting the rucksack on with both straps, she went back to the kitchen where she let up the blind and put on the radio. Leaving it gently playing, Danni let herself out and locked the back door. She dropped the rubber gloves into a neighbour's bin and returned to the caravan park.

'We've sorted out the taxis,' said Gary.

His suitcase was packed and waiting by the door. Danni threw the rucksack at Les, then headed for the bedroom. She gathered her few clothes into the holdall, picked up her pink backpack and returned to the living room.

'What time is the train?' Danni asked Les.

'Ten fifteen,' he said. 'It will take half an hour to get there.'

Danni checked her mobile. It was almost eight thirty. She had spent more time sorting this out than she'd wanted to. 'What time for the taxis?'

'Mine will be here soon. Yours will be here about nine. I wanted to get away before the laughing squad came back.'

'OK. You better be at the station when we get there.'

'I will.'

The taxis turned up as ordered. Les ran to the park gate as if he was under sniper fire, half bent over and taking a zigzag route.

There's no one to see, Danni thought, *and it makes him look suspicious. I'm dealing with an idiot.*

She and Gary left hand in hand, dragging the suitcase behind them as if they were leaving at the end of a holiday. As the driver helped Gary put the case in the boot, Danni took a last look around the park. The sky was looking stormy. She could hear the sea breaking in large waves, and the wind was getting up again. Whatever happened next, Danni was glad to be leaving.

CHAPTER 42

Sara knew that Great Yarmouth had a bit of a reputation for being run-down, with a population that could sometimes be difficult. According to the press, it was a hotbed of vice and deprivation. The two things often went together, in Sara's experience. She seriously doubted that they would find Dan Wade at his elderly mother's house, and couldn't help thinking that they could have asked a local uniformed officer to go and check. But once the DI had a bee in his bonnet, he didn't trust anyone else to follow it up.

She gazed out at the town as they drove along the seafront. Even on a Sunday morning in December, most of the shops and attractions had lights on. It just seemed like a typical seaside resort to Sara, and she said so.

'It gets a bum deal sometimes,' said Edwards. 'It's not as bad as they say, although there is more than the average amount of crime. The trouble is, it's been left behind.'

'I've never been here,' she replied. 'Should I have?'

'Why not? In the summer it's a great place.'

She checked the map on her phone. 'Along here on the right.'

Edwards turned them into a crescent, and their destination, Peggotty Road, turned them again. Small terraced houses ran along both sides of the road, hunched together to save space and turn a quick profit for their original builders. Even so, Sara sensed the pride of the occupants. Each house had clean windows, and the outside walls were nicely painted. Steering the car between the ranks of vehicles that were parked bumper-to-bumper on both sides of the road, the DI finally found a space, which he neatly manoeuvred into. They walked back along the road to find the house they wanted.

It had a white double-glazed front door with a brass knocker. Like all the others, it opened straight on to the street without even the benefit of a strip of garden to make it more private. Sara knocked, pulling out her warrant card while they waited. Wade would surely have vanished by now. She didn't want to upset his mother if she was as ill as Mrs Wade had suggested. She knocked again, more loudly this time. They waited some more. Edwards tried to peer in the window next to the door. He held his hand up to shield his reflection from the glass.

'Damn these nets,' he said. 'I can't see a thing.'

Sara knocked again, as the neighbour's door was flung open. A well-muscled man, with tattoos rippling down his arms and a bulldog expression, looked out.

'What do you want?' he demanded.

'We'd like to speak to Mrs Wade,' said Sara. She proffered her warrant card, and the man sneered at her.

'I guessed you was coppers,' he said. 'Stand out a mile. What do you want with the old lady?'

'We're just trying to find her son, Dan Wade,' explained Sara.

'Then best you go to the hospital,' said the pugnacious man. 'He was here last night when she had a massive stroke. Ambulance came, took them both up to the Paget.'

He slammed his front door. Sara looked at Edwards, who in turn looked surprised. 'You think he'll be there?' she asked. 'I'd have put money on Wade having done a runner.'

'Me too,' said Edwards. They walked back to the car and had barely managed to get it out of the small space before another car was waiting behind them to fill it.

The James Paget University Hospital was only a few minutes' drive away, though they had to go back into the town to find a river crossing and head for Gorleston, Yarmouth's conjoined neighbour. It was a modern, purpose-built place. The receptionist quickly located Mrs Wade for them, directing them to the rear of the hospital to an ICU for older patients.

Dan Wade was sitting by his mother's bed, in a small room next to the main ward. He held her hand and was gazing at the monitors that surrounded her. Their approach disturbed him, and he looked blankly at them. Sara felt a rush of compassion for him. Whatever he had intended to do last night had been derailed by his mother's situation. Edwards jogged her in the ribs with his elbow, which these days meant he wanted her to lead.

'I'm sorry to disturb you, Mr Wade,' she began. He nodded vaguely, flickered a glance at Edwards and returned his gaze to his mother. 'You may have heard our message to you? About searching the garage?'

Wade grunted in reply. Sara continued. 'We've found a vehicle there, Mr Wade. Hidden behind a false wall. Can you tell us about it?'

'Les Myers,' said Wade. 'It belongs to Myers. He asked me to hide it.'

'When?' asked Sara.

'Can't this wait?' Wade asked, his voice low, the tone anguished. 'My mum's dying here. We need some peace.'

Sara looked to Edwards for clarification. He hesitated, then said, 'It can wait, Mr Wade. But I must make sure you don't leave until we can interview you. I'll have to put an officer in here.'

Wade frowned. 'Just leave me alone, will you?'

'They would be outside,' Sara assured him. 'Perhaps you could call your wife? She might be able to come and support you.'

Wade seemed to take a moment to consider this, then picked up his mobile from where it lay on the end of the bed. Sara pointed into the corridor, encouraging Edwards to follow her. 'Let's give him some privacy.'

'You stay here,' replied Edwards. He also dug out his mobile and wandered into the corridor away from the ward to request backup. Sara sat on a chair opposite the side room. Wade made his call and went back to holding his mother's hand. The DI was gone for some time, returning with two takeaway coffees and a uniformed officer. With a brief instruction and a nod to Wade, they left.

'Who knows how deep he is in this,' said Edwards. 'He might be in the centre, or just helping out a mate. We'll have to be careful.'

He called ahead to request a search warrant for Myers's bungalow, as they sped along the Acle Straight back to Norwich. If Sara had thought north Norfolk was flat, this was even flatter. The fields were below the level of the road. The horizon seemed to stretch beyond her view.

'Whatever his involvement, we can't drag him away from his dying mother's bedside. His lawyer and the press would have a field day.'

'You're all heart, sir,' said Sara. Edwards laughed, but not unkindly.

Skirting Norwich, they arrived back at the HQ in Wyndham just before lunchtime. Aggie was sitting in the office waiting for them. She had the paperwork for the warrant ready on her desk. 'I've tracked down the duty magistrate,' she said. 'He said he'd be there at half past two.'

'Time for a quick sandwich, then,' said Edwards. He handed Sara a tenner, and she took their orders.

As she crossed the glass atrium to the canteen, Sara could see into the car park. With a start, she watched as a convoy of several cars swung in, and the Drugs squad piled out of them.

I wonder if their raid has been successful as well, she thought.

It seemed a pity because she still didn't think the Lodge was a centre for drug dealing. In fact, she would have laid good money on the possibility that the housefather had been one of the good guys, trying to make a difference. When they pulled Matt Morgan out of one of the cars, handcuffed and protesting, Sara stopped in her tracks. She was even more shocked when she saw Ellie unload the schoolteacher, Sophie Bailey, from another car.

The team marched the pair inside the building towards the interview rooms. Ellie saw Sara standing near the reception desk and grinned. 'You just never know, do you?'

No, thought Sara, *you don't, and what has all this to do with Callum?*

CHAPTER 43

The last thing Danni had done as they left the caravan was to take the euros, passport and tickets from the kitchen drawer and hide them in her bag. Gary had been struggling with his suitcase, and she was almost certain that he hadn't seen her do it. He hadn't mentioned it.

Gary did still have the wad of cash that he'd taken from Muscleman in his jacket pocket. He used it to pay off their taxi at North Walsham. Danni suggested he shouldn't be waving that much around as it drew attention. She took a twenty to buy their train tickets from the self-service machine in the platform. The station was tiny and unmanned, the line running locally between Norwich and Sheringham. Dozens of people were waiting when the train arrived. Les climbed into the front carriage, while Danni followed Gary into the rear of the second.

The line wound its way through small villages and across rivers. At one station a large sign said *Welcome to the Broads National Park*. The train stopped three more times before reaching Norwich. Danni remembered the station from her previous trip, and as they got out through the barriers, she scanned the entrance hall until she spotted Les. They fol-lowed him across the car park, down the station approach and across a busy junction. Danni and Gary hovered at the back of the crowd of people waiting for the lights to change.

Les crossed a second road, on a bridge over a river. He didn't look behind to see if they were there and when he suddenly turned down the side of a pub, Danni wondered if he was trying to lose them. She watched him over the bridge wall as he crossed the timber decking outside the pub and vanished down a set of metal steps. Hurrying Gary along, she could see Les walking along a footpath through a garden with a river on his right.

'Can you manage that suitcase down here?' she asked. Gary looked at the path and nodded. She realised with a flash of anger that they were looking conspicuous, trundling along a riverside garden walk dragging the thing along on the grass. They kept their distance. Les vanished again, this time down the side of an old building. When they reached it, she could see that the path veered behind it. Passing with difficulty through a metal kissing gate, they came out in a small lane that ran away from the river. Les was already halfway along it. At least this had tarmac, and they lengthened their strides to cut the distance between them. The place was too quiet for Danni's liking.

The lane widened past a row of old houses. It opened on to a green, and the cathedral loomed over the roofs. She remembered it from the day she had arrived. Now they were right underneath it, and silently Danni was rather impressed by the grandeur.

'Why are there so many people?' asked Gary. They wove between the groups and couples who were all heading in one direction. In answer to his question, the bells in the cathedral rang out.

'It's Sunday,' said Danni. 'They must be going to Mass.'

'Mass? You a Catholic, then?'

'Would it bother you if I was?'

'Don't think so,' said Gary. 'Most of my family are Catholic.'

'I'm not any religion.' *Not anymore*, she thought. 'Are you really Italian?'

'Yeah. Well, my dad was. My mum was a Londoner.'

Les walked under a stone arch out of the cathedral grounds and headed into the pedestrianised centre of the city. The shops were beginning to open for Sunday trade. The place was clean, and the shops and cafés looked expensive. Glancing up, she could see CCTV cameras everywhere. What was the idiot doing?

'You said "was"?' Danni probed, as they forked right on to a cobbled street. The suitcase bounced along behind Gary. 'Where are they now?'

'Dead,' said Gary. His voice was surprisingly without emotion. 'I was only young. Lisa has been looking after me ever since.'

'On her own?' *That would explain their closeness*, she thought.

Les turned into a large department store. They had difficulty following him without bumping into the displays of expensive handbags, perfume stands and high-end make-up concessions.

'We lived with my uncle Frank.' Les was leaving the store by another door. They came out opposite the market. 'Francesco. My dad's brother. And my auntie Lily.'

'Is he still around?'

'They both are,' said Gary. Les was climbing a rise behind the market, which led to a large official-looking building. They followed him along in front of it, then between a modern glass-and-steel library on one side and another huge church on the other. They had been walking for ages. 'Where the hell are we going?'

'I don't know,' said Danni. 'But if we don't get there soon, I'm going to catch up with the bugger and ask.'

'Let's not,' said Gary. He nodded at a passing police car. Les turned away from the city and across a small park.

'You have family in Naples, then?'

'That would be my *nonna*.' Gary smiled. 'She's lovely.'

'Why don't you want to go to her, then?' asked Danni.

'I love Nonna. It's not her. It's the rest of them.'

As they crossed another busy road, Danni realised she ought to know where she was. That other large church, the one with *The Narthex* over the door, was on their right and ahead of them blocks of flats rose above the older buildings. Les turned and twisted several more times before they got to the square where Nick had brought her. Les had already vanished yet again, and Danni had to rack her brain for several moments before she could remember which block they needed.

As they approached Nick's maisonette, the front door was unlocked. There were angry voices and, pushing open the door to look through the tiny hallway into the kitchen, she could see Les. He was being held down in a chair by Muscleman, who was pulling both of Les's arms up behind him. Les was squirming in pain. Striker was leaning on the kitchen table.

'You better not have lost them,' said a female voice.

Gary froze next to Danni, his eyes wide, mouth open.

'He hasn't,' called Danni.

She pushed Gary inside, dragged the suitcase into the hallway and shut the front door behind her. At the same time, Muscleman let go of Les, who lurched on to the floor at Striker's feet. Striker casually pulled back one heavy boot and landed a kick in the middle of Les's back. Les rolled away, banging his head on the kitchen door as he went. Nick was standing part-way up the stairs, watching the scene and wringing his hands anxiously.

'We're here,' said Danni.

'Thank God for that,' said Nick.

'Go on, then,' she said. 'Look who's come to see you.'

Gary ran into the kitchen, a huge smile on his face. As Danni followed, she saw him run into his sister's waiting arms. Hugging him possessively, Lisa London looked over his shoulder at Danni.

'Everything's all right now,' she crooned, rocking Gary gently. 'Everything's going to be all right now.' She fixed Danni with a stare. 'You did well.'

Danni nearly wet herself with relief. Then she grinned. This was exactly what she had been hoping for.

CHAPTER 44

By the time Sara had returned from the canteen, the Drugs squad were all in their office, joshing one another. Ellie, the only woman in the group, stood to one side, looking uncomfortable.

Edwards looked surprised when Sara told him what she'd seen in reception. 'I wouldn't have thought that of him.'

'I agree,' said Sara. 'They must have some evidence, or they wouldn't have brought them in. And what about the teacher, where does she fit into all this?'

'Let's go find out,' said Edwards. 'If Morgan is dealing drugs, then this puts a new spin on who might be responsible for Callum's death.'

The Drugs team didn't notice them coming into their office. Edwards interrupted DI Powell to request an update, which Powell seemed reluctant to give him.

'You better ask Ellie,' he said. 'We're going to the pub for lunch.'

'When will you be interviewing?' Edwards asked.

'Later on,' replied Powell. 'Let the pair of them sweat a bit. DS James.' He shouted this last, quieting the group. Ellie turned around. 'You go with DI Edwards and liaise.' His voice was loud, and he sounded smug. 'Come on, you lot. Let's grab a quick one.'

With a scowl, Ellie followed them back to their office, while the rest of the Drugs team headed off to the pub without her. She stood by the spare desk, her arms folded. 'Sir?'

'The faster you fill us in, the sooner you can join your new friends,' said Edwards.

'My team, you mean.'

Ellie outlined the raid, saying the boys had all been cautioned at the home and released again. With relish, she told them about the scene outside in the driveway, and Sophie Bailey's Saint-Peter-like denial of Matt Morgan's assertions. Powell had arrested both of them, she finished.

'Are the boys alone up there?' asked Sara.

'No, some social worker was called. The one from the school, you remember her? Lives local and got there pronto.'

'What made you arrest Morgan in the first place?' asked Edwards.

'The sniffer dogs,' said Ellie. 'We had a pair of them lined up to search as soon as we got everyone outside. Morgan's office was one of the first places they went, and sure enough, we found wraps of coke in his jacket pocket.'

'What about the rest of the place?'

'Clean as a whistle,' said Ellie. 'At least, that's the news so far. Still got the outbuildings to do.'

'I bet you find traces in young Callum's little workshop,' said Edwards. 'Do you think the coke does belong to the teacher? Why would Morgan have it if it did?'

'Don't know, sir,' said Ellie. 'DI Powell will get to that when he interviews them later.'

'Let me know when he does,' said Edwards. 'I'd like to watch, in case there's anything else to help trace Callum's murderer.'

'I'll ask DI Powell.' Ellie's tone was verging on mutinous.

'Then tell him from me, I want to watch the whole thing.' Edwards headed into his office, calling over his shoulder, 'If he has a problem, he can talk to me about it. Or ACC Miller.'

It's all to do with turfs, thought Sara. Turf wars and gang behaviour. They were almost as bad as the street criminals they were fighting. What was the point of making an issue out of it, when they weren't going to be here? They would be going out to search Myers's place any minute now. Sara followed Ellie out of the door. 'Which room is the teacher in? Can you show me?'

'If it's quick,' snapped Ellie. They headed for the interview suite, where a private viewing area stretched behind three standard interview rooms. Sara shut the door as they went in to look.

Sophie Bailey was in the first. Slumped in a chair, she was rubbing at her arms through her jumper. She paused to sip the cup of drink in front of her, then began rubbing again. Matt Morgan was in the second, pacing the floor. He held his plastic cup in his hand, drops of grey machine coffee spilling on to his fingers each time he changed direction. A stone-faced uniformed officer stood in each room. Sophie ignored her female companion. Morgan kept glancing periodically at his male one, as if he wanted to ask a question but knew there was no point in trying.

'You say you found wraps of coke?' Sara asked. 'Were they like the ones in Callum's bedroom?'

'Identical,' replied Ellie.

'Were there many of them?'

'About a dozen.' Ellie shuffled as if she felt uncomfortable.

'Is that all?' Sara was surprised. 'That could easily be for personal use, then, rather than dealing. Could he have confiscated them from Callum?'

'Or given them to Callum to sell.'

'You remember that school friend of Callum's?' Ellie nodded, facing Sara for the first time. 'He said that Callum had an older, richer friend somewhere. He thought that Callum would cycle off to meet him.'

'Go on.'

'We think it might have been a man called Les Myers, lives out at Walton. The lad also said it had something to do with Wade's garage in the town.'

'Where you were this morning?'

'Yep. And guess whose car we found there? Les Myers's. We're going to search his place this afternoon. The DI is organising a team as we speak. You should come with us. If he's as deep into this as I suspect, there could be something in this for your team.'

'You think he could be the dealer, not Morgan?' Ellie asked breathlessly.

'It's possible,' said Sara.

'Oh, I'd love to come with you,' said Ellie. Her eyes lit up. 'That would be a real coup for me.'

'Good.' Sara turned to look at Sophie Bailey again. 'You know what? I think she's a user. Look at her.'

The teacher had rubbed her arms until blood had stained her pretty jumper. Now she was scratching at the back of her neck with one hand. With the other, her fingers beat an arhythmic tattoo on the table. Sweat was forming on her face.

'She's getting withdrawal symptoms, if you ask me.'

'Could be,' said Ellie. She turned to leave the observation room, but Sara stepped in front of her.

'Are your new team giving you a hard time?' she asked. She kept her voice low, moving close to Ellie. 'I know what that's like. You know I do.' Sara had been subjected to resentment, a nasty piece of hazing and a degree of racism when she had first joined the team back in August.

Ellie nodded. 'I'm the only woman.'

'Just plain old sexism, then?'

'More of a macho culture than anything outright.' Ellie sighed. 'I can handle myself, you know I can. They don't believe me.'

'Meaning that you have to go in twice as hard, to prove the point.' Sara had been in this situation herself, before she had left the London Met to come to Norwich. 'Makes you edgy and angry, doesn't it?'

'I suppose. If you're right, then this search would be great for me. Prove I can do something special and they should give me less hassle.'

'What's Bowen's beef, then? I know he can be a bloody dinosaur, attitude-wise, but I thought you both got on.'

'We did.'

Sara waited for Ellie to continue. Sometimes silence was the best way to draw someone out. Ellie seemed to be weighing her up. Finally, she spoke.

'We're mates, right?'

'I certainly think so,' said Sara. She schooled herself to be patient again.

'Can you keep a secret? A personal one? It's really important to me.'

'Of course, if you want me to.'

'Mike saw me,' said Ellie. 'Off duty. On Thursday night. I was coming out of the Loft. With my new girlfriend.'

CHAPTER 45

'I'd guessed,' said Sara. Ellie stepped back. In the interview rooms, Sophie Bailey's face ran with sweat, and Matt Morgan continued to pace the floor.

'How?'

'When we went out for drinks,' said Sara. 'You would be eyeing up the other women in the bar, not the men. I'm not saying you made yourself obvious, but watching body language is part of our training. I read what I saw.'

'It didn't stop you coming out with me?'

'Why would it?' Sara asked. 'We're just friends, right?'

'You didn't think I would try to hit on you? That's the excuse I've been given before.'

'Not at all. Besides, that's a man thing, isn't it?' She mimicked a blokey voice. '*All they need is a good man, that would sort them out.*' Ellie laughed, and Sara was glad she had taken it as a joke. 'Is that the sort of bollocks they say in Drugs?'

'Exactly right,' said Ellie.

'Some things don't change, do they?' Sara asked. 'It's nobody else's business.'

'It's different with Mike.'

'He hadn't guessed?'

'No, he was shocked.'

206

'I reckon he's been carrying a candle for you for years,' said Sara.

'I know,' sighed Ellie. 'I never encouraged him, though I appreciated his support over the promotion thing. He seems to like Aggie these days, so I thought I was off the hook.'

'Give him time,' suggested Sara. 'You know how old-fashioned he is. You were too young for him, anyway.'

Sara led Ellie back to the SCU office, where Edwards was waiting for them. 'SOCOs are bringing Myers's car in this afternoon. There are fingerprints everywhere and lots of trace samples to be had. It looks like Wade just hid it and didn't do anything else with it.'

'Surely Myers must have cleaned it before he took it there?' Ellie asked.

'He would have tried,' replied Edwards. He turned to Aggie, who was packing her stuff to go home. 'Thanks for coming in, it's been a great help. Now, let's get this warrant for Myers's bungalow signed off.'

He didn't question that Ellie was tagging along when she grabbed her bag from the other team's office. The magistrate lived in a large Georgian terraced house in an exclusive crescent in the centre of Norwich. Edwards joined the duty magistrates' clerk at the door, and they went inside. Within ten minutes, he'd emerged with the signed warrant. They drove out to the coast, where a SOCO team, Bowen and Noble were waiting outside Myers's bungalow. Bowen scowled when he saw Ellie climb out of the back seat of Edwards's car.

He turned his back on her and spoke to Edwards. 'I've knocked twice, boss. We had a wander around the back garden. There's a radio on in the kitchen, but no other signs of life. I don't think there's anyone here.'

Edwards knocked at the front door for the form of it. Curtains twitched in one or two of the neighbouring properties. There was no reply, and Edwards waved Noble in with the door ram. The old wooden door smashed open with the first hit.

Noble looked at the ram in his hands with surprise. 'I didn't hit it that hard.'

'It's old and knackered,' said Bowen. 'You're young and strong. Suit up, kid, and let's have a look.'

They pulled on the necessary protective wear and did a quick sweep around the small house, before letting the SOCOs in.

'Pull the place apart,' ordered Edwards. 'I want to know what this man's been doing. Look for anything. Drugs, cash, what's on the computer.'

Immediately the photographer began to take positioning shots and a searcher went into each room. They opened drawers and cupboards, lifted cushions and mattresses, and emptied waste bins. The first shout came from the SOCO who was standing by Myers's ancient-looking computer. It stood on a table in the corner farthest away from the front window. Edwards and Sara looked over his shoulder.

'It was already on.' He sounded excited. 'Only had to push the mouse. His search history is vast.' He clicked through the computer files. 'This thing is an antique, too. Easy enough to go through, no passwords, no protection.'

'Anything in particular?'

'Lots of porn.' The man scrolled down a long list. 'Suspect stuff, if you ask me. Look at this.' He clicked open the site.

Sara gasped at the images that slowly downloaded. It was hardcore. The participants were older men and young boys, their bodies free from pubic hair.

'They could have been shaved,' said Edwards. His voice was soft, though Sara could hear the anger radiating from it. 'Or they could be underage. Either way, we need to speak to Les Myers. Has he been acting on this? Is Callum his victim? Save this stuff, bag everything up and get it back to the lab. Let's see how much of this he watches.'

The officer pushed a memory stick into a wonky portal and looked delighted when the computer recognised it. Settling in the chair in front of the screen, he streamed data on to the backup.

'Are we sure Myers is the friend that Callum used to visit?' Sara asked.

'Fingerprints,' shouted Edwards. His frustration was boiling over. 'I want clear fingerprints and anything that will give us DNA samples.'

Another officer was dusting the door frame. 'Some good ones here. I'll get them on to the system as soon as I can.'

They heard Bowen call from the bathroom door. Sara followed Edwards as he hurried down the narrow corridor. Bowen held up a toothbrush and a hairbrush in separate evidence bags. 'This should cover Myers.'

'What about anyone else?'

'I'll check the kitchen,' said Sara. 'Unwashed crockery?'

She was out of luck. The SOCO working in there pointed to a plastic draining rack, where Myers had left his washing up to dry. There were no dirty dishes. The washing machine stood empty, the door partly open.

'You never know,' said the SOCO. He ran a swab around the inside of the rubber door seal. 'Let's see what he's been washing recently.'

'Sir?' Sara heard Ellie call from one of the bedrooms. They crowded through the tiny door. Ellie was looking at the bed, where several clothes hangers were scattered. 'This place is really neat. He even makes his bed. So why are the hangers thrown here? Those might be gaps in the wardrobe.' She pointed to the line of shirts and trousers hanging on the rail inside. 'He may have done a runner and taken clothes with him.'

Before they could consider this, a woman's voice called from the bathroom. 'DI Edwards?'

The officer was kneeling on the floor. When they clustered in the doorway behind the DI, she sat back on her heels and dropped two numbered evidence markers in place. The first stood next to a basket in the corner of the room. The second leaned against the base of the ceramic shower tray.

'I can't be sure until I get this lot back to the lab,' she said. 'But?'

'That's Lloyd Loom.' She pointed to the basket. 'Hard to clean because of how it's constructed. I think there are blood traces in the weave.'

'Not unusual to cut yourself in a bathroom,' said Edwards.

She nodded and pointed to a break in the edge of the shower tray. Two sharp points of porcelain loomed up like canine teeth on either side of the damage. Someone had tried to fill the gap. The old grout looked discoloured.

'Someone's tried to clean this area. But they didn't do a very good job. This looks like a tiny bit of blood and hair. Someone's banged their head on this, and recently.'

CHAPTER 46

Despite loud objections, Les left with Muscleman, and instructions to work out a plan to solve the problems in the Marlham dealing chain. Nick had fussed around Lisa London like a tugboat docking an expensive cruise liner. Assuming she would be staying there that night, Danni took her holdall upstairs to the spare bedroom, peeping into the living room while she was up there. Nick's study looked lived-in. The computer was running an outer space screensaver. A wad of paper at least two inches thick lay in the printer's out tray. Piles of used mugs, plates and empty food packets littered the desk and the living room. The muse must have been driving the writer's side of Nick ever since they had gone up to the caravan park.

Danni returned to the kitchen.

'Time to go,' said London. She pointed at Danni. 'You'll come with me, for now.'

Nick was evidently happy to shut the door as the four of them went outside. Danni wondered where they were going, as Gary walked beside her, holding her hand possessively. London's black saloon stood in a tree-lined side street with expensive-looking Victorian terraced houses on either side. Striker drove them around a one-way system until he reached a tiny hotel behind a large white wall. He spoke into an intercom, the gate opened and they drove into the gravelled car park.

Danni had no experience of hotels, except from the outside. On occasional trips into the centre of London, she had gazed enviously down the private road that led to the Savoy, where taxis dropped uber-rich people outside the front door, and doormen in uniforms sprang to help them out. As they walked into the lobby of this elegant hotel, she greedily breathed in the heady atmosphere of luxury and looked with jealous eyes at the antiques that stood on side tables and shelves.

Striker and Gary were despatched to a separate room, while Danni followed London upstairs. The bedroom seemed large to Danni. Two tall, narrow windows overlooked a formal garden. In the bay of one stood a pair of chairs and a low table already laid with a tray of hot coffee and a selection of exquisite miniature cakes. Danni stared round in amazement and longing. How wonderful it must be to live like this. She thought of the untidy, dank flat she shared with Johnny and made a vow that she was never going back to that kind of life ever again.

'Sit there,' commanded London. 'Tell me what's been going on. Leave nothing out.'

Danni did as she was told. London interrupted with the occasional question, such as 'Did you sleep with him?' or 'How did Gary react?', but largely let Danni talk. When she'd finished, London passed Danni a coffee cup. 'You have great observation skills.' She maintained eye contact for an uncomfortably long time.

Danni fiddled with the china cup and saucer. 'This is a nice place.'

'It was recommended to me,' said London. 'You haven't asked about your boyfriend.'

'Johnny? I haven't thought about him much,' admitted Danni. Putting the drink back on the tray, she decided to go for broke. 'He's a loser, isn't he?'

'I'd say so,' replied London. 'It's not clever to steal from the company you work for, no matter what the business. It was bound to get back to me.'

'What's happened to him?'

'Let's just say he went a couple of rounds with a friend of mine and has seen the error of his ways.'

Danni took this to mean Striker, although no doubt he also had minions who would be happy to do that kind of thing. Easy enough on those estates to find a thuggish alt-right geezer who'd enjoy a bout with a young black man, especially if the meeting was secret and no police likely to arrive. Striker wouldn't have to get his own hands dirty. She didn't want to go back to that estate — even the place where Nick lived was nicer than that. Heart pounding, Danni looked at London.

'I think Gary trusts me,' she said. 'I don't want to go back to that estate, or Johnny, any more than he wants to go to Naples.'

'Gary will be going to Naples, whether he likes it or not,' snapped London. 'You're going to help me make sure that happens tomorrow morning, first thing. He doesn't have his passport. Do you know where it is?'

'It's in my holdall, at the other place.'

'Striker will collect it.'

'What will happen to me after that?'

'We'll see. You seem to have half a brain. I might be able to use you if I can trust you. What do you want out of life?'

Danni looked around the beautiful room, turned the cup around on its paper-thin china saucer, and looked at London's elegant figure. Her designer clothes, the expensive scent, and the aura of being in complete control. That was what Danni wanted, and she didn't much care how she got it. She held up her hand, palm outwards in supplication.

'All this,' she said. Her voice was breathy with excitement. 'I want nice things like this. I want good clothes, not cheap shit from a chain store. I want meals in restaurants, not McDonald's, and holidays on beaches with cocktails to drink. I want the money it takes to get those things. I want to be like you.' She stood up. 'I don't want to go back into all that useless shit.'

'What size are you?'

'What?' The odd question stopped the flow of Danni's excited talk. 'Sorry?'

'What dress size are you?' Danni heard the impatient edge creeping into London's voice.

'Ten.'

'Lucky you. Go and get a shower. Put a face on. Hurry.'

It delighted Danni to do as she was told. The towels were soft and absorbent. The gels and lotions had a heavenly scent. As she dried her hair, London came into the bathroom with a handful of make-up, which Danni began to use. She returned with a beautiful pale-blue, floaty floral dress and a pair of matching shoes. The dress had a designer label, a brand whose Regent Street shop window displays intimidated Danni when she walked past. The shoes were a bit big, but Danni didn't mind. The outfit made her feel like a princess.

'Come on, girl,' called London. 'I'm hungry.'

Danni burst out of the bathroom, ecstatic at the transformation.

London looked at her calmly. 'It will do for a start.'

'Thank you,' breathed Danni.

'If you like the good life, what will you do to get it?'

'Anything,' said Danni. She meant it. Anything — mule work, high-class prostitution, bringing drugs in a suitcase from abroad. She didn't care. 'Absolutely anything.'

'Here's the deal,' said London. 'You help me get Gary to the airport tomorrow and then we'll see. If you think he trusts you, let's put that to the test.' She threw a pale-pink pashmina to Danni, who ran its soft folds through her fingers and draped it around her shoulders. They went down to the lobby. Gary was wearing a sharp-cut suit and a silk shirt with a high-buttoned neck. He looked amazing.

'Did you get a private room?' London asked. Striker nodded.

'Where are we going?' asked Gary. They went out to the car.

'The Holly,' said London.

'My favourite,' said Gary. His brow wrinkled in thought. 'You mean, in London?'

'No. There's one here in Norwich, and they have shepherd's pie, just the way you like it. Will that do?'

Gary laughed with pleasure as Striker drove them out of the car park.

CHAPTER 47

They kept Sophie in the interview room for hours. At one point, a kindly, older uniformed officer came in and offered to get her a sandwich, which she gratefully accepted. Eventually, the female officer near the door agreed to take Sophie to the toilet. She found it troubling that the officer waited inside the ladies while she used the cubicle. After she washed her hands, Sophie inspected the welts on her arms.

'Do you need something for that?' the officer asked.

Sophie nodded. The nice older officer returned to the interview room with a first aid kit.

'I'm Sergeant Jones,' he said. Sitting next to Sophie, he cleaned the scratches with antiseptic wipes and held up a tube of Savlon. 'You OK with this and plasters?'

'Yes,' said Sophie. Sweat bubbles formed on her face and dripped down the back of her neck.

The man placed the tube and some plasters on the table, watching as Sophie rubbed on the cream. 'Some people are allergic, you see.' Plasters in place, the sergeant pointed under her forearm. 'Can I?' Sophie nodded, and he rotated her arms to inspect her veins. 'Not injecting, then?'

'No,' said Sophie. Instinctively she sniffed, rubbing at the base of her nose.

'I see.' Pulling the sleeves of her jumper down to cover the injuries, he packed up his first aid kit. 'My daughter's a teacher. Didn't they say you're a teacher too?'

'Yes. At Marlham Academy. English literature, mostly.'

'My girl teaches biology,' he said. Standing up, he tucked the kit under his arm and went to the door. 'It's very stressful in those high schools, isn't it?'

'Sometimes.'

'Need a little help to get through the workload?'

Sophie couldn't reply. She stared at the table in front of her, ashamed to admit anything to herself, let alone to this kindly, soft-spoken sergeant. He'd seen through her immediately. Of course he had, it was his job to be able to do that, and no doubt he'd known plenty of other people like her before.

'There's places, or people can help you with that,' said Sergeant Jones. 'It's not too late to change, you know.'

Then he was gone, and the waiting continued. They'd taken Sophie's mobile away when she'd been arrested, so all she could do was watch the digital clock high up on the wall as it silently ticked away the minutes. It felt like torture. It also made her angry, even though she guessed that they were doing this to her on purpose. More tea arrived. Sophie got taken to the toilet again. Finally, she became drowsy, and her chin sagged on to her chest. Suddenly, just after 4 p.m., the door opened with a bang and two officers came into the room. They turned on the recording machine and began. The man spoke rapidly, reiterating her caution and offering a duty solicitor. Sophie didn't understand half of it and shook her head.

'DI Powell and DS Ellie James,' said the man. 'Say your name for the recording.'

Sophie complied. She gave her address and details about where she worked.

'A high-school teacher?' Powell asked. 'These lads at Lyndford Lodge were your pupils, then?'

'Some of them,' she agreed. 'Depends on their streaming.'

'You were at the Lodge when the drugs were found in the boy's room.' This wasn't a question.

'Yes,' said Sophie. 'One of my pupils was Callum Young. He hadn't been into class that morning, and I was worried about him.'

'Was this boy a regular attendee at school?'

'Not always, but he seemed to like my classes.'

'Have you ever gone to find a missing pupil during your lunch break before?' DI Powell waited until Sophie shook her head. 'What's special about Callum Young?'

'Apart from the fact that someone murdered him?' Sophie snapped. 'I was right to be worried about him.'

'Did you have any reason to suspect something might have happened to him?'

'Not really.' Sophie kept her voice low.

'Then why did you go to the Lodge?' Powell persisted.

'Did you know him outside school?' asked DS James. Her tone was less judgemental. 'About his life? What about his friends?'

Sophie couldn't answer either of those questions. The sweat was increasing, her breathing was shallower, and her head swimming.

'What sort of company did this boy keep?' Powell asked before Sophie could collect her thoughts.

'I don't know,' said Sophie. Fuzzily her brain flashed up something about good cop, bad cop. Her lips smiled before she could control them.

'You find this amusing?' Powell leaned back in his chair, an arrogant smirk on his face.

'What about Matt Morgan?' asked DS James. 'How long have you known him?'

'A few days,' replied Sophie. 'I met him for the first time when I went up to the Lodge to ask about Callum.'

'As you may be aware, we found cocaine powder in his possession.' The DS paused for Sophie to reply, but she didn't. 'Matt Morgan is adamant that these wraps are your property.'

Sophie put her arms around herself in a defensive hug. It was no use. Had they guessed why she was looking for Callum? Matt had called her 'cruel', she suddenly remembered. He didn't deserve her protection.

'No,' she said. It was more of a wail.

'He says that he was keeping them for you,' said Powell. His look seemed condescending, as if he knew he had caught Sophie out in a stupid lie. 'We'll have to investigate this claim. Do you understand?'

'Yes,' said Sophie.

'We will have to search your home. What will we find, do you think? Or would you prefer to tell us now?'

Sophie tried to shake her head, only to feel her whole body shake. In a panic, she looked up at the nicer, female officer. Her jaw seemed to be locking, and she couldn't speak.

'What do you take?' asked DS James. Her voice was almost as quiet as Sophie's had been. 'Are you missing it now?'

'Look at you,' DI Powell sneered. 'Going cold turkey, are we? Who does the coke in Morgan's jacket pocket belong to? Is it yours?'

She was shaking hard. Releasing her arms with a jerk, Sophie gripped the edge of the table.

'Who did you get these drugs from?' Powell's voice echoed in Sophie's ears.

'Sophie, do you feel unwell?' asked DS James. Sophie felt her body stiffen as she struggled to control the shaking and the noise in her mind. She just wanted them to shut up. She needed to breathe and couldn't while they were grilling her like this.

'Sophie, did Matt Morgan give you the drugs?' It was Powell again.

Sophie shook her head once.

'Did you get them from someone else?'

One nod.

'Can you name them? Was it always the same person?'

One shake. Sophie thought her head was going to explode.

'More than one person, then?'

'Yes.' Her voice had become a high-pitched rasp.

'Who then?'

'Was it Callum Young?' demanded the impatient Powell.

'Sometimes.'

'Who else?' asked James.

'Gary. Gary Barr.'

'Who the hell is that?' Powell turned to James. 'Is he at the home too?'

'I think we need to leave this for now. She doesn't look good.'

Sophie's world began to spin. Her rigid muscles released all at once, and she slipped sideways off the chair on to the floor. Curling up in a foetal position, she sobbed into her chest. Her voice grew louder and louder. 'I want my father! I want my father!'

'For fuck's sake,' shouted Powell. 'Get a first-aider.'

Footsteps pounded out of the room. Someone put their hands on her, and tried to pick her up.

DS James's voice was low but brisk. 'Sophie? Sophie. Can you sit up? Sophie, have you called anyone to help you?'

'Dad! Dad!' Sophie pulled herself into an even tighter ball. She beat the side of her head on the floor. 'Get off me. Leave me alone. I want my father.'

CHAPTER 48

Edwards and Sara had watched DI Powell from the observation room as he'd interviewed Matt Morgan and then Sophie Bailey. Morgan had continued to claim that the coke belonged to the teacher.

'I've been trying to help her,' he'd said. There had been no colour in his face and he'd sat rigidly, looking Powell in the eye. 'She's in trouble, takes too much of the stuff. Ask her.'

'We will,' Powell had said. 'Don't worry about that.'

'I need to get back to my boys. They need me.'

'Social Services will deal with them,' Ellie had said. 'They'll be fine.'

'You'll stay here until I say otherwise.' The pair had moved next door to where Sophie Bailey had been nodding asleep. They'd watched without comment as Powell had browbeaten the teacher until she'd fallen on the floor in hysterics.

Edwards stood to leave, as Sara watched Sergeant Jones rush to help Sophie. 'That won't stand up in court.'

'No, sir,' agreed Sara. Powell slammed out of the interview room and stomped away to the Drugs team office.

As they went back to their room, Edwards said grimly, 'Powell won't be allowed near her until tomorrow at the earliest. Nor will we.'

'At least we learned one thing,' said Sara. 'Sophie Bailey was buying coke from our victim Callum Young. And who is Gary Barr? Why haven't we heard about him before? I'm still not sure about Matt Morgan, though.'

'I suspect he's telling the truth. He's a do-gooder. I think he must have known that she was getting the stuff from one of his charges and he didn't see fit to tell us. That gives us grounds to interview him too.'

'Now, sir?'

'No,' said Edwards. 'Let the fuss die down a bit. Then I'll tell Powell. He'll need to know.'

'Right, sir,' said Sara. 'Will they take Bailey to hospital?'

'I would think so. Speaking of which, can you check up on Mr Wade and his mum?'

Noble had loaded the coffee machine in readiness. Bowen was working through the various police databases for mentions of Les Myers, without success, while Sara rang the James Paget Hospital.

'Forensics have sent off the toothbrush for DNA testing,' Bowen said. 'That will take a couple of days, I expect.'

'The SOCO team have brought the car back into the forensics garage,' said Noble. 'And they're going over Wade's garage for anything else.'

Sara put the phone back in its cradle. 'Mrs Wade senior is seriously ill. The nurse thinks she won't make it through the night. Mrs Wade junior has arrived, and they've had some big row.'

'I wouldn't be at all surprised,' said Edwards. He smiled wryly. 'It doesn't pay to keep secrets from your partner. I can tell you that from personal experience.'

'Damn right,' said Bowen. He angrily opened Aggie's cake tin, then, turning the base upside down, added gloomily, 'All gone.'

But you weren't Ellie's partner, thought Sara, *so you don't have any right to know. He needs a few home truths delivering.*

Sara wasn't convinced that being Ellie's friend gave her the right to speak out, nor did she want to spoil the truce between Bowen and herself. But if they didn't sort themselves out soon, she knew she would have to say something.

'Shame,' she said. 'I do miss Aggie when she's not around.'

'Mike, do you have the list of names for the residents at Lyndford Lodge?' Edwards asked. 'Is there a Gary Barr?'

Bowen pulled a sheet from his tray and scanned down it. 'No, sir. I didn't think I remembered the name from our interviews.'

'Fingerprints are in, sir,' said Noble. He had been monitoring his computer while they had been filling their coffee cups. 'There are three different sets.'

'Good, let's see what matches we have,' said Edwards.

Sara pulled up the email on her screen and ran the search. The first set belonged to their victim, Callum Young.

'We know he was in the bungalow,' said Sara. 'There's no match for the second set, even though they seem to be everywhere.'

'If Myers has no reason to be on any databases, then we won't get a match,' Edwards pointed out. 'Bet we get some from the car to match him. What about the third set?'

'Nothing locally, sir,' said Sara. She logged into the National DNA Database. The programme ran for a couple of minutes until it threw up a match with an *urgent* flag. 'Sir. Look at this.'

'Met flag?' Edwards leaned forward. 'Bring it all up. Let's see what's going on.'

Sara opened the tabs to bring up a mug shot of a handsome young man, with short dark hair and a surly expression. He looked about twenty-four or twenty-five years old, and underneath the charge number, he was wearing an expensive shirt and designer jacket.

'He was charged with dealing in a nightclub raid.' Sara read off the entry. 'Pockets full of weed, but no class A drugs. Brought in and charged, released pending a court date. Never turned up. Missing since early August. Name of Gary Barnet.'

'Not Gary Barr?'

'No, sir, but the prints are a definite match. There's a direct line number here.' Sara dialled the number and realised she recognised it. 'Think I might know this officer.'

'One of your old Met mates, eh?' Bowen asked.

'I think we worked a big case together. I doubt he'd be in on a Sunday.'

They were all surprised when a brusque man answered after a few rings. 'DS Mead.'

'Mead, is that really you?' asked Sara. She put the phone on speaker.

'Who is this?'

'It's Sara, Sara Hirst. We did the Gillies investigation together.'

'Sara?' They listened as DS Mead searched his memory. 'Sara, erm, Sara Hirst. Oh God, the tall lass from Tower Hamlets? Really? I thought you'd left.'

'I have, at least I left London. Working for the Norfolk force now.'

Mead laughed. 'You'll regret that. Nothing interesting ever happens up there.'

Sara looked at Edwards, who shrugged his shoulders, and Bowen scowled into his coffee mug. 'It's happening now. What are you doing in on a Sunday anyway?'

'Lost at darts,' said Mead. 'And the same back at you, Sunday working. Why are you ringing?'

'I think we might have a trace on a missing con for you.' Sara explained about the match. Mead sounded excited at the news. 'We think he's calling himself Gary Barr up here.'

'Is it recent? Is he still up there?'

'Can't be sure at the moment.'

'God, I hope you find the little bugger,' said Mead. 'I was furious when we lost him.'

'Surely it was a relatively low-grade offence?' Sara was puzzled. 'That amount of weed is too much for personal use, but hardly a major dealer.'

'No, it isn't. His sister is the dealer.'

'What?'

'Gary Barnet—' Mead couldn't keep the excitement out of his voice — 'is the little brother of Lisa London.'

Bowen sucked in his breath and cold coffee with it, sending him choking out of the room. Noble looked at Edwards in puzzlement, as the DI stood up.

'Different names,' Sara pointed out.

'Sure, but they all have a raft of names. You know that. We've been after Lisa London for years, ever since her uncle set her up in business. Never been able to prove a goddam thing, of course. Far too clever for that.'

'How do you know he's related?'

'We knew she had a little brother, though he didn't seem to be active in the firm. There's a huge file on her, and when we got a familial match on the DNA, we thought that we'd finally got something on them we could make stick. You know, put him away for the lesser crime, and expose her somehow. Of course, by the time we realised who he was, it was too late.'

'He'd gone?'

'We traced Big Sister's car as far as the motorway services near Stansted Airport the day after the raid. Assumed she'd sent him back to Naples.'

'Naples?'

'Who's that?' Mead asked.

'My boss, DI Edwards.'

'Hi, DS Mead,' said Edwards. 'Thank you for your help. Why Naples?'

'The family originate from there. Their father died twenty or more years ago. He was stabbed in a gang fight. The two children went to live with their uncle, who's a legit kind of guy. At least, we think he is. Runs the best Italian coffee bar in Soho.'

'Her uncle who set Lisa London up in business?'

'Not the same guy,' said Mead. 'It's a big family. They waited all that time, then came over in a pack to take out the gang that had killed the father. Lisa took over the turf. Totally ruthless, except where her brother is concerned.'

'Looks like he washed up in north Norfolk. We only know where he has been, not where he is now.'

'Good enough for a start,' said Mead. 'I'm going to get hold of my boss. He'll want to know everything you got.'

DS Mead took down their details, and Sara agreed to email over the fingerprints for a double-check. 'Thanks for all this. It's a breakthrough for us all. I do remember you, Sara. When we raided the Gillies warehouse, you felled that big lad with a single punch. You can handle yourself.'

'Thanks, I think,' said Sara.

'Just be careful, won't you?'

'I always am.'

'No, I mean, be really careful. These people are dangerous.'

'How so?'

'Lisa London is Elisabeta di Maletesti of the Maletesti Camorra family.'

CHAPTER 49

The Holly was the classiest restaurant Danni had ever been in. Not that there was much in her experience to compare it to. The three of them were sitting at the bar, sipping cocktails. Danni's had a sprig of lavender in it, a flower she could only identify because it was listed on the menu.

Striker waited in the lobby until their private dining room on the first floor was ready. The manager was a slim, tall and elegant woman, wearing the version of the staff uniform that indicated her status. She took them upstairs, introduced their private waiter and left them to look at the menu. Striker sat on a chair outside in the corridor, looking every inch the personal bodyguard that he was. Gary took all this in his stride, opening the bottle of champagne that was chilling in a bucket on the table with a skill Danni would not have credited him as having. She felt as if she had fallen through a trapdoor into an alternative universe. This was how the other half lived. It was worth breaking her no-alcohol rule for drinks as lovely as this.

London encouraged them both to have anything they wanted while she sipped the fizz gently and ordered low-calorie everything. Danni was confused by the menu, so she fell back on a cliché she'd seen in old movies. 'I don't know what to have,' she said. Smiling at Gary, she folded the menu and put it next to her plate. 'You order for me, will you?'

Gary blushed with delight and studied the menu closely. When she glanced at London, the big sister was wearing a smug expression that Danni chose to interpret as approval. She ended up with exactly the same as Gary. Soup that arrived with cooked baby tomatoes in the bowl and the liquid poured over them by the waiter. The shepherd's pie was luscious, as was a sweet called crème brûlée that was more creamy than anything she had ever tasted before. While they ate the meal and drank more champagne, it grew dark outside. Danni watched open-mouthed as London paid the bill in cash and tipped the waiter with a fifty-pound note. It was a short walk along the cobbled street to meet Striker, who brought the car round to pick them up.

London took Gary into the hotel, leaving Danni in the car. Striker studied her in the rear-view mirror, his face impassive. She felt as if he was trying to read her mind or memorise her features for future reference. After a short wait, London returned, and they drove off.

'Where are we going?' asked Danni.

'You didn't think you were staying there, did you?' London laughed, and Danni bowed her head in embarrassment. She had been hoping that she would. 'You can keep the clothes and shoes. I won't touch them again now.'

They drove along a suburban road with parades of shops and fashionable bars. Striker turned up a side road, which wound into a housing estate and stopped outside a small park. He peeled pairs of surgical gloves out of a box and handed them round. Danni followed London's lead and pulled them on. The park gates were locked, but Striker led them a short way along the metal railings to where a maintenance building was set into the fence. A narrow alley ran down the side to a large metal gate. Striker put his arm through the rails and turned the handle from the inside. The gate swung open.

Danni followed the pair into the park. Her first thought was that she might ruin her new shoes. Her second thought was that the pashmina wasn't enough to keep her warm, and her third was to wonder what the hell they were doing here.

It grew darker away from the street lights. Striker flicked on a small torch. The path led them beside a formal ornamental lake to a circular, single-storey white building with a colonnade running around the circumference inside and out. Striker turned down the inside colonnade, where doors and windows alternated at set spaces, indicating rooms inside. The doors all had bars across them, and the windows had padlocked shutters. Stopping outside the only door without a bar, Striker rapped on the solid wood panel. There was a scuffle inside, then the door opened slightly. The occupant was checking them.

Satisfied, Muscleman let them in and locked the door. The room was clearly a store for a café, with tables and chairs piled up to one side and boxes of crockery or supplies to the other. A pair of strip lights flickered in the ceiling. Striker stood with his back to the door, hands folded in front of his groin. Danni stood beside him, slumped against the wall in horror. Tied to a chair in the middle of the room was Les Myers. His hands and legs were strapped to the sides of the chair with cable ties. His face was bruised and cut. A trickle of sticky blood congealed on his left cheek. Muscleman stood behind Myers, hands on his hips.

'Cameras?' asked London.

'Dealt with,' said Muscleman.

London stood in front of Myers. 'I'm feeling generous, and I'm going to give you a deal—'

'I don't need a deal.' Myers looked furious. 'I was doing fine on my own until you showed up.'

Muscleman slapped him hard across the back of the head. Myers grunted as his head rocked forward with a loud crack from his neck. Slowly, he looked up.

'I paid you to look after Gary,' said London. Her voice was measured, though the tone hinted at anger underneath.

'And I tried,' replied Myers. One eye was twitching with an involuntary spasm.

'You didn't do a very good job.'

'He kept going off on his own. I didn't know what he was doing. Took half my stock with him sometimes.'

'I didn't pay you to be his jailor. I paid you to keep him safe.' She nodded at Muscleman, who slapped Myers hard on the ear. Myers squealed in pain, and Danni bit her lip to stop herself making an involuntary sound. 'Shut him up.'

For one horrible moment, Danni thought London was ordering one of them to kill Myers, until Muscleman pulled out a roll of black gaffer tape, and plastered a strip over the man's mouth. Myers started to hyperventilate. Danni could hear his breath struggling in and out of his nose with the sticky accompaniment of blood-flecked snot. He shook his head to clear his nose, and the mucus flew in the air, spattering a few gobbets on London's gorgeous suit jacket.

'Will you look at that.' She took a dainty lace handkerchief from her pocket and wiped at the spots. 'Dirty fucking animal.'

Muscleman grabbed Myers under the chin and turned his face up to look at London. She grabbed Myers's face. Snot flew everywhere, and blood-filled mucus ran down London's fingers. The tension in her hand turned her knuckles white, as she squeezed hard, fingernails piercing into his cheeks. Tiny beads of blood bloomed and ran. The man could barely catch enough air and tiny mewling noises issued from his throat.

'Dirty. Fucking. Animal.' She laughed in his face and let go. Myers sucked in air and phlegm, coughing into his sealed mouth. His eyes rolled in panic as he tried to swallow and breathe at the same time. London took the lace hanky and wiped her hand. She dropped it gracefully into Striker's waiting hand.

'As you failed to keep my beautiful brother safe—' London raised a finger and glanced at Muscleman — 'you have one last chance to redeem yourself.'

With his free hand, Muscleman pulled a knife from his jacket pocket. He held it against Myers's neck, making sure that it nicked the flesh. Just as Striker had done to Johnny, Danni remembered.

London leaned over Myers, bringing her face close to his. 'You claim that Gary killed this boy. Why would he do that?'

'Accident,' Myers tried to mutter even though his mouth was sealed and his jaw clamped from below by Muscleman's rigid hand.

'Sure, it was an accident,' said London. 'One that you caused, and then you tried to blame my poor, defenceless brother.' Myers's eyes widened. 'Here's your deal. When the police catch up with you, and they will, believe me, you tell them that you had a fight. That the boy fell and banged his head, just like you told me. You admit that the punch came from you. There was no one else in the house.'

Myers gargled something that might have been 'No, no, no,' until Muscleman cut another large wound in the struggling man's neck.

'It will be manslaughter,' said London. She stretched up, took a step back from Myers and pulled out her mobile. She opened an app with a code. 'You can say that you moved the body in a panic. You have no previous, and I'll make sure you have a good lawyer. With luck, you might get a suspended sentence. Either way, it's unlikely to be more than three or four years. Depends on the judge.'

She stepped to one side of the chair, and Myers did his best to lean away from her. Muscleman slapped Myers's other ear, grabbed the chin again and twisted Myers's face round to London. The man was making fearful animal noises and openly blubbering. London held up the mobile.

'See this?' Muscleman prodded Myers in the throat with his knife until he nodded. 'You see how much this is? Can you see where it is?'

Myers squinted at the screen. He looked at London without understanding.

'This is for you,' she said. 'If you deny Gary's involvement, and take the blame on yourself, it will be waiting for you in an account that only you can access once you have accepted whatever sentence they give to you. Three years? Maybe four? And then you will be a rich man. Do I have your agreement?'

Muscleman released Myers's head and put the knife back in his jacket, wiping it with a tissue first. The imprisoned man's head lolled forward in relief.

'Well?'

Myers nodded.

'Good,' said London. 'I'm done here. Striker will come back to help you move, Mr Myers, after he has taken me back to my hotel.'

Danni looked in horror at the figure of Les Myers slumped in the chair, only the cable ties held him upright. That could have been her or Johnny. Muscleman unlocked the door. Striker checked outside, then held it open for London. For a moment Danni wasn't sure what to do.

London crooked an imperious finger and Danni ran after them. Muscleman shut and locked the door as they walked down the colonnade.

Her heart was racing, her body covered in a sheen of sweat. The ill-fitting, high-heeled shoes clacked on the concrete of the footpath by the ornamental lake. London frowned at her. She was making too much noise, it might attract attention. Fearfully trying to walk on the grass next to the path, Danni stumbled along.

Her mind spun with the scene she had just watched. What was she involved in? Why had London wanted her to witness that? Was it to see her reaction to the violence? Was it so that Danni could be placed at the scene if London wanted to turn her over in the future? Danni had seen fights before, of course. Living on the Hayridge, you couldn't really avoid seeing them. Never before had she seen anyone who seemed to relish cold-hearted violence as much as Lisa London.

It was too late now. This was the world she had just begged London to be allowed to join. Danni shivered, and it wasn't with cold.

CHAPTER 50

Mead's boss was DCI Lambert. Sara remembered him and it seemed he also recalled her. He rang back ten minutes after they had finished speaking to DS Mead, and arranged to be in Norfolk HQ the following morning.

'I need to talk to this Myers urgently,' said Lambert.

'If we find him, I'll let you know,' replied Edwards. 'Our other contacts are all second-tier until we track him down. See you tomorrow.'

There was little else they could do until Forensics had completed their work in the house and on Myers's car, so they finished for the day. When Sara reached her flat, she was surprised to find Chris already in the kitchen. They had exchanged keys some weeks before with the understanding that they didn't take advantage of each other's personal space too much. How much was too much had yet to be negotiated.

'I thought you might be working late.' He opened the oven door. 'I was going to leave this here on a low light. I know how tired you are when you get in sometimes. Shall I sod off now?'

'No, that's OK,' said Sara. There was a fresh crusty loaf on the worktop, which Chris cut into large slices. She brought two bowls and shared out the casserole.

'I felt I owed you an apology,' said Chris. They settled on to the sofa to eat. 'About last night.'

Sara ate a few mouthfuls of food before replying. 'I can't help my hours. They're always going to be difficult.'

'I know,' said Chris. 'I can accept that, if you try to understand about my acting. It's important to me, even if it is amateur. I'm not going to give it up any time soon.'

'There will be times when we might not see each other for weeks on end, then?'

'Probably,' said Chris. He put down his bowl of food. 'I'm still happy to give this a go if you are.'

'I need to think about it.' From the look on Chris's face, this wasn't the answer he'd wanted.

'Let's carry on as we are,' he said after a pause. 'How was your day?'

'I think we're making good progress,' said Sara. She ran a chunk of bread round the gravy on the side of the bowl and ate it appreciatively. 'I'm just not sure where it's all heading.'

'Can you talk about it?'

'Not directly. Besides, it's not the crime itself. It's more about my professional judgement. I think my personal feelings have got in the way again.' Sara put her empty bowl on the coffee table and wiped her fingers with a tissue.

'What do you mean?'

'The victim is under sixteen,' she said. 'He's been in and out of homes, mother was incapable and his father nowhere in sight.'

'You feel an affinity because he has no father figure?' asked Chris.

'Yes, I guess so,' said Sara. 'I was so busy feeling sorry him that I forgot to look at how he behaved. What the boy got up to, the choices he made that might have influenced the outcome.'

'He got into something nasty, did he?'

'Deep and difficult,' she said. 'We haven't got to the bottom of that yet. It looks like he went off the rails about six months ago and nobody noticed.'

'He isn't like you, then, is he?'

'In what sense?'

'You had your mum and your grandparents, for one thing. You could just as easily have taken a wrong turning, but you didn't. Wanting to find out about your dad was natural, you know. You shouldn't keep feeling guilty about that.'

'Shouldn't I? Mum still won't speak to me. Now she might be ill.'

'What do you mean?'

'She's been referred to the cancer clinic,' said Sara.

'You never mentioned this,' he said. His eye's searched Sara's face with concern. 'When was this?'

'Javed called me during the week.' Her shoulders slumped, and Chris pulled her into a strong hug. 'They're waiting for the appointment.'

'You can't go down to see her because of the case? Is that it?'

'Partly,' she admitted. She pulled away. 'I'm still not sure I'd be welcome.'

'You know what? I think you should ring your mum, whatever you worry that she might say. In my opinion, this has gone on long enough.'

'What if she puts the phone down on me again?'

'You're a grown-up. Call her back.' Chris collected the dirty dishes. 'I know it's none of my bloody business. Your mum must be very worried at the moment. It seems to me that you miss her, and I bet she misses you. She could do with your support, even if you can't get down there right now.'

He went into the kitchen. She knew Chris was right. It was easier to hold the argument at a distance than to deal with it. One of them had to make the next move, or it would get engrained and much harder to change.

Sara went out on to the little balcony that was her private outdoor space. It was quiet in the street below. Many of the independent restaurants that lined the pavements didn't open on a Sunday evening. The Christmas lights twinkled in the wind that gusted up and down between the buildings.

235

She dialled her mother's number. It rang several times before Javed answered it. He sounded pleased to hear from her. 'I'll try,' he said.

Sara listened as he went off into the house, trying to persuade her mum to come to the phone. For once, he succeeded.

'Hello, Sara?'

'Hi, Mum. How are you?'

'Tired,' said Tegan. 'It's late. What do you want?'

'To talk to you.' Her throat tightened with emotion. 'I spoke to Javed during the week. He told me about what's happening.'

'He had no right. That's private.'

'Of course it is. But he's your partner, Mum, so he does have some rights. He's worried about you.'

'What about mine?' snapped Tegan. 'He rang you without telling me.'

'Mum, I don't want to argue anymore. I just wanted to say that I'm worried for you as well. If you want to talk about all that other stuff, we can do it later. For now, it's your health that matters and nothing else.'

Sara paused, worried that Tegan hadn't already interrupted her. She heard sniffing.

'I love you, Mum,' she said. 'I'm here for you, even if I can't always get away from work.'

'I love you too.' Sara could barely catch the words, her mum's voice was so quiet. 'I'm really frightened.'

CHAPTER 51

Striker dropped Danni off with the instruction to be ready at four the following morning, and took Gary's passport with him. Nick gave her a cup of tea and headed back to his computer. 'No talking, no music,' he said. 'It disturbs my train of thought.'

'Play going well, then?'

'Television drama,' he said. 'Best thing I've ever done.'

His fingers tapped at the keyboard. Danni realised he wasn't paying any attention at all to her, and went to bed. The burner mobile had an alarm function, which she set for half past three.

Not that she got to sleep. Behind her closed eyes, all she could see was Les Myers and Lisa London in that tiny room. She was grateful that the violence was being inflicted on someone else. As long as it continued that way, she could harden her heart against it. Her shock had passed by the time they had dropped her off, hadn't it? Maybe she was as tough as Lisa London after all. When the saloon pulled up in the street outside, Danni was watching from the bedroom window. She'd packed the pretty clothes in the holdall — she wasn't going to leave them behind.

'Bye, then,' said Danni. Nick jumped in his computer chair, making a snorting noise. She had woken him up.

'You off?'

'My lift is here,' she said. 'Thanks for everything.'

Nick nodded dreamily, too sleepy to be coherent. 'Any time. Around here, I mean.'

'Sure, thanks again.' She slammed the front door to the maisonette, vowing that this was somewhere else she was never going to come again if she could help it.

She got into the back seat next to a yawning Gary. He smiled at her, putting his hand over hers where it lay on the leather upholstery. London sat in the front passenger seat, staring out of the windscreen. She didn't acknowledge Danni. Striker took them through the backstreets out to the ring road. No one seemed to have any energy until they turned away from the city on to the Cromer road. Gary sat up, suddenly paying attention.

'Where are we going?' His head swung from side to side, looking at the houses. He let go of Danni's hand and began to tap his fingers on the car door. At a set of traffic lights, he read the road signs. 'No, no, no. I'm not going. You can't make me. Where are you taking me?'

'Naples, babe,' said London. She didn't turn her head and kept her voice soft.

'I want to go home.' The panic was rising in his voice. 'I don't like flying.'

'I know that,' said London. 'I'm coming with you.'

'All the way to Naples?' Gary asked. His tapping fingers stilled.

'Part-way,' promised London. They reached another set of traffic lights and turned into Norwich Airport.

'You said you liked Nonna,' Danni said.

Gary looked at her. 'You don't know my *nonna*. I don't like her. I *love* Nonna.'

'You're right,' said Danni. 'I don't know her, but she sounds like a wonderful person.'

'She is.'

'It would be nice to visit her, wouldn't it?'

'Not in Naples. Not with her horrible family.'

'She wants you to stay with her,' said London. Striker parked the car in the visitors' area. London and Danni stepped out into the cold, dark morning. Gary clung to the handle to keep the door shut. London leaned inside the car. 'Come on, Gary. No more messing about. Do as Lisa tells you.'

'Danni, Danni,' he called. Danni went round to the other side and tapped on the window glass. With a smile, she tugged at the door handle. Gary let go and tumbled out, sending Danni skittering backwards across the car park. As she struggled to catch her balance, he ran after her, face crumpled. 'I'm sorry, I didn't mean it.'

'I know you didn't,' she said. Gary reached out, and she took his hands in hers. 'Let's get your bag.'

Striker had pulled out Gary's suitcase, slammed the boot lid and locked the car. The party headed for the building. Danni had only seen airports in those endless fly-on-the-wall documentaries. In comparison to Heathrow, this one was tiny.

A single open space housed a handful of checking-in desks down one side, and a café next to a wall of windows. A door marked *Rig Departures Only* stood by the windows, while a customer service desk staffed by two sleepy-looking attendants faced the entrance. To their right was the passport control and search area, which led to the main departure lounge.

Gary rocked gently from one foot to the other, clutching Danni's hand, as London pulled the paperwork and passports from her handbag. She smiled at Gary. 'Desk number three, look.'

'That says Amsterdam.' His tone was sullen.

'That's right,' said Danni. 'You have to change there to get to Naples.'

'Two planes? I don't like planes.'

'This is no longer about what you like,' said London. Her patience was wearing thin. 'You have to go.'

Danni jumped in before Gary could say anything else. 'Nonna will be meeting you. Won't she?'

'Yes, she will,' said London. If it hadn't been true before, Danni knew that someone would make sure it was going to happen before Gary landed. 'Let's check in, shall we, and get a drink?'

Striker dragged the suitcase up to the machine, then stood back with Danni while London went through check-in. Gary stood with his head bowed. The beautifully made-up uniformed lady behind the desk handed over two boarding passes. Danni wondered how they managed to look as good as that so early in the morning. London looked even more classy.

'We have a little time,' said London. 'Before we have to go through to the gates.'

Gary looked at the security guards on the boarding checkpoint. He grasped Danni's hand again. 'Can't you come with me?'

'No,' said Danni.

'Why not? I want you to.'

'I don't have a passport,' she said. 'They won't let me go without one, now will they?'

Gary shook his head and thought for a moment. 'You could get one and come and join me later.'

'She could,' said London.

'I want her to.' Gary turned to his sister. 'You can sort it out. You need to look after Danni now. Make sure nothing happens to her.'

A wave of nerves ran through Danni. Could she trust Lisa London once Gary was safely in Naples? The commitment was all on her side. London hadn't promised her a thing.

'Let's get a coffee, shall we?' London's voice was neutral.

They followed her. Gary and Striker joined the queue for breakfasts. London chose a table by the window, indicating for Danni to sit opposite. Through the glass wall, she could see two planes on the tarmac. One belonged to a holiday company, and the other had a huge KLM logo on the side. Being this close to an aircraft was another new experience for her.

'So far, so good,' said London. 'You've been helpful.'

'Thank you,' said Danni. 'Helpful enough?'

'We'll see. It depends where you are when I get back.'

London took an envelope from her bag and pushed it across the table. Danni took it and slid it into her backpack without opening it.

'That will get you home and Johnny out of trouble,' said London. 'Or it could take you on a shopping spree in Norwich, and Striker will bring you back here to meet me later this afternoon. You don't need to decide until he drops you off in Norwich.'

'If I come back here . . . ?'

'Things might improve for you.' London glanced up to check where Gary had got to. Danni saw that he was by the coffee machines.

'What happened to Les?'

'How disappointing,' said London. 'I thought you were clever.'

'It's not that I care about him,' said Danni. This was the moment she knew she had to play her ace, win or lose. 'I just want to know the consequences for me.'

'Were you shocked by what you saw last night?'

'At first,' admitted Danni. 'Then I realised that he had let you down. He got what he deserved.'

'Have you got the stomach for that kind of thing? Could you do that to someone?'

'I'm not strong enough. Physically, I mean.'

'Would you order it?'

'If it was necessary.' London looked at Danni, her lips pursed into a pretty pout as she weighed up what she was seeing and hearing. Danni held her gaze. She couldn't afford to back down now. 'I'm glad I've been able to help get him away,' she said. 'They won't find him once he gets to Naples, will they?'

'The family will take care of all that,' said London. 'And he speaks Italian like a native.'

'They'll keep him safe? He won't cause any more problems in your business?'

'There's no question of you going to Naples to join him.'

'That's fine. We could visit together one day, maybe.'

London laughed softly. 'I think you'll do after all. I'm going to Amsterdam with Gary. I'll put him on the connecting flight and be back here on the return flight that arrives just after four o'clock. Now it's your choice. Use the offer, or leave and go back to Johnny.'

Gary and Striker approached with two laden trays. Gary placed his on the table between them with a big smile.

'Look,' he said. 'Pain au chocolat. My favourite.'

CHAPTER 52

Sara was in early on Monday. The investigation had gathered impetus over the weekend, and now had the velocity of a landslide. She wanted to make sure there was no collateral damage in the hunt for any Camorra family members or the drugs rings they must be operating. It seemed that Callum was turning out to be less of a victim and more a willing participant. Nonetheless, he deserved justice like anyone else. Nor did Sara believe that Matt Morgan was anything other than an enthusiastic social worker or Sophie Bailey a victim of addiction. The more she thought about it, the more DI Powell's treatment of the pair had enraged her.

She had the coffee on and a tray of bacon butties ready before the rest of the team assembled. Ellie settled at a spare desk. Bowen made a point of working at his computer with his back to the rest of the room.

DS Mead and DCI Lambert were in the room by nine o'clock, tucking in with the rest of them as the DI brought them up to speed on their progress. Edwards had a file with some of the forensic results.

'As you know, the DNA results will take a couple of days. Fingerprints confirm the presence of Myers, Gary Barnet and Callum Young inside the property.'

'Does Myers have any previous?' DS Mead asked.

'Not that we can find,' said Edwards. 'If he's a known dealer, then he ought to be on DI Powell's radar. Ellie tells us that he isn't.'

'No, sir,' said Ellie.

DCI Lambert scowled. 'Why wasn't this man in your sights?'

'Most of our work is in the city, sir,' she replied. Sara watched Ellie choose her words carefully. 'There are several outlying hot spots where we know small-time dealers work, and these get watched sometimes. The Marlham area wasn't one that we regarded as needing resources. At the moment, we are interviewing two people who may have been involved in the Marlham chain.'

It was a masterclass in protecting her team leader, Sara thought. Especially given how Powell allowed the rest of his team to treat her so dismissively. DCI Lambert replied with a dismissive guttural sound and turned his attention back to Edwards. 'What else have you got?'

'Initial forensic results this morning confirm traces of various illegal substances in the house and also in Myers's car. So far, fingerprints in the car unsurprisingly match the ones in the house that we assume to be for Myers. There are also partials for Gary Barnet and several others, which so far have no match. Noble, I want you to trawl through traffic and council cameras to see if you can find any activity for Myers in the last week. Start with anything in the vicinity of his house and then the roads to and from Marlham.'

Noble's shoulders fell. That would be a mammoth task.

'We also need to do house-to-house with Myers's neighbours,' said Edwards. 'It's not that big a place. We may get lucky with that. At least we can build a picture of activity, especially visitors out of season. Bowen, I want you to get cracking with that. Ellie, can you go with Mike? I think the results might help your team.'

Ellie reluctantly put down her coffee mug. Bowen looked furious but nodded in agreement.

'Sara. With DCI Lambert's permission, I want you and DS Mead to work together.'

'Fine by me,' said Lambert. 'Let's see if we can trace Lisa London in the area. If her brother is here, she will be too. Whatever you can think of, check it.'

'Sir?' Sara asked. 'What about Matt Morgan and Sophie Bailey?'

'We'll deal with them later,' said Edwards. The team began their tasks. The DI led Lambert into his corner office, where they settled down to talk. Ellie went to retrieve her coat, while Bowen gathered up his stuff for the morning. As he went past her desk and out into the corridor, Sara followed him.

'Mike?' Sara didn't often use first names. Bowen turned to face her, looking resigned.

'What?'

'Please don't be too hard on Ellie,' said Sara.

'It's none of your business.'

'I know. But I think of you both as my friends. I don't like to see you at odds like this.'

'Has she told you?'

Sara nodded. 'To be honest, I wasn't surprised. You're right. It's not my business. Not yours either.'

'You don't know anything about it.'

'I have eyes,' said Sara. 'I saw that you had a soft spot for her.'

'That's one way of putting it.'

'They're giving her a hard time in there.' Sara gestured towards the Drugs team's office.

'Why doesn't that surprise me?'

'So she's keeping personal stuff to herself. She doesn't need your wounded ego trampling about as well.'

'Don't tell me how to feel.'

'I'm not. I'm asking you to be kind.'

Bowen looked at Sara thoughtfully. If there was one thing she was sure about, it was that Bowen wasn't an unkind man. She was banking on it.

Ellie returned with her coat and bag. 'Come on then, Mike.'

Bowen smiled at Sara. 'Ready when you are, Ellie. Who's driving, me or you?'

The pair set off for the car park and Sara returned to the office. DS Mead had set up a laptop on the spare desk behind her and was logging into the national system.

Sara swung her chair round to face Mead. 'Where shall we start?'

'I think Lambert's correct. If Gary is up here, the odds are that Lisa is too. The question is why.'

'When did you arrest him?'

'Beginning of August.' Mead settled himself at the desk, giving Sara his full attention. 'I wasn't on the raid. I've been working on Lisa London's empire for nearly twelve months. It only flagged to me when Gary was identified.'

'How long did that take?'

'Nearly a week.' Mead sighed. 'You know how it is with standard DNA tests. He hadn't been on our radar before that. We thought he worked in the coffee bar with his uncle. Of course, he'd vanished by the time we realised. Traced Lisa's vehicle to Birchanger Green Services on the M11, after which it vanished until they got home the next day.'

'Not even at Stansted Airport?'

'No. We assumed he had got a taxi from the service station to the airport. There was no reason to think he would be hiding up here.'

'I bet he came up here with all the other holidaymakers,' said Sara. 'In August there is an insane amount of traffic on these roads. They all head for the coast.'

'Then we put the flag on and continued to watch Big Sister. She changed her car, of course. But we have the new details. Shall we start there?'

'I suppose,' said Sara. 'What about other things we could do? We know Gary was going into Myers's house, and it would seem that our teacher from Marlham was getting some supplies from Gary. Presumably, he was staying in the area. Would Lisa have stayed with him?'

'Not her.' Mead laughed. 'Considers herself too good for seaside resorts. She'd be in a posh hotel.'

'We don't have too many of those,' said Sara. 'It wouldn't take long to ring them up and ask. Does she have an alias?'

'Several that we know of.'

'The other thing is, why now?' said Sara.

'Something Myers did?'

'Or something Gary did to Myers? Or in Myers's house?' Sara leaned forward excitedly. 'I bet this has something to do with our victim, Callum Young. What if Gary was involved in some way, or saw something? Then London would have to move him again.'

'You've got a handy airport,' said Mead.

'Yes, you do,' said Sara. 'It's not very big, but it does international flights.'

'We thought London would get Gary out to Naples, to be with the family. He'd be hard to find in those backstreets and under their protection. Do you have flights to Naples?'

'No.' Sara swung back to her computer screen and began a search. 'We do have regular flights to Amsterdam. KLM use it as a hub. My boyfriend's mum goes to Vancouver to visit her family that way. Get on in Norwich, connecting long-haul flight from Schiphol. Easy as pie, she says.'

DS Mead came round to stand next to her desk. 'It's just like old times. Us two brainstorming together.'

Sara brought up flights and connections for Naples, and they both checked the list. An early morning flight to Amsterdam could easily connect to a mid-morning Naples flight at Schiphol. 'That looks promising. We need to check the passenger manifest. You got that list of names?'

'Never! Surely not?' DI Edwards's voice was suddenly raised. Sara and Mead looked at his office. He was on the phone. 'We're on our way.'

Edwards signalled to DCI Lambert, and they came into the main office. Everyone was staring at them.

'You'll never guess what the SOCOs found this morning at Myers's house?'

'Drugs cache?' asked Mead. Logical and expectant.

'Body in the garden shed?' asked Aggie. Dramatic and imaginative.

'Solid evidence about Callum's murder?' said Sara. Practical and hopeful.

'Nope.' Edwards surveyed them all with a grin. 'They found Les Myers. Bound and gagged, and dumped on his bed.'

CHAPTER 53

Edwards and DCI Lambert shot out of the office, leaving Sara and DS Mead behind.

'They'll be ages bringing him back,' she said. 'The journey times here are similar to trying to cross London in rush hour.'

Mead laughed. 'That good, hey?'

'How do we know that Lisa isn't still in her house in London?' Sara asked.

'We keep an eye on her place through the traffic cameras. I called the surveillance team last night. They confirmed that she left yesterday morning and hasn't returned. If Gary has got into trouble or needs moving on, she would do it herself.'

'If you think Naples is the most likely destination, we should go up to the airport first. What time did Lisa leave her home?'

Mead checked his notes. 'About half past seven in the morning.'

'The only Sunday flight is at half past nine,' said Sara. She pointed to the flight charts. 'With the best driver in the world, they would have been pushed to make it.'

'You don't have the best road system in the world, do you?' said Mead.

'There are three flights most days,' said Sara, ignoring him 'Early one at 6.30 a.m., the holidaymakers' one at 9.30 a.m., and an evening one at 5.30 p.m.'

'Bet they went on the first available one.'

'You know all London's assumed names? Do you have a picture of the pair of them?'

Mead pointed to his laptop. 'I've got all the known aliases and photos on this.'

'Bring it, then,' said Sara. 'I'll get us a pool car.'

It took half an hour to get to the airport with the rush-hour traffic. The place was busy and noisy. An Aberdeen flight had just landed and two holiday flights were due to board. Business people and numerous holidaymakers milled around, getting in the way of the rig workers trying to access the heliport. One family with a large pile of suitcases were blocking the middle of the check-in area, looking confused. Sara and Mead tried the customer services desk first, showing their warrant cards and asking for the manager. He arrived swiftly and ushered them into his office down a private corridor.

'I'm Geoff Harris,' he said. 'How can I help you?'

'We are trying to trace two people who we think may have used the airport early this morning,' said Sara. Mead opened his laptop and pulled up the two photos. Mr Harris looked at the pictures and shook his head.

'I don't recognise them,' he said. 'The girls on the desk might.'

'We think they may have boarded the six thirty Amsterdam flight,' said Mead. 'Could we see the passenger manifest and security camera footage?'

'Security is in my remit,' said Harris. 'I'll get one of my team to run through it with you. We open at four thirty, which gives quite a short time frame.'

'And the passenger list?' asked Sara.

Mr Harris frowned. 'That belongs to the airline. We'll need permission from their head office.'

'Can you get that for us?'

'I'll try.'

'What about the boarding staff?' asked Mead.

'The same shift should still be here,' said Harris. 'They change at midday. It's busy out there, so I can't take them all off at once. It should clear in half an hour or so. Would that do?'

It felt like a plan, so Sara agreed, and they went with Mr Harris into the security office. Banks of screens flickered with live images from various parts of the airport buildings. From a variety of angles, they could watch the check-in desks, café, security area, departure lounge and duty-free. More cameras covered the entrance, exit and car parks. There were eight check-in desks for the airlines and two for the heliport.

'We're one of the main heliports for workers on the gas rigs,' explained the security guard stationed in front of the screens. 'These are the airline check-ins.' He gestured across four cameras.

'Do you keep a backup, or is it all live?' asked Mead.

'Seven-day retention,' said the security guard. 'It will be in one-hour batches.' He moved to a table with a separate computer and screen. Sara outlined the times, and Mead pulled up a chair. 'There would only be three desks open for KLM first thing in the morning. Try these.'

'That passenger manifest, Mr Harris?' prompted Sara. Harris nodded and left the room.

The recordings were fast-forwarding, just enough to cut down the search time without cutting the information. After a few minutes, Mead stabbed a finger at the screen, and the security guard paused the video.

'There, look,' Mead said. Sara looked at the frozen image. A tall man in a suit and dark glasses was putting a suitcase on the weighing machine. Next to him stood both their targets. The timestamp said 4.37 a.m.

'Who's that?' asked Sara. Mead squinted at the fuzzy picture on the screen.

'Known associate of Lisa London,' replied Mead. 'Italian by the name of Luca Sinagra. Cousin of Lisa's, several times removed. Officially, he is her chauffeur. I doubt that's all he does for her.'

'Also part of the family?'

'Naturally.' They ran the video on in real time. The chauffeur left the case and walked back into the waiting area, as London handed over two passports. The young man stood next to her, keeping his head bowed as if to hide his face. London didn't seem to be concerned. 'She knows there will be cameras. It's a pity we can't see the boy's face clearly.'

'They both seem to be getting on the flight,' said Sara. 'It looks like there are two boarding passes and passports. What do they do next?'

'We'll need to change cameras,' said the security guard. 'They've gone out of range for the check-in desk.'

He flicked through a selection of images with the same timestamp. First, he paused in the café, pointing to the bulky figure of the chauffeur in the coffee queue next to the young man. Their faces were still unclear.

'Looks like him, doesn't it?' Mead asked, hopefully. 'Not good enough for evidence, though.'

They picked up London on another screen sitting at a distant café table with a young woman.

'Who the hell is that?' asked Mead. 'I don't recognise her at all.'

As they worked through the cameras, London and the young man moved through security into the departure lounge, while the chauffeur and the mystery girl went to the car park.

'London's latest model,' said Mead. They watched the car pause at the barrier to pay the exit fee. It headed off-site. At 6.15 a.m., the pair got on the KLM flight, which left on time for Amsterdam.

'Fuck,' said Mead. 'We've lost them. We need that manifest to find which names they are travelling under. Then we can contact border control in Schiphol.'

Promising to make copies of the recordings for them, the security guard took them back to see Mr Harris. He was on the phone, speaking in a language Sara guessed was

Dutch. The conversation was getting heated. With a grimace, he slammed down the phone.

'They say they'll try and get it over this morning,' he said. 'It should have quietened down out there by now. The TUI flight is boarding, and the Aberdeen passengers will have been picked up.'

The check-in area was almost like a ghost town. The departure screen showed no new flights for the next three hours. Mr Harris took them behind the counters to a staff rest area. Several beautiful, slim women and one smartly dressed man in travel company uniforms were sitting there eating salads, unwrapping sandwiches and sharing out drinks from a vending machine. Their friendly chatter ceased as soon as Mr Harris walked in.

'I'm sorry to disturb your break,' he said. He introduced DS Mead and Sara, and explained who they were looking for.

'Do you mind if I put my laptop on here?' asked Mead. A leggy blonde moved from her seat at the table to sit on a sofa. Mead flipped up the screen to show the pictures of London and Gary. 'These two were on the six thirty to Amsterdam. Can any of you remember checking them in?'

'It will be in the manifest,' said a woman in a KLM uniform. Her tone indicated boredom, not to mention an assumed superiority.

'Yes, Julie,' said Mr Harris. 'We've asked your head office for that. We need to identify them more quickly than that. Which one of you served them?'

The KLM crew gathered around the computer to check the pictures. After a little debate, one woman said, 'I think that was me. The boy was a little odd, wouldn't look at me or speak at all. The woman did all the talking and paperwork.'

'Can you remember their names?' asked Sara. The woman shook her head.

'Not especially,' she said. 'If it matches the passport then we're happy.'

'Anything else you can remember?' Mead tried to encourage her. 'What about the passports?'

'That was the other odd thing, now I think about it.' The woman tapped the young man's picture on the screen. 'If that is him, his passport was Italian. Hers was British. They both looked brand new.'

'Were they flying on from Amsterdam?' asked Sara.

'He was,' said the woman. 'Connecting flight to Naples.'

'I'll get on to Border Control immediately,' said Mead. He snatched at his mobile.

'No point in contacting Schiphol.' The KLM woman shook her head. 'The Naples flight will already have boarded or left. There's an hour time difference. Naples might be able to meet him.'

'And the woman?' asked Sara.

'She was booked on the return flight from Amsterdam, the one that gets in at 4 p.m.'

CHAPTER 54

As the hysteria ran its course, Sophie's screams subsided, and she accepted help from the kindly Sergeant Jones. He'd got her back on the chair, brought tissues for her to clean herself up with and brought her mobile.

'I think you should call your father immediately.' Sophie did so.

It was the hardest call she'd ever made. Her father was an unforgiving man, used to being in charge. He frightened her — he always had. In the background, she could hear her mother break down in tears, as the news was relayed.

'I'll sort it out, I suppose.' Her father's voice was clipped with anger. 'Will they keep you in there tonight?'

As it turned out, and despite Sergeant Jones's attempted intervention, DI Powell had no intention of letting her go home or to the hospital. They shut Sophie in a holding cell for the night. They took her shoes at the door, fed her through a hatch and left her on her own. The lights stayed on all night. The hatch was opened regularly, then shut again. Sleep was impossible.

The next morning, they brought her a bacon sandwich, which made her retch. Eventually, a custody officer appeared and took her up to an interview room. This one had sofas and easy chairs. It was rather different from the place Sophie had been in yesterday. Her father was standing in the room, looking angry. His hands jingled loose coins in his trouser pocket, a sure sign to Sophie that he had been shouting about something. A smartly dressed woman, with dark hair pulled into a chignon, sat on one of the sofas.

'Dad? What are you doing in here?'

'I might say the same to you.' Her father sounded grimly determined. 'When did this all start? The drugs, I mean.'

'At uni,' said Sophie, bowing her head.

'Then it took over?'

'Got worse, couldn't seem to stop craving it.'

'And you couldn't talk to me about it? Or your mother? For God's sake, Sophie. What did you think we'd say?'

Sophie cringed and sank on to an easy chair. Her father leaned over her, lowering the volume of his voice with a visible effort. 'Have we ever let you down?'

'No. I've let you down. I've become a monster.'

'The drugs will have changed you,' he said. 'They often do, or so Mrs Curtis here tells me.' He indicated the other woman, who smiled and offered Sophie her hand. It took some effort for Sophie to reach out and accept it. 'After you rang me, I came straight up here. On the way, I found you the best lawyer in Norwich.'

'You got here last night?'

'I tried to get you out, but they wouldn't agree.' Sophie's father looked slightly shamefaced. 'I put up in a hotel. Anyway, Mrs Curtis is already on your case.'

'I'm a junkie, Dad,' said Sophie. 'I'm guilty of possession. Class A drugs.'

'You are someone who will be seeking medical assistance in dealing with an addiction.' He paused and looked at Sophie quizzically.

She nodded. 'I'll do whatever you say, Dad.'

Her gaze flittered away from his face and through a window. Sophie could see an interior courtyard with a gravelled garden, with people sitting on benches enjoying a smoke or a drink. Her stomach churned, and her thoughts raced. Had her father tried to have her released last night? Knowing him, he had probably felt that a night in a cell would do her good. She rolled her head down to hide her tears. 'The police will charge me.'

'We'll see about that, although you may have to put in a court appearance. An apology will go a long way, I think you'll find. I have that on good advice. Mrs Curtis?'

'Thank you, Mr Bailey.' The lawyer looked across at Sophie. 'To proceed for you, I need to ask you a few questions. Is that all right?'

'Yes.'

'In your own words, tell me what happened yesterday.'

Sophie explained about her arrest at Lyndford Lodge, being kept in the interview room for hours and the hectoring manner of DI Powell. 'There was a woman detective. She was nicer.'

'And then?'

'I felt faint, and like I was going to throw up. It all got weird. Then I fell on to the floor.'

'Exactly,' said her father. 'They treated you badly, despite being ill. More care should have been taken.'

'I'm sorry, I feel tired.' Sophie's eyelids drooped.

'Pay attention, young lady,' he snapped. 'We're doing our best to help you.'

'I won't trouble you for the full details at the moment,' said Mrs Curtis. She balanced a briefcase on her lap and pulled out a small pile of papers. 'I can confirm that I've requested a copy of your interview. The police are not being very cooperative at the moment, but I can apply to the court if they don't send it to me. I want you to try and remember three things for me.'

'Yes?'

'Were you cautioned when you were arrested?'

'Yes, outside the Lodge.'

'When they started your interview, were you asked if you felt well?'

'They just asked me to give my name and address.'

'Finally, did they tell you that you could have a solicitor present while you were being interviewed?'

'I don't remember that.' Sophie chewed her lip as she tried to dredge up the memory. 'I was very confused.'

'Fine,' said Mrs Curtis. 'When I get the full transcript or recording, we should be able to get any charges cancelled.'

'How?' asked her father.

'If they haven't followed the correct procedures or checked on Sophie's welfare when she was plainly unwell, their interview will not be admissible in court. In addition, we can file a complaint about her treatment. If Sophie is getting help or going to rehab by then, I doubt they will try to do more than issue a caution.'

'No,' said Sophie. She felt determined about one thing, and it was going to take all her courage to say what it was. 'I won't do it if it means Matt gets the blame for the drugs. I don't want them pinning it on him.'

'Mr Morgan is insistent that the cocaine in his possession was yours,' said Mrs Curtis. 'I've spoken to the duty solicitor who is helping him. They managed to offer one to Mr Morgan this morning.'

'The drugs were mine,' admitted Sophie. 'He was trying to help me. He took my stash and was giving it to me in small doses.'

'And you agreed to this?'

'I thought it might help me. I couldn't kick the stuff on my own.'

'Why didn't you come home?' Her father sounded offended.

Sophie looked down at her knees. Her cravings were kicking in, her arms itching. She gripped at her thighs to stop herself scratching at the wounds. 'I was too ashamed.'

'Addiction is an illness,' said Mrs Curtis. 'Your father has already agreed to stand as your mentor when you go for help.'

'As soon as the paperwork is processed, we're leaving,' he said. 'I'll get you all the help you need once we get back to Sussex.'

'Take your father's advice,' said Mrs Curtis. 'You are very lucky to have him, and I think you'll be in the best place you could be, under the circumstances.'

'I know,' said Sophie. 'I still don't want Matt to get the blame. It wasn't his fault. It was mine.'

'Mr Morgan seems to have disowned you.'

'I don't care,' Sophie insisted. 'I want to do the right thing for once. He's kind, and I just got him into more trouble. As if Matt didn't have enough to cope with enough as it is. Poor Callum.' She began to sob.

Her father patted her shoulder with an awkward gesture. 'It's going to be all right. There's no need to feel guilty about that man. I'll look after you.'

Mrs Curtis took her leave. Sophie's father demanded cups of tea for the two of them from the officer outside. The bail papers were signed by the time they had drained their cups. In the car park, her father's executive Jaguar stood out like an expensive sore thumb.

'Are we going back to my flat?' Sophie asked. She fastened her seat belt and collapsed into the passenger seat.

Her father shook his head. 'We're going home.' Within minutes, they were on the A11 heading south.

'What about work? I can't just walk out on them.'

'I've spoken to your headmaster,' he said. 'Explained that you need sick leave. Once I've got you back safely, we can decide what to do next.'

'But my flat?'

'I've arranged for a professional cleaner to go in. They will pack up your clothes and send them on. The rest of the stuff can go to charity shops.'

'Apart from my books,' said Sophie. 'I don't want to lose them.'

'If we must. Mrs Curtis will sort out the notice on your rental.'

'My car?'

'Already dealt with. A professional driver will bring it down at the end of the week.'

He's thought of everything, Sophie thought, *except how I feel.*

The Jaguar purred along, cocooning Sophie from the world outside. He had little else to say to her, now that he'd dealt with the practicalities, and Sophie was glad to sit quietly, watching out of the window. Her cravings came and went. The itching subsided. They had almost reached the M11 when the console lit up with an incoming call. Her father tapped a button on the steering wheel.

'Mrs Curtis. How have you got on?'

'I've spoken to DI Powell,' said the solicitor. 'He asked how Sophie was.'

'Kind of him.' Her father's tone was deeply sarcastic. 'Did you mention the complaint?'

'I didn't have to. He apologised before I could bring it up. Says that there will be no possession charges, so long as Sophie is seeking help. I assured him that she was. He asked for a guarantor.'

'That will be me, as we agreed,' said her father.

'DI Powell indicated that would be acceptable.'

'What about Matt?' Sophie interrupted.

'How are you, Miss Bailey?'

'I'm OK,' said Sophie. 'You told them I admitted that the wraps belonged to me?'

'I spoke about Mr Morgan.' The solicitor's tone was cautious. 'DI Powell is of the opinion that Mr Morgan is, and I quote, "an interfering social worker who was stupid enough to do something like that".'

'Will they charge him?'

'It seems that they have decided not to. They have accepted his word that the items belonged to you, without my having to confirm it. Unfortunately, I think it might not be enough to save Mr Morgan's job.'

'I only want your legal opinions,' snapped Sophie's father.

'Thank you, Mrs Curtis,' said Sophie. She curled up as small as she could on the luxurious car seat and returned to gazing out of the window. She felt sleep begin to wash over her. At least she was safe now. Her father finished the conversation with Mrs Curtis.

'All sorted,' he said. They pulled on to the motorway. 'Do you want a stop?'

'Yes, please.'

'There's a service station in a few miles, I'll pull in there. After that, we'll soon be home. I've taken care of it all for you, just like I always do.'

Apart from Matt Morgan, thought Sophie. *Well, I tried my best for him. I didn't ask him to interfere. Besides, he said I was cruel.*

The car sped along, lulling her with the *tick-tick* of the concrete road surface. As she dozed, her brain tried to sort out her confusion.

Sophie would have to go to rehab or counselling or something. Her father would arrange it all. Daddy would take care of everything. The school could find another mug to teach their rural tearaways. She'd send in her resignation after a few days' rest. Matt would be all right, he'd find another job. She never ever wanted to go to Norfolk again.

As they pulled into Stansted Services, Sophie realised that she could no longer remember what Matt looked like, she was so tired.

CHAPTER 55

Aggie and Noble were grinning like the cats that got the cream when Sara and Mead got back to the office.

'Ian has done really well,' said Aggie. They were sitting at Noble's desk, examining CCTV traffic footage. 'He spotted Myers's car going to Norwich on Friday morning and returning in the early evening.'

'You remember where we saw Callum leave Marlham on his bike?' Noble asked. Sara nodded, looking at the grainy image on the screen. 'That junction near the agricultural showroom is an accident black spot, so there's a traffic camera there, despite it being a B-road.'

They showed the two times when a silver car pulled up at the junction, heading for Norwich in the daylight and turned back towards the coast after dark. The outward journey was clear. They could read the number plate and see two figures in the front seats. The quality of the evening shot wasn't great, so they had to examine the image closely.

'Is there a third person in the back seat?'

'We think so,' said Noble. He added with a triumphant grin, 'It comes back again. Look.'

He opened a third file. There was little traffic once the city workers had returned to their village homes, until just after 8 p.m. Moving at speed, Myers's car came past the junction and headed towards Marlham.

'That must be when he took it to Wade, and they hid it,' said Noble.

'Why didn't he just torch it?' Mead asked.

'I suspect it's because that type of crime is rare here,' replied Sara. 'Cars get stolen, of course, but rarely burned out. It would be too much of a coincidence, look too suspicious if that particular one suddenly got stolen and fired.'

DI Edwards and DCI Lambert joined them as Aggie made a celebratory round of coffee. Sara brought them up to speed.

'Myers is in the rape suite,' said Edwards.

'Rape?' Mead was shocked. 'Why?'

'It's our only contamination collection unit,' said Edwards. 'He has been beaten up, bound with cable ties and gagged with gaffer tape. He needs medical care and feeding before we interview him. I'm not making the same mistakes as some around here.'

'What about Bailey and Morgan?' asked DCI Lambert.

'Bailey's been released on bail. We can interview Morgan another time, Powell had to let him go this morning. There is one person we can deal with, however. Sara, you'll be with me for this one.'

'Sir?'

'Unfortunately, Mrs Wade senior died early this morning. Mr Wade has agreed to come in and be interviewed. Great Yarmouth have already brought him over.'

They went to the observation room first. Dan Wade was sitting in interview room one, and Sara was pleased to see that the duty solicitor was with him, offering quiet advice. Unsurprisingly, Wade looked upset, although he appeared to be listening to what the solicitor was saying. His face looked drawn, and he held a cup in unsteady hands.

'By the book,' murmured Edwards. 'Besides, I suspect this is a sprat to catch a mackerel. I'm not sure he had anything to do with Callum's death.'

They went into the interview room, started the recording and carried out the formalities. Wade squared his shoulders and looked at Edwards, then Sara.

'Mr Wade, can you tell us why we found a car belonging to Les Myers hidden at your garage?' Edwards began.

'He called me late on Friday evening,' said Wade. 'Said he needed to get rid of it urgently.'

'Did he say why?'

'No, only that he had to get rid of it.'

'Why would you agree to this?'

Wade looked at the solicitor, who folded his hands on the table. 'You don't have to answer any questions, Mr Wade. It is entirely at your own discretion.'

Wade thought for a moment, then reached into his pocket and pulled out a set of garage keys, which he placed on the table between him and Sara. 'You'll need these.'

'Why?' asked Sara. She didn't touch the keys.

'A year ago, I lost a lot of money,' said Wade. 'My trade took a long time to pick up after the last recession. Classic cars are a niche market at the best of times.'

'May I ask how this loss occurred?' Edwards asked.

'Most of my work is with local collectors. It's steady stuff, but I do get the occasional large project. About eighteen months ago, I was approached by someone I had no previous dealings with. He had bought a 1960s Chevy, and he wanted me to restore it.'

'A big project?'

'Very big,' said Wade. 'I laid out quite a bit on auction sites, got vintage parts from America and put a lot of hours into it.'

'He never paid?' Edwards guessed.

'He was cleverer than that.' Wade grimaced. 'I was taken in. He gave me a few small interim payments, just never the full amount. By the end of the job, he owed me more than thirty grand. Claimed he had paid me by bank transfer and I believed him. Took the car away and vanished.'

'So where does Les Myers fit into this?' Edwards asked.

'I like to smoke a joint sometimes,' admitted Wade. 'It calms me down. Myers sold me a bit of weed. Sometimes we would share a spliff. I told him what had happened, and he recruited me.'

'To do what?' Sara had already guessed the answer.

'To sell weed.' Wade poked at the bunch of keys until he brought up a small one with a yellow dot on it. 'It was cash in hand, no questions asked. I know you're searching my garage. This key opens the cabinet where I keep the goods.'

'Why would you help Myers hide the car?' Edwards insisted.

'Said he would report me to the police as a dealer if I didn't help.'

'What about Callum Young? Was he involved in any way?'

'Yes, he was,' admitted Wade. 'He seemed to know Myers already when he came to me. Sometimes he brought the goods to me, sometimes Myers would bring it. They were as thick as thieves.' Wade winced when he realised what he had said.

'Thank you, Mr Wade,' said Edwards. 'You have been very helpful. We need to continue our investigations, and I think you have enough to cope with at the moment. I'm going to release you on police bail pending further enquiries. I'll need a DNA sample for elimination purposes.'

'Yes, no problem.' Wade sighed with relief. 'Then I can go?'

'Yes, Mr Wade,' said Edwards. 'I strongly recommend that you get further legal advice.'

The recording was officially closed, and they left Dan Wade to finish his drink. Sara booked out a swab test from the store, returned to the interview room and took Wade's sample. When she got back to the office to log it, the rest of the team, including the visitors, were gathered around the incident board.

'Sara, just in time,' said Edwards. She pulled her chair forward and joined them. 'More discoveries at Myers's house. Forensics turned their attention outside this morning. They've discovered where Myers keeps his goods. The resourcefulness of this man is amazing. He has a secret panel in his boat.'

'There isn't a boat,' said Sara.

'It's amazing what we walk past and take no notice of, isn't it?'

'Sir?'

'In the back garden, there's a rockery.'

Sara examined the garden in her mind's eye. A rowing boat, with peeling blue paint, had been in plain sight, stacked on top of the rockery, filled with soil and dead plants.

'The old blue boat?' Sara asked.

'Yup,' said Edwards. 'There's a panel in the side nearest to the kitchen door. SOCOs found it this morning. Inside there's a cavity, probably made of an old plastic storage box, and it's full of just about every illegal drug that has a value on the street.'

CHAPTER 56

Danni had made her decision before Gary and his sister had
vanished through the security gate to the departure lounge.
As Striker drove them away, she pulled out the envelope and
counted the cash. Three thousand pounds. He stopped at a
taxi rank in the centre of Norwich. It was still early, and few
shops were open.

'Well?' asked Striker.

'I'm in.'

'Here. Three o'clock.' He drove off as soon as Danni
had shut the door.

She surveyed the shops and colourful market stalls. The
beautiful department store that they had struggled through
with Gary's suitcase stood on one corner. Streets full of independent shops, boutiques and cafés radiated from the market. After a coffee, Danni explored the best of them through
their windows before making up her mind and going into
the department store as the doors opened. It was the most
amazing day Danni ever had. She felt like Julia Roberts in
Pretty Woman.

She started with a new haircut, had a makeover from
a trendy concession stand, and a manicure at a small nail
bar. Department by department she upgraded her shoes, her

underwear and her clothes, peeling the cash from her newly acquired leather purse and matching handbag. By midday, Danni looked as close to Lisa London's chic appearance as could be managed in one store. In one of the changing rooms, she took time to repack her purchases in the store bags. She put the old clothes, the pink parka and the small backpack that Mrs Strong had given her into a spare carrier.

Outside, she walked around the market until she found a set of commercial wheelie bins in an alley behind a pub. Checking that the passage was empty, she lifted the lid and threw her old things away.

After lunch she walked further and found more shops. She bought branded sportswear and a new phone. Weighed down with carriers, she met Striker at exactly 3 p.m. He made no comment, opening the boot for her to deposit the spoils of her spree. Danni felt like a celebrity when she climbed into the back seat and Striker closed the door for her.

A man she didn't know was sitting in the front. He looked in his fifties, with neatly trimmed greying hair and manicured fingernails. He balanced a bulging briefcase on his lap. They were not introduced.

The flight was on time, and Danni stood with Striker and the other man at the doorway for the arrivals lounge. Several other people waited with them, meeting family or business colleagues. A cluster of three people, two older men and a tall woman stood together. If Danni had to hazard a guess, she would assume they were the police. In her limited experience, all police officers had an air about them, even when they weren't in uniform. She didn't doubt that they were here for Lisa London. But how had they worked it out so quickly?

Danni took a couple of steps back, until she was behind Striker's bulk. He allowed her to hide. She would wait and see what happened next. Perhaps London would stand by her or perhaps she would try to throw her as bait to the police. She still wasn't sure she could trust her. Sweat broke through Danni's lovely makeover. She didn't want to forfeit all that shopping in the back of the car either, if she could help it. She checked out the terminal exit doors. If things were about to turn nasty, Danni figured she could always blend in with the crowd of passengers and get away.

As the passengers began to trickle through Customs, London appeared carrying half a dozen elegant shopping bags. Glancing round, she spotted the greeting party and waved them forward. Striker gripped Danni at the elbow and steered her to the front of the group. As they met, London handed the bags to Danni.

'Look after these for me,' she said, while the three police officers moved towards them.

It was too late now, Danni realised. It was obvious that Lisa London knew her. The police had seen them together. All thought of leaving unobserved had to be abandoned. She would have to stick this out to the end. London looked at her, one eyebrow raised quizzically.

'Enjoy your day?' she asked. 'Nice make-up, by the way.'

'Thank you.'

'If you get yourself a passport, next time you could come with me.'

Danni desperately wanted to believe her. The police group had reached them.

'Lisa London,' said the older of the officers. 'We're arresting you for perverting the course of justice. Come with us.'

London smiled. 'I don't think you are. Let me introduce you to my legal advisor, Mr Gray.'

The mystery man nodded at the officers. Inwardly Danni laughed. London had thought of everything.

The officer looked angry. 'We are going to interview you under caution,' he said. He grabbed London's arm.

Mr Gray shot forward. 'You may not touch my client,' he said. 'We will cooperate with you in whatever investigation you may be undertaking. We refute any charges without exception. And if you attempt to touch my client again, I will sue you for damages, whoever you are.'

The man let go of London and introduced himself as DCI Lambert of the Metropolitan Police. He introduced the other two officers as belonging to the Norfolk force, and gestured to another man who stood hovering nearby. Curious passengers stopped to watch, one or two pulling mobiles from their pockets. Without further comment, they were all led down a private corridor to an office that said *General Manager* on the door.

The other man must be the manager, Danni thought. He couldn't wait to leave the room, and pulled the door shut behind him as he hurried away. Once they were all seated, London looked at the three officers with a calmness that impressed Danni. 'Allow me to introduce my remaining staff,' she said.

'Luca Sinagra we already know,' said DCI Lambert.

'My chauffeur,' said London. 'My legal advisor you have already met. This young lady is my new personal assistant, Danni Jordan. Oh, Danni, that one is for you.'

London pointed to one of the shopping bags at Danni's feet. She peered inside at a carefully wrapped box nestled in crumpled tissue paper.

'An addition for your Clarice Cliff collection. I thought you'd like them. Now, what can I do for you, DCI Lambert?'

It was a perfect piece of theatre. Striker stood next to Danni to emphasise her allegiance.

'At six thirty this morning,' began DCI Lambert, 'you travelled to Amsterdam in the company of Gary Barnet.'

'That is partly correct,' said London.

Mr Gray leaned forward. 'My client is not under caution and is cooperating as a gesture of good intent.'

'Would you like to be under caution, Miss London?' asked the woman.

DCI Lambert frowned to silence her. 'Why is it only partly correct?'

'I have indeed been to Amsterdam,' said London. She wafted a languid hand over the bags. 'The shops there are so much more exclusive.'

'You went shopping?' The DCI sounded incredulous. 'I don't think so. You took your brother to catch a connecting flight to Naples so that he could escape justice.'

'I'm afraid I have no idea where my brother is,' said London. 'I haven't seen him since August when he was falsely arrested and wrongly charged by the Metropolitan Police. We would have put in a formal complaint, but when my brother vanished we couldn't. Perhaps you had something to do with that?'

The atmosphere in the room changed. London was on the attack, and the police officers realised it. She was also lying, as Danni was well aware. If London could do this with her consummate acting skills, the least she could do was to look as impassive as possible. She locked her jaw to prevent her face muscles from twitching.

'You haven't seen your brother since August?' asked the DCI. His disbelief was obvious.

'No.'

'We have evidence showing the pair of you boarding the flight this morning.'

'No, you don't.'

The other police officer snorted in disbelief. DCI Lambert held up his hand in a restraining gesture.

'You admit you got on the flight?'

London nodded.

'Then who was with you?'

'I think when you check, you'll find that my cousin, Giovanni di Maletesti, accompanied me.'

'Your cousin?' The DCI laughed out loud.

'I can understand your error.' A smug smile tugged at the edge of London's mouth. 'He looks rather like my brother. Giovanni has been helping me to look for Gary, sadly to no avail. We can't find him any more than you can.'

'You expect me to believe that.'

'We expect you to present proof to the contrary,' said Mr Gray. 'Otherwise, I think this interview is at an end.'

The two Norfolk officers conferred in a whisper and the woman headed out of the office.

'Why would you use a regional airport, when you could have flown from London?' Lambert persisted.

'My client does not have to explain her choices to you,' snapped Mr Gray. London nodded in agreement.

'It seems an odd choice to me,' said Lambert. 'Won't you satisfy my curiosity?'

'No,' said London. 'Have you finished?'

'I haven't even begun.'

'Then you'd better get some evidence before you harass my client again.' Mr Gray stood up, offering his hand to help London stand. Danni gathered up the shopping bags.

'You'll wait until we've checked the manifest,' said Lambert. He also stood up, pointing to the chair London had vacated. 'Sit down.'

For a moment, Danni wondered if the situation would get out of hand. She stood aside as Striker took a pace forward so that he stood behind London. Mr Gray opened his mouth to object. The door opened, and the woman came back in, holding a sheet of paper.

'Show me,' demanded Lambert. The woman pointed to a name on the list. 'Of course. Giovanni di Maletesti. Travelling on an Italian passport.'

London smiled sweetly. 'Goodbye, DCI Lambert.'

The manager was waiting in the corridor as they left the office. Before the door shut, Danni glanced behind her to see DCI Lambert throw the paper angrily on the desk and curse. They were politely led back into the main airport, where the manager stamped their parking ticket as a courtesy.

Danni proudly followed London across the car park. The woman had elevated herself to the status of a goddess in her eyes. It had been a masterful display of power and control. She could have fallen and worshipped the ground London walked on. There was nothing in the world that Danni wanted to do more, than to emulate Lisa London.

Striker drove through the suburbs of Norwich to the A11. Mr Gray sat in the back next to Danni.

'You had a good day's shopping, I see,' said London. She sipped a bottle of water as she watched out of the window. 'Quite the makeover.'

'Yes, thank you,' breathed Danni.

'I like your hair,' London said casually. 'How old are you? Be honest.'

'I'm twenty,' said Danni. 'My birthday is in January.'

'Perhaps we'll have a party.'

'Did you mean it?'

'What?'

'You said I was your personal assistant. Did you mean it?'

'Yes.' London turned in her seat to look at Danni. 'For a trial period to begin with. Does that suit you?'

'Oh, yes. Please.' Danni nodded her head so hard that it felt as if it might rock off her neck.

'We'll work out your duties as we go, shall we?' London turned back to watching the road.

As they joined the dual carriageway, Striker gunned the saloon down the outside lane. London's eyelids fell shut, and Mr Gray was answering emails on his mobile. Danni unwrapped the present that London had given her. It was a Clarice Cliff salt-and-pepper set with the 'Crocus' pattern on it. She grinned. This was just the start of her new life. She had Lisa London looking after her now and so long as she kept her boss happy, there would be many more days like this. Who cared what the cost might be?

Danni looked at Striker in the rear-view mirror. He glanced at her, winked, and slowly pulled one finger across his throat.

CHAPTER 57

Sara was grateful that it was DI Edwards who was driving them back to HQ, not DCI Lambert. The latter was fuming. His language was ripe and his face bright red. God knows what speed they would have been doing if he had been in control of the car.

'She's taking the piss,' snarled Lambert. 'Fucking laughing at us.'

'The burden of proof is still ours,' said Edwards. 'We can prove he was at Les Myers's house and in his car. But not why, until we interview Myers.'

In the back seat, Sara silently wished him good luck in trying to calm down the DCI.

'What about these security videos? Sara?'

'They were all a bit distant, to be honest,' she said. 'I guess they could be enhanced. Trouble is, they're not intended for facial recognition, they're to keep an eye on movement.'

'What about Naples? Did you try them?'

'Mead got someone at your office to make contact, sir,' she said to Lambert. 'I don't know the outcome.'

Unfortunately, the outcome had been poor. When the team reached the office, Mead confirmed that although

Naples Customs had been approached, they'd had the wrong name. Consequently, they hadn't stopped or questioned anyone from the Amsterdam flight. Privately Sara wondered if the local Customs officers would be prepared to go up against the di Maletesti family. They were the ones who would have to live with the consequences if a family member was arrested and not their British counterparts. Gary Barnet, or Gary Barr, or Giovanni di Maletesti, or whoever he was, would be safe in the backstreets of Naples where his family could protect him.

'What about Myers?' stormed Lambert. 'I want him. He must know about this bloody family. He's at the end of their chain.'

'DCI Lambert, a word, if you please.' Edwards led the angry detective into the glass corner office. They all heard the raised voices, and the argument about patches and rights until Lambert calmed down.

'Poor bugger,' said Mead. He was slumped in his chair, looking grim. 'We've been after this lot for years, and we were so close this time. Now they'll be even more on their guard. Where is Myers, by the way?'

'Interview room one,' said Noble. The young DC had been watching the row open-mouthed.

'What about Ellie and Bowen?' Sara asked.

'They're on their way back,' said Aggie.

'They said that only half of the houses are occupied at this time of year,' said Noble. 'The rest are holiday places. One neighbour said that she saw Callum visiting Myers regularly, recognised the photo and the bike. Claimed he had been going up there for months. Moaned that the lad never had any lights on his bike.'

Edwards offered a courtesy to DI Powell, despite Powell's lack of courtesy to the SCU team. He sent Noble to invite Powell to join in the interviewing of Les Myers, since he was a suspect in both investigations.

The viewing room was packed when Edwards and Powell went in to interview Myers. Sara sat next to Lambert. Mead stood behind his boss and Ellie behind Sara. Bowen and Noble were the last ones in. Sara wondered what had been said, because once the preliminaries were dealt with, Edwards took the lead. Myers looked worried, despite the smartly dressed lawyer that sat beside him. He wore a white temporary coverall, and there were red marks on his wrists and mouth. Edwards checked that he was well enough to continue and cautioned him.

'Mr Myers,' said Edwards. 'I have several questions regarding your association with Callum Young. Can you begin by telling me about the nature of your relationship?'

'He was my friend,' said Myers.

'There was a huge age difference between you.'

'I know, but it's not easy to make friends here. I was grateful to him.'

'How did you meet?'

'I don't remember.' Myers's eyes shifted sideways to the lawyer. He straightened himself up again.

'Did he buy drugs from you?' Powell jumped in. Sara saw Edwards stiffen, though he managed to stop himself from speaking over the other DI.

Myers didn't answer.

'Did you get him to sell them for you?' Edwards took back control. Myers still didn't answer. 'Mr Myers, are you aware that we have found a large cache of drugs at your property?'

'No.' Another flicker of the eyes to the lawyer. Edwards listed the substances they had found.

Myers's eyes grew wider with each addition. 'That can't be mine.'

'What do you mean?'

'Weed,' said Myers. His voice oozed with panic. 'I sell a bit of weed. That's why the boys come to me.'

'And cocaine?'

'A bit of marching powder, now and then. But not all that other stuff. I won't touch that sort of gear. I don't know where that all came from.'

In the viewing room, Lambert spoke. 'I bet I do. London will have had it left there.'

'How would she know where the hiding place was?' Sara asked. Lambert shrugged.

'I don't doubt that she took her brother to Amsterdam this morning, but we can't prove it. So where has he been all this time? Staying with Myers? His fingerprints were in the house. If so, he'd know where the stuff was kept.'

Much to Powell's annoyance, DI Edwards had moved away from asking about the drugs and was focusing on Callum.

'We know that Callum was a regular visitor to your house,' said Edwards.

Myers shrugged.

'Did he only come to collect drugs?'

Still no reply from Myers.

'Can you tell me what happened on the night of Tuesday the fourth of December? Did Callum visit you that night?'

'Yes,' said Myers. 'Yes, he was there.'

'And another young man, called Gary Barr or Barnet?'

The lawyer placed his hand on a notepad lying on the table between himself and Myers. It looked like a signal to Sara.

Myers shook his head. 'Gary comes round sometimes. Not that night.'

'What happened, Mr Myers?'

'We were drinking.'

'You are aware that Callum was too young to drink alcohol?'

'Yeah,' said Myers. 'It was only a bit of lager. I suppose he wasn't used to it and he got drunk.'

Myers faltered. The lawyer put his other hand on the notepad, winding his fingers together slowly. Myers watched them with fascination and looked up at the impassive face of his counsel.

'And then?' Edwards prompted.

'It all got a bit out of hand,' said Myers, his eyes still trained on the lawyer's face. 'He started getting difficult.'

'What do you mean by that?'

'I thought he felt sick, so I sent him to the bathroom. When I went to check up on him, he had taken his clothes off. Started coming on to me.'

277

'Coming on to you?'

'Yeah, you know, like sexual advances. Grabbed at my dick, but I was dressed and he couldn't. Then he tried to kiss me.'

'Only that?'

'It was enough,' said Myers. 'I didn't like it and . . .'

Both rooms fell silent. They all watched Myers, who looked at the lawyer. No one moved until the lawyer gave the briefest of nods. Myers turned away and gazed at the table.

'I hit him.' Myers's voice was quiet. It was hard to catch his words. 'We had a bit of a struggle. I punched him. He fell backwards and smashed his head on the shower tray. When he didn't get up, I thought he was mucking about. I left him there for a bit because I thought the cold would bring him round.'

'It didn't?'

Myers shook his head. 'When he was still there after a couple of minutes, I went to check. He'd stopped breathing. I didn't mean to hurt him. It was an accident.'

'Why didn't you ring for an ambulance?' Edwards asked.

'I got into a panic. I knew they would call you lot and I didn't want that. So I wrapped him up and moved him.'

'I understand what you are saying,' said Edwards. 'I still have one question. If Callum approached you for sex and you were offended by this, can you explain to me why we have been able to match your DNA with some our pathologist found inside Callum's body?'

At this, the lawyer sat upright with a jerk and turned to look at Myers. This was news to him too.

'In his back passage.' Edwards's face was grim, and even Powell looked at his fellow officer in surprise. 'As if he had just had anal sex with you.'

Myers shrank into his seat.

'Did you have a sexual relationship with Callum?' Edwards carried on remorselessly. 'And if you did, were you aware that Callum Young was only fifteen years old?'

278

CHAPTER 58

The team came in at a more normal hour on Tuesday morning. DCI Lambert and DS Mead had returned to London empty-handed the previous evening.

They'd said their goodbyes in the car park.

Mead had shrugged. 'We'll get her next time. Bound to make another mistake one day soon. It was good to work with you again. Thanks for all your help.'

The morning meeting was a joint affair, with DI Powell and all his team perched around the SCU office. Sara wondered if ACC Miller had waded in to prevent the two teams being at odds. Aggie seemed to have anticipated this, and put down two cake tins instead of one.

'Didn't have much time last night,' she said. She'd stayed late to begin the long stream of paperwork for the prosecution. 'Help yourselves. Banana bread or jam sponge.'

DI Powell and DI Edwards stood together by the incident board. Powell began. 'This is how we see it. Myers was running a small-scale operation selling weed and cocaine to supplement his income. According to the neighbour we interviewed yesterday, there was a stream of young men who visited him, presumably to collect stuff to sell on. In other words, he was a small-time middleman.'

'Where did he get his gear from?' asked Ellie.

'We don't know,' said Powell. 'I'll be interviewing him about that this morning. Forensics are trying to find fingerprints on the packages in the boat cavity. Myers's prints are all over a couple of bags of weed. Remarkably, there are no prints at all on the other packages.'

'Planted, sir?' asked Ellie.

'Almost certainly,' replied Powell. 'Safety net against Myers. No prints, and we can't prove without doubt that it was his stuff, especially as he denies it. I'll ask again this morning.'

'We don't know any of his Norwich contacts at all?' Ellie sat heavily on the edge of a desk in defeat.

'We can't be sure,' said her boss. 'Maybe one day we will be able to link it up from another investigation. Unfortunately, that fancy lawyer of his has already arrived again, and I don't expect to get anything from Myers except "No comment". If he's at the boot end of a Maletesti family chain, he's unlikely to reveal anything else.'

'Who is this lawyer?' Sara asked. 'I don't recognise him as one of our duty team.'

'He's from some upmarket firm.' Powell's voice had a sour note. 'Was waiting in reception when Myers was first brought in. He doesn't have to say who is paying for his time, but I'd lay good money on the fact that it's Lisa London.'

'A chain that begins with London and ends with Callum Young,' said Sara.

'That's a thorny one,' said Edwards. 'There are more forensic results this morning. You remember that our sharp-eyed SOCO found blood in the bathroom? The sample on the shower tray is Callum's. Some of the blood in the Lloyd Loom basket weave is a match for Gary Barnet.'

A murmur ran around the room.

'Myers has confessed to the unlawful killing of Callum,' continued Edwards, 'so he will be charged with it. I expect it will be involuntary manslaughter during a fight. Who Young fought with is another matter. Unfortunately, we can't pursue anyone else as Myers has come forward with a reasonable explanation. I'll be passing this information down to the Met team, to see if they can make anything out of it.'

'Why would Myers confess, if he didn't do it?' asked Noble.

'Fear? Money? Blackmail?' said Edwards.

'Money,' said Sara and Ellie together. The teams laughed, and some of the tension in the room dissipated.

'And the underage sex?' Sara asked.

'I think that was Myers's biggest secret,' replied Edwards. 'I don't think that his fancy lawyer or Lisa London knew anything about that. I suspect he paid Callum for it. We never did explain that extra wodge of cash.'

'Saving up to go to London,' said Sara. 'His school friend said it was all he talked about.'

'Myers will also be charged with rape of a minor, even if he thought he was sixteen.'

'He'll get stick in jail,' rumbled Bowen. He was standing at the back of the room with DC Noble. 'They give any paedo a tough time.'

'Indeed.'

'Bailey and Morgan, sir?' Sara addressed DI Powell.

The Drugs team leader looked uncomfortable. 'Sophie's father took her home. He's standing guarantor that she will get rehabilitation treatment. As a consequence, I am not pressing charges for this as a first offence.'

Sara thought of the botched interview and knew that Powell would be unlikely to persuade the Crown Prosecution Service to take it on.

'Lyndford Lodge was clean,' continued Powell. 'We have done blood tests on Morgan, and he's clean.'

'Sir, why did Morgan keep the stuff when he must have realised we might be keeping an eye the Lodge?' Ellie asked.

'He said he thought he'd thrown it all away, but was distracted when he got back to the Lodge and forgot about it.'

'Do you believe that?'

'Maybe,' said Powell. 'I do believe his story about Bailey. Morgan is one of those bleeding-heart liberals, who can't resist a cause.'

Sometimes, Sara thought, *I despair of the attitude of these guys.* 'And Dan Wade?'

'We'll be looking into charges in his case.'

'So that's where we are,' said Edwards. 'I can't see any further prosecutions coming out of this, so best we get on with the paperwork.'

The two teams went back to their desks to begin the paper trail. Ellie was the last to leave. She stopped by Sara on her way out, keeping her voice low. 'Thank you for speaking to Mike.'

'You two made up? Are you friends again?'

'We talked about it when we were out yesterday,' said Ellie. 'We're friends again, as far as that goes.'

'I'm glad,' said Sara. And she meant it. 'We must all go for a beer soon.'

'That would be great.'

Sara felt pleased that Ellie sounded more cheerful as she left the SCU office. Aggie cleared up the debris from the team meeting, while Bowen and Noble started on the evidence log for the CPS.

Edwards swept out of his room. 'Come on, Hirst. One more thing to do before this is closed.'

They discussed the case as they drove to Marlham. Neither were sure they had the right person for Callum's death, but also knew they were unlikely to be able to prove anything against Gary Barnet. He was in Naples, under the protection of his family, and the Italian police would be lucky to find him, let alone send him for extradition.

When they pulled into Lyndford Lodge, a rental van was standing in the drive with its back doors open. Inside, they found the door to Matt Morgan's office open. Morgan was talking to a young man who neither of them recognised.

'DI Edwards,' said Morgan. He patted the young man on the shoulder to comfort him. 'Go and make us all a cuppa, Tom. We'll sort it out later.'

'What's going on, Mr Morgan?' Edwards asked. The office was full of supermarket boxes and packed bags filled the hallway outside.

'I've lost my job,' said Morgan. He sighed. 'I know you aren't charging me, but the management company think that my handling of Callum was poor and that I've brought them into disrepute. So out I go.'

Sara knew this was unfair, that Matt had no idea what Callum had been up to. She also remembered that the management company had cut back on his staff and resources. Matt Morgan was collateral damage, just like Dan Wade. Wade had been trying to save his business, and Morgan had been trying to save his young charges. Unfortunately, no one ever said that life was going to be fair.

'We came to tell you that we have Callum's killer,' said Edwards. 'He says it was an accident. That he hit Callum, who fell and injured his head.'

'Not murder, then?'

'Manslaughter. He'll do time for it. He was also supplying Callum with the drugs that he was selling.'

'Then he deserves what he gets, I guess,' said Matt. Tom returned with a tray with mugs of tea balanced on it. Matt shared them out as Tom wandered back to the kitchen.

'What will you do?' Sara asked. 'You lived in, didn't you?'

'Yes,' said Matt. He stared into his mug for a moment, then smiled at Sara. 'There's an Indian takeaway in the town. I went in there sometimes to get a treat for the lads, and I often chatted with the owner. We became mates in a way. Rajid asked me the same question yesterday.'

They sipped their tea, waiting for him to continue.

'There's a small empty flat over the restaurant. Rajid says I can have it for a while until I get on my feet. I'm taking Tom with me.' Matt pointed towards the kitchen. 'He's the one who has been sleeping in my office, who isn't officially living here anymore. There isn't anywhere else he can go, and I won't see him on the streets.'

'What will you do for work? Will—' Sara stopped herself. 'I'm sorry, it's none of my business.'

'That's OK,' said Matt. 'Tom has just started an apprenticeship at Hotel Wroxham. He can do that and share the flat. As for me? Well, I don't have many qualifications. You see, I'm a product of the system that this lodge is part of. I left school without anything much and worked my way back here.'

Which is why, Sara thought, *you are such a good advocate for these youngsters.*

'I've decided to get some qualifications. Rajid says I can work in the takeaway in the evenings, taking orders and all that. I've signed up for a course at City College, starting in the new year. I'm training to be a substance misuse counsellor.'

As they drove back to HQ, Edwards seemed even quieter than usual.

'All done then, sir?' Sara asked.

'It's the little people who always seem to get hurt, isn't it?' he said.

'Yes, sir. It is.' Sara thought of all the people besides Callum who had been affected by their investigation. Even her relationship with Chris had taken a battering.

'While the Lisa Londons of this murky world get away with everything. Their money protects them.'

'At least Sophie Bailey is getting help, and Matt Morgan is moving on. I think he'll make a great counsellor.'

'So do I,' agreed DI Edwards. 'We need more people like him on our side.'

CHAPTER 59

After Tuesday's meeting, the two teams began to gather the evidence for the joint operation, as it was now being styled. Sara decided the result was more to their credit in SCU than it was to DI Powell's Drugs squad. At least the experience appeared to have made both teams less tribal than before. That evening, her mum called to say that her visit to the cancer clinic was scheduled for Friday afternoon. Sara offered to go down to be with Tegan, but her mum preferred Javed to go with her.

'I don't want to make too much fuss,' she said. 'We'll call on Friday evening. You have so much to do at work.'

For a day or two, Sara felt hurt by this. If she was honest with herself, she had often used work as an excuse in the past. She didn't tell anyone at the office what was happening. It would only add to her stress.

On Friday evening, Sara cooked her favourite Jamaican brown stewed chicken and invited Chris to share it with her. It was as close to an apology as she was able to go.

Chris was slicing chunks of fresh-baked granary loaf to dunk in the stew. 'Guess what? I've got an unexpected day off.'

'How did you manage that?'

'I should have been rehearsing on Sunday afternoon,' he said. 'The director cancelled at the last minute.'

'Shouldn't you be going to the café, then?'

'I should.' He smiled. 'I offered, and the girls declined. Said they were happy to cover for my rehearsal, so they were happy to cover for me to have a day off. I love my staff.'

'Sunday off? Me too — tomorrow as well.'

After they had finished their meal, which Chris declared delicious despite the amount of chilli in it, they sat on the balcony. Sara's mobile sat between them on the table as they waited. It was cold, though not freezing, and Chris had made them luxury hot chocolate to keep out the chill. When her phone rang, Sara had to wipe a creamy moustache from her top lip. She felt surprisingly nervous.

'Hi, Mum. How did you get on?'

'It's fine!' Laughter bubbled over for the pair of them. 'It was just a cyst. I had one of them mammogram things. My goodness, they hurt.'

'Worth it, though,' said Sara.

'You think so? I do too. Shan't miss a screening again. Anyway. They stabbed me in the boob with a big needle, and they drew off all the liquid.'

Sara winced. 'Did they give you an anaesthetic?'

'Nah. But Javed held my hand. That liquid was dark brown. The doctor said it was blood, which was natural and not to worry. Now I got to keep checking on me boobs, and he showed me how.'

'That's amazing, Mum,' said Sara. Tears of relief trickled down her cheeks. Chris leaned over the table and gently took her hand.

'All this made me think,' said Tegan. 'About our argument.'

'Yes, me too.'

'I would like it if you came home to see me and we can talk it through. Would that be all right with you?'

'Very much,' said Sara. She squeezed Chris's hand. 'How about Sunday? I have a day off on Sunday, and there's someone I'd like you to meet.'

She smiled at Chris, as Tegan laughed.

* * *

On Saturday morning, Chris left Sara's flat early to open the café. Sara knew they would be busy, as there were only two Saturdays left before Christmas. Once she had gathered up enough energy, she also needed to go shopping. Sara wanted presents for Tegan and Javed, and cards for the extended family, neighbours and friends in Tower Hamlets. She didn't even have any tape or wrapping paper.

The city centre was heaving. The narrow lanes were packed, and it wasn't easy to weave her way through to her favourite store. Jarrolds was the first department store she had ever fallen in love with. It reminded Sara of Harrods but felt more welcoming to her than the Knightsbridge store had ever been. As she worked her way through the various floors, she found everything she wanted. A new jumper and pocket handkerchiefs for Javed. Perfume and a colourful silk scarf for Tegan. A new diary for herself and a lovely leather satchel for Chris. If she could persuade him to use it, perhaps he would stop wandering across the road with handfuls of paperwork from the coffee shop to his flat. With an armful of bags, she headed for the top-floor restaurant. There was a queue, which was no surprise. Sara tagged on the end of it. A tap on her arm made her swing around.

'Sara Hirst!'

'Mrs Barker! How are you?'

'I'm well, thank you,' said Mrs Barker. 'I haven't seen you in weeks. Not since your father's funeral.'

'I've been busy. Work, you know.'

'I imagined so. Your father always seemed to be busy.'

Mrs Barker lived at one end of a terrace of cottages on the outskirts of Happisburgh. The house Sara's father had left her stood at the other.

'I thought you might have moved in by now,' she said.

'I've been waiting for probate,' explained Sara.

Mrs Barker nodded sadly. 'I do miss your dad. The other cottages are holiday lets, you know. I'm on my own now.'

'It's through, now. The probate. I collected the keys during the week.'

'How lovely.' Mrs Barker cheered up immediately. 'When will you move in?' Sara hesitated, and Mrs Barker's face fell again. 'Or do you intend to sell it?'

Sara had been thinking about this for days, without making a decision. She understood why Chris wanted her to sell it. If she moved so far out of the city, then they would see even less of each other than they did now. She had worked out the commute times, which were no worse than they had been in London, and weighed up Chris's desire to continue working all day and acting every evening, given a chance. Even so, the emotional pull of living in her estranged father's old home was huge. He had obviously come to love living here and enjoyed the country life. Perhaps she would too.

Sara smiled at Mrs Barker, who was watching her hopefully.

'Do you know, Mrs Barker,' said Sara. 'I don't want to sell it.'

'Oh, how lovely,' declared Mrs Barker. 'Please call me Gilly if we're going to be real neighbours.'

'I can't move in yet — there's so much to do.'

'How much?'

The queue moved nearer to the entrance of the restaurant.

'It's desperate for a clean, and I will need to sort through all my father's things.'

'The furniture's still in there? Forgive my curiosity. I'm a nosey old thing, but it doesn't look empty.'

'Everything is still there.'

'Then it just needs a good clean, and you can move straight in. Sort it out and replace the furniture when you have time.'

'I guess so,' said Sara. She'd think about how she felt about living among her father's things another time.

'I could get a couple of my chums to come and help,' offered Gilly. 'We clean at the church together, like all good WI members. If it would be any use?'

'That would be wonderful,' said Sara. 'I have Christmas off, from the twenty-second.'

'Great. I can have a cleaning party organised by then, no problem. Then you can be in your own home in time for Christmas Eve. Shall we share a table?'

Sara agreed and, with a smile, followed her new neighbour to select from the giant pile of scones that made the restaurant so famous. *Finally*, she thought, *things are working out.*

Norfolk was beginning to feel like home, and Sara couldn't have wished for a better Christmas present.

THE END

ACKNOWLEDGEMENTS

I would like to thank my beta readers. Antony Dunford, Karen Taylor, Louise Sharland and Wendy Turbin for notes and encouragement that went beyond the line of duty! Jayne Farnworth and Clive Forbes, two former DIs from the Met and the NCA respectively, for police procedural advice. Any incorrect procedures are there because I made an executive author's decision (or mistake!).

My gratitude goes out to Jasper Joffe for welcoming me to Joffe Books, thank you for your belief. Also to Emma Grundy Haigh, Cat Phipps and Elodie Olson-Coons for helping me improve the novel with very helpful edits and generous comments. My grateful thanks to the rest of the Joffe Books team for all your work and support.

Last but not least, my family. My husband, Rhett, who is always there for me whatever happens, even more so during the writing of this book during the 2020 lockdowns and beyond. My daughter, Gwen Lexmoke, really a computer games designer, but always there to help me when I've messed up on my PC. Thank you for your continued support and love.

THE JOFFE BOOKS STORY

We began in 2014 when Jasper agreed to publish his mum's much-rejected romance novel and it became a bestseller.

Since then we've grown into the largest independent publisher in the UK. We're extremely proud to publish some of the very best writers in the world, including Joy Ellis, Faith Martin, Caro Ramsay, Helen Forrester, Simon Brett and Robert Goddard. Everyone at Joffe Books loves reading and we never forget that it all begins with the magic of an author telling a story.

We are proud to publish talented first-time authors, as well as established writers whose books we love introducing to a new generation of readers.

We have been shortlisted for Independent Publisher of the Year at the British Book Awards three times, in 2020, 2021 and 2022, and for the Diversity and Inclusivity Award at the Independent Publishing Awards in 2022.

We built this company with your help, and we love to hear from you, so please email us about absolutely anything bookish at: feedback@joffebooks.com.

If you want to receive free books every Friday and hear about all our new releases, join our mailing list: www.joffebooks.com/contact

And when you tell your friends about us, just remember: it's pronounced Joffe as in coffee or toffee!